MAGIC UNDER STONE

ALSO BY JACLYN DOLAMORE

Magic Under Glass
Between the Sea and Sky

MAGIC UNDER STONE

JACLYN DOLAMORE

BLOOMSBURY

NEW YORK BERLIN LONDON SYDNEY

First published in the United States of America in April 2012
by Bloomsbury Books for Young Readers
www.bloomsburyteens.com

For information about permission to reproduce selections from this book, write to
Permissions, Bloomsbury BFYR, 175 Fifth Avenue, New York, New York 10010

Library of Congress Cataloging-in-Publication Data
Dolamore, Jaclyn.
Magic under stone / by Jaclyn Dolamore. — 1st U.S. ed.
    p.   cm.
Summary: Star-crossed lovers Nimira and Erris seek the sorcerer Ordoria Valdana hoping he
will be able to free Erris from his clockwork form, but Valdana has
vanished and as Nimira studies his spell books she realizes the terrible danger
that could come from returning Erris to real life.
ISBN 978-1-59990-643-0 (hardcover)
[1. Magic—Fiction. 2. Robots—Fiction. 3. Princes—Fiction. 4. Fairies—Fiction.
5. Genies—Fiction. 6. Wizards—Fiction. 7. Fantasy.] I. Title.
PZ7.D6975Maj 2012   [Fic]—dc23   2011025659

Book design by Donna Mark
Typeset by Westchester Book Composition
Printed in the U.S.A. by Quad/Graphics, Fairfield, Pennsylvania
2 4 6 8 10 9 7 5 3 1

To my sister Kate.

I don't miss my childhood that much ... but I do miss ours.

THE HALL OF OAK AND ASH, TELMIRRA

Ifra became aware of his body like a prisoner waking to find himself in chains. One moment he was liquid smoke, hot with magic, and the next, his feet were touching the floor. He felt the weight of fabric on his body, the golden cuffs at his wrists, the cool air on his skin. This was the fifth time, his fifth master, and he still wasn't used to it.

His arms were dappled with green-tinged shadow, and his first vision was of forest—trees growing tall as towers around him, their leaves whispering—but the sound was wrong. Too closed, like the indoors.

The man standing before him drew a slight breath and turned to a younger man beside him. "A jinn. It really is a jinn. I do believe you've proven yourself enough for two lifetimes, my son."

"It's my honor, Father." The younger man stared with clear pride at the golden lamp in his father's hands.

Ifra remembered his training and swept into a graceful bow. A new language came to him with magical ease. "Master. You have released me from my bondage, and for that, I shall grant you three wishes within my formidable powers."

The older man was beautiful, with his high cheekbones and full, almost androgynous lips. His dark red hair was chin length and worn loose beneath a simple crown of gold that matched his gold waistcoat and the gold embroidery on his green velvet coat. The younger man resembled him strongly, only his hair had more blond in it, his clothes were simple and travel worn, and his expression held a hint of desperation.

Ifra saw now that he was, in fact, in a vast room with trees growing within its walls, curving in a circle around a stone throne. The flagstones beneath his feet were scattered with fallen leaves.

"I see the beauty of the Hall of Oak and Ash impresses even a jinn," the man said. "But perhaps you are used to the desert."

"Jinn roam far and wide. I grew up in the hills," Ifra said, already breaking one of his tutor's rules: *Make your master believe you had no other life before him.* Breaking a rule on his second sentence, that was probably a record.

"Well, there is much I do not know," the man said, with a slight shrug. He smiled affably. "My name is Luka. I am the king of fairies, known as King of the Longest Day, but you may call me Luka. And this is my son Belin."

A king. Kings didn't usually brave the treacherous ruins to find a jinn, but it seemed his son had done it for him. What would a king wish for, when he already had riches and power? Most people looked for a jinn to give them a king's life.

"Do jinn eat?" Luka asked. "You may know our wine is the finest in the world." He clapped a hand on Ifra's arm, turning him to meet a young woman who emerged from the hawthorn bushes growing along the walls, as if she had simply materialized, with a cup in each hand.

"Master Luka, there is no need for all this," Ifra said, trying to sound stern, but his hand moved to the cup. His tutor had warned him that accepting favors was likely to reveal vulnerability, and free people were not to be trusted, but Ifra already missed food and drink and kindness.

Luka shook his head. "Please. A token of my gratitude for your powers."

Ifra sipped the wine, tasting blackberries.

"Now," Luka said. "Tell me. What are the rules? What is within your power? I know jinn like to trick people."

We don't trick people, we just exercise our right to interpret sloppy wishes, Ifra thought, but he said exactly what he'd been taught to say. "Many things are within my power. I can twist the threads of fortune to your favor. I can sense people's hearts and steer their thoughts. I'm difficult to kill, my senses are keen. I can be a healer or a destroyer. What I can't do is bend the laws of nature or change things that are beyond one man's grasp, no matter how powerful that man may be."

"Is it true," Belin said, "that we could forfeit our three wishes in exchange for your lifelong loyal servitude? That is, my father's wishes?"

Ifra's gut twisted. *Of course, you knew this would happen at some point. How many jinn are ever set free? That's why there are so few of us.* "It's true," he said. He couldn't lie about the wishes. "But I can no longer grant magic for you that I couldn't grant for myself. I'll lose most of my ability to manipulate events."

"But is it true what they say about jinn?" Belin continued. "That you're nearly invincible? That you are never ill? You're stronger than most men? And loyal to your master?"

"Yes," Ifra said softly.

"Kings always need loyal men." Luka's expression was not unkind.

Please let him be kind, if this is to be my fate.

"Especially in a time like this. I have the humans to deal with, the lost heir, even my own people threatening rebellion. If they only knew all I've done to protect them these many years . . ." The king shook his head. "I'll be good to you, you can be assured of that. Fairies don't keep slaves, and it's not in me to treat any man poorly."

Maybe—maybe it was best this way. At least if he remained in one place for the rest of his life, he might have friends; maybe he would even gain his freedom when the king died. His mother, after all, had conceived him while in servitude, and when her master died, she would be free.

"Father?" Belin turned to the older man. "You should bind him not just to you, but to the throne. That way when you're gone, he won't disappear."

"Yes, but what if . . . it's usurped?"

"That won't happen." Belin glanced at the stone throne. "Bind him to the Graweldin family, then."

"But Erris's mother was a Graweldin. I'm not sure it would prevent . . . There are dozens of Graweldins. It's too vague. No, I think you're right, I think we must bind him to the one who sits on the throne."

Belin nodded.

With every word out of their mouths, Ifra's fate sounded more real. Bound to the fairy throne? He might serve any number of kings, then, before he died, and who knew what they would ask him to do.

"Wait," Ifra said, his voice almost shaking. "What about a bargain? I'll serve you faithfully, if—if you don't wish. I'll serve you just as I would if I was bound to you."

Belin frowned. "Sounds like jinn tricks to me."

"All my men say they are loyal," Luka said. "Sometimes they lie. I need someone I can trust."

"It wouldn't be like that," Ifra said. "I'm still your servant. Only, you would have your three wishes, waiting in reserve, should you need them, along with my loyalty too."

"I still think it sounds like a trick," Belin said. "Father, if you die, we'll lose the jinn. What's the point of allowing him freedom if he's going to behave as if he's our servant in the first place, except that he can plot your demise?"

Luka, however, was regarding Ifra with eyes that looked somehow too old for his face. "I understand," he said. "I do believe you just want some sense that you're your own man. I can't blame you for that. And you're right—you still wouldn't really be free, but it would be a gesture of trust on my part. Can I trust you? Or are the myths about your people true?"

"Are the myths about your people true?" Ifra said, barely breathing. "I *do* mean it."

"I believe you," Luka said. He put a hand on his son's shoulder before he could protest. "I'd rather earn loyalty than force it, but with times being as they are, know that I won't tolerate tricks."

"I won't disappoint you, Master Luka."

Luka made a faint nod, and Ifra felt the tension drain from him—at least for now.

Luka turned to his son. "You've done very well."

Belin looked slightly impatient, but he lowered his head deferentially. "Thank you, Father."

"Now, jinn, if you'll follow me, I'm eager to find out what you're capable of." Luka moved toward heavy wooden doors carved with trees and animals. A waiting guard dressed in black and scarlet opened them to reveal a garden.

Just outside waited two other young men who bore a strong resemblance to Belin. One had a young woman hanging on his arm. The other man was grinning, but Ifra detected aggression in his eyes.

"What, no greeting for your brothers, Belin?" the grinning man said.

"I came straight to Father," Belin said, glaring.

"Who's this?" Belin's brother was staring at the golden cuffs at Ifra's wrists. The smile was gone now.

"Whoever he is, he's beautiful," said the woman, looking at Ifra with open interest.

Belin paused, then replied, "He belongs to Father now, and he is Father's to introduce."

Ifra fought back a sick feeling in his gut, hearing himself referred to as a possession. Somehow, granting three wishes and then departing never felt like this. Or had it? His memory of his first few masters was already fading.

"It's quite obvious, I think," Luka said, stepping forward. "Belin has brought me a jinn. Jinn, these are my other sons, Tamin and Ilsin, and Ilsin's wife, Elsana."

Tamin's eyes narrowed slightly. "A jinn, eh? I'm surprised you made it out of the ruins alive, Belin."

"Well, I did," Belin said with cool hostility. Luka gave him a sharp look, and he bowed quickly. "Father, I shall leave you to enjoy your gift."

"Thank you, Belin." Luka smiled almost apologetically at Tamin. "Big risks must be rewarded, you know."

Tamin's nostrils flared. He didn't say anything; he merely tapped Ilsin on the shoulder and both of them left. Only Elsana said good-bye.

Luka resumed his stroll through the gardens. Vegetables grew alongside flower bushes. A young woman in a plain lilac dress walked the edge with a watering can. Vines, some of them as thick as a wrist with age, climbed the surrounding walls on all sides.

"Is Belin your youngest son?" Ifra asked, not entirely understanding the exchange he had just seen. Ifra imagined he must be the youngest, to be allowed to travel to the vast ruins, full of caved-in corridors, narrow tunnels, and traps, where all jinn dwelt until they were freed or permanently enslaved. Once a jinn finished his or her service, his or her lamp or vessel reappeared in the depths of the ruins. Over time, a city had built up around them, an entire tourist trade catering to intrepid adventurers and desperate men who wanted three wishes. Thousands of people braved the ruins, so while some jinn still slept for decades, waiting to be found, most jinn were awakened every few years. Ifra hadn't gone six months without a new master.

"By some minutes, yes. The boys are triplets."

"What fortune!" said Ifra. With the ranks of jinn ever dwindling, news of twins born to a jinn mother might travel for hundreds of miles.

Luka grunted. "It killed their mother. She was already dead when the midwife took Belin from her womb. And it hasn't made things easy for me. Who do I give the kingdom to when I'm gone?

That's why I told them each to go forth and bring me back a gift, just like in the old days. Whoever's gift was the greatest treasure would inherit. It'll go to Belin, now. His brothers returned a good year or two before him, one with a very fine antique sword and one with a sacred wine cup that never runs dry. But I'd say a jinn beats them both. Swords and wine, I have."

"Ah . . ." Now Ifra understood the hostility from Tamin. "I'm sorry about your wife."

"Probably better for her," Luka answered. "They were certainly a trio of little scamps, and they all wanted the throne like they want everything, but if something isn't done, none of them will have it."

They had crossed the covered path cutting through the garden's center, and now entered a common hall. While the throne room had been hushed and ancient, this equally vast room bustled with life—a crackling hearth, gentlemen playing cards, ladies in gowns of trailing silk strolling past the carved wooden support columns in close conversation, a harpist in the corner providing gentle music, even a palm reader tracing the lines of a girl's hand. Even here, small trees and flowers sprung from breaks in the tiled floors.

"How do the trees grow indoors?" Ifra asked, still curious about the throne room.

"Oh, the trees in the Hall of Oak and Ash have an ancient lineage. When we came across the ocean five hundred years ago, fleeing the humans, we had to leave the old trees behind, but we brought saplings. Those trees grew from the saplings. As long as anyone can remember, the throne of our people has been protected by the sacred trees. The king's trees. They don't need light or water to grow, only the presence of their king, and they lend him wisdom to assure that the king always acts for the good of his people—if he's not too stubborn to listen. The last Tanharrow king..." Luka scoffed.

"What did he do?"

"Well, you must understand, we were on this continent first. The humans in the old world were running us out of the forests for the lumber and the animals, so we came here. We had almost two hundred peaceful years before human greed and human ships caught up to us. They've driven us out of the eastern ports over the years, and then thirty years ago, we went to war and lost our trade route up the Great Serpent River. Now all we have is the southern passage. The Tanharrow family was working toward a truce when the humans wiped them out. But the humans don't really want peace and neither do I. It's us or them. My sons will inherit a conflict that won't end until we wipe them off the continent."

Ifra had followed Luka down a hall to a smaller chamber. Now Luka drew keys from his pocket and unlocked the door to an office. A map was spread across a table, and a desk was strewn with papers.

"Which brings me to you," Luka said.

"What do you ask of me?"

Luka crossed the room, opening a drawer. He rummaged there a moment, then drew a nearby chair underneath him to sit while he continued his search.

"For five hundred years on this continent and beyond," Luka said, "this kingdom passed from father to son—or sometimes daughter—an unbroken chain of Tanharrows. Remarkable, isn't it?

"But the Tanharrow clan—every last one of them—died in the war. Or so everyone supposed. The soul of Erris Tanharrow, the ninth son, was trapped in the body of a clockwork man. He has recently been found and the clockwork given gruesome animation.

But it's not really life. He could hardly be fit to rule. He was five years younger than me when he was trapped, so he's never had a chance to grow beyond the seventeen-year-old dandy I remember. Besides that, I doubt he has the strength of character to hold up under trying circumstances."

Seventeen . . . and trapped. I know what that feels like. Ifra, like all jinn, had gone into his vessel to begin granting wishes on his seventeenth birthday. Now he aged only while he was granting wishes. If he continued to live a month here and a month there, hundreds of years might pass before he died of old age, and it would be a life without attachments, without family. While Luka spoke, Ifra gazed out the window, at a view of gently sloped land covered in forest. A young couple walked hand in hand on a sun-dappled path woven through the woods.

"Still," Luka continued, "those who disagree with the way I've handled things think the restoration of the Tanharrows would solve all our problems. My first request of you is to bring Erris Tanharrow to me, intact and unharmed, without alerting anyone to your mission. Can you do that?"

Ifra turned from the window—and briefly started when he saw not Luka, but a man with pallid skin clinging to delicate bones, his red hair cropped to his skull and peppered with white. And then it was gone, a trick of the eye.

Ifra remembered to answer. "I—I should be able to manage it. Does Erris Tanharrow have any magic I should be wary of?"

"Oh, he never paid attention to his studies. I highly doubt he'll be a threat, but he was staying in the human city with the new ambassador of magic, Dr. Greinfern, who is a necromancer. If he's still there, you might have some work ahead of you, but if he tries to come back here . . . You should be able to nab him in our borders."

Luka frowned. "You see through my glamour, don't you?" His voice was low.

"Only . . . glimpses," Ifra admitted. "You don't look well, sir."

"I'm not. I have a wasting sickness and none of the healers know how to fix it. But I'm not on my deathbed quite yet."

"You won't use one of your wishes for your health? I might be able to—" Ifra shut his mouth. *A jinn should never suggest wishes to his master.*

"It doesn't matter to me if I die. I'm ready to join my wife. I have a lot of burdens here, and death seems the only way to lay them down. I just want to make sure my sons will take care of things and protect the kingdom." Luka stood, and what Ifra had taken for stately movements now seemed merely the slowness of age. "I think they know what needs to be done."

"What will you do with Erris Tanharrow when you find him?"

"Depends what shape he's in." Luka sounded weary, but beneath it was hard resolve. "Why don't you bring him here first, and then I'll decide."

I'm not sure what is worse: failing to save someone or saving him only halfway. That question kept me awake nights and followed me into the mornings, when I awoke to the weight of a silver key around my neck.

I still wore my nightgown as I slipped from my room into his. Erris was sleeping—if you could call it that—on his stomach, clothed except for his jacket. His shirt was slit down the back to expose a keyhole surrounded by clockwork that was mostly concealed by the shirt.

It was hard to believe that just weeks ago, he had been a true automaton, with a painted wooden face and articulated fingers that moved stiffly along the keys of a piano. His soul, the soul of the lost fairy prince, had been trapped inside, unable to speak. He had been my secret, a tragic secret that tore at my heart, and yet I had never had a secret like that. It made me feel alive. I would be the one to set him free from his prison. I would be the one to summon the Queen of the Dead and give Erris life.

I hadn't realized my efforts would gain him only a half life and make me the keeper of his prison. His face and hands looked supple as flesh, felt supple as flesh, and he moved like a living man, but beneath his clothes he was still just clockwork, and every night when he wound down, he had to trust that I would be there in the morning to help him wake. It was not exactly the romance I had hoped for.

Each morning, a wave of profound loneliness swept over me. The key was a burden no one would understand.

He was still, like someone who had passed away in his sleep. Not a breath or a twitch. I put the key in the keyhole and twisted five and a half times, the length we had determined would give him a full day before he wound down. The key, as always, almost seemed to have a mind of its own once it was slotted in place. There was none of the tension a clockwork toy would have.

I pulled out the key and slipped from the room. I was out the door in three ticks.

I used to wait while he awoke. I thought he would want to see a friendly face. But sometimes he cried out as if he had seen something awful in the realm of dreams. Other times he lay motionless, haunted eyes staring before they met mine. He never seemed to come to peacefully. At first, he would try to smile and tell me of his nightmares, of his lost family or being chased by strange beasts or any number of other awful things, but one day he snapped at me not to ask him what he saw ever again. So I started to leave and he didn't tell me to come back. I think it made it easier for him to pretend he woke like a normal person.

I returned to my room. Karstor's maid helped me dress in a fetching silk gown of dark blue with green velvet trim and cummerbund and pulled my hair back in soft wings over my ears, with a knot at the nape of my neck. Even fine clothes weren't enough to make things feel proper and normal anymore.

I joined Karstor at the breakfast table. He had a book opened against the rim of his plate, but he looked up from it when I entered the room.

"Good morning, Nimira."

"Good morning, Dr. Greinfern." Erris called him Karstor, and that was how I thought of him, but of course I was not so presumptuous to refer to the head of the Sorcerer's Council, the ambassador of magic, by his given name.

The table was already spread with good, simple food: a basket of bread, a plate of large slices of golden cheese, a crock of yellow butter, and a pot of coffee. I could hear the cook, Birte, singing in the kitchen as she often did.

Erris wouldn't join us; his clockwork innards would not accept food.

"Ready to set out tomorrow?" Karstor asked.

"I suppose so. I will miss you, sir." I had known, of course, that Karstor was a busy man. He had just ascended to the head of the Sorcerer's Council after the revelation of the crimes of his predecessor, Mr. Smollings. He had never expected to take in boarders, I was sure, especially not a long-lost fairy prince. It would likely be a conflict of interest, considering the political tension between the people of Lorinar and the fairies. Still, some deep-down part of me had hoped he would look upon us as the children he never had, because it stung to go away.

"I will miss you too," he said softly. "But Ordorio Valdana will know more than I do."

"Is he the most powerful sorcerer in Lorinar, do you think?"

"He is, at least, the most powerful necromancer," Karstor said. "And that is what you will want. Besides that, he was involved in the war when Erris was cursed. Maybe he will know something."

I put my hand to Hollin's letter. I kept it in my dress pocket at all times, even though I knew every word by heart now. *If anyone knows how to help Erris, it might be Mr. Valdana.* They were not the most hopeful words, with the "if" and the "might." The suggestion had come from Hollin's wife, Annalie, who could commune with the spirits. *The spirits told Annalie that Mr. Valdana was once married to a fairy woman. Melia Tanharrow . . . Erris's sister.*

I wished it were Erris's sister we were going to see, but she was dead. His whole family had died during his years imprisoned in an automaton.

"Don't despair," Karstor said, noticing how I had begun to pick at my food. "Look how much you have already done. You have helped Erris so now he can move and speak."

"Yes, but . . ." I stopped. How stupid I would sound, to say what I worried was true—that Erris seemed to care for me more *before* I helped him.

"He needs time to grieve," Karstor said. "It takes time." Karstor had lost something too, I reminded myself. His dear friend Garvin had been murdered by Smollings.

I almost wished I had something solid to grieve. Every day I told myself to be strong for Erris, but it was hard to be strong so unceasingly. "I know," I said.

"It's not all you have done. You helped prove that Smollings murdered Garvin, and removed him from the council. You can't know how much that means to me, Nimira. Have I ever thanked you properly?"

I made a vague sound. I couldn't remember. "I didn't do anything with the thought of being thanked."

"Of course," he agreed. "But you should remember that your bravery helped more people than just Erris. You brought me peace, knowing that Garvin was avenged, and that is no small thing."

I smiled, just a little, at that. Sometimes my bravery only brought me trouble, and it was good to know that it could bring someone peace.

"I know it all must look a little bleak right now," Karstor continued. "But we never know what fate has in store for us."

It was true. A year ago, I was just a foreign girl of no importance, dancing in a cheap show, and today I was having breakfast with one of the most powerful men in the country. Tomorrow, I would be on a train north to find a man who would, I hoped, be more powerful still.

The train brought us as far as Cernan, the northernmost stop on a route that stretched almost the entire length of the coast. This place was a far cry from where we had begun, the grand station in New Sweeling, with its golden halls and stairs, statues and glittering gaslights.

There was no one to meet us, of course, although plenty to stare at us. The train station was hardly more than a shack, and the few people who had gotten off with us were quickly met by their relations. At least, I assumed they were relations because they looked the same, but as I glanced at one lean, weather-beaten, dark-haired individual after another, I wondered if the entire town wasn't related.

I halted to check my map. "I didn't think this town would be so small. I hope we can hire a hack."

Erris was quiet, as he had been for most of the journey. We had started out talking about the sights flying by our windows, and he had made jokes, but I could tell he was relieved when I fell silent for long stretches.

A young man approached, perhaps only a year or two older than my seventeen years. He hitched up his trousers with the hand not grasping a cigarette. "You people looking for something?" He placed a subtle emphasis on *you people*. I wondered if he could tell Erris was a fairy, but perhaps not, for I was the one who seemed the focus of his scrutiny. Fairies looked much like Lorinarian humans, but my black hair and brown skin marked me as a foreigner.

The man at the ticket counter, the porter, the families greeting each other—all their attention subtly shifted to see what we would say.

"Yes, we are," I said, folding my map halfway. "Ordorio Valdana."

You could have heard the trees growing in the ensuing silence.

An older man who had just stepped off the train marched into the conversation. "Ordorio Valdana? What would you want with him? What's going on?"

Erris finally spoke. "We've come a long way, from New Sweeling, looking for Mr. Valdana."

We could have told them the ambassador of magic himself had sent us, but the less talk we left in our wake, the better.

The younger man took a drag on his cigarette. "The minute I saw them, I said to myself, I bet they're here to see that old lunatic. Well, he's not even home, so you might as well get right back on that train."

I had grown sadly accustomed to being condescended to ever since I'd arrived on these shores. They'd have to do better than that to get rid of me. "When will he be back?"

"Probably not until spring," the older man said.

The older man's wife had been waiting behind him, but now

she joined his side and the conversation. I half expected the man in the ticket booth to abandon his post and trot out his opinion as well. She said, "You know that man sold his soul to the devil?"

"Come again?" I didn't know if she meant it literally, or if the fact that Mr. Valdana was a necromancer had biased the town against him.

The men nodded. "You don't want anything to do with him if you know what's good for you."

"What's good for us?" Erris repeated. "No, we certainly don't know that. Where does Mr. Valdana live?" he pressed.

The townspeople exchanged looks, as if deciding to wash their hands of our fate. The old woman pointed toward the bald-topped mountain looming north of the train station. "On the shore by the mountain."

"Thank you," Erris said, bowing in a courtly way that left them flustered. "Come on, Nimira."

I was relieved to see him taking charge, but then, finding Mr. Valdana was the only thing he cared about since learning that his sister had been married to the man. Melia's husband was, in a sense, the only tie Erris had to what once had been a boisterous royal family of ten children. Yet, I was terrified that after we met Mr. Valdana and heard the fate of Erris's sister, he would have nothing else to live for.

I didn't delude myself that I might be enough. Never mind that he was all I had too. It had been a long time since I'd had anyone to care for.

Erris carried both our bags to a waiting hack. "We're headed for the shore, by the mountain."

The driver's eyes narrowed. "Mr. Valdana?"

"Yes."

The driver snorted. He could have been a brother to the old man we'd spoken to a moment before; they shared the same large nostrils and jutting chin. "You've got money?"

"Of course." I patted my pocketbook.

When the man pointed his eyes forward again, we took that as permission to board. Erris gave me a hand. He touched me only sparingly now, perhaps ashamed of what he was, and yet every time our skin met, my body betrayed me with tingles.

I settled my skirts as Erris climbed up beside me, the weight of the clockwork skeleton beneath his clothes making the bench groan, but the driver didn't notice.

"You young folks know that Mr. Valdana's sold his soul to the devil, don't you?" he said, snapping the reins.

"Truly?" I asked. "How do you know?"

"His parents were good people," the man continued. "But Valdana was always a strange one. When he came back from New Sweeling after all those years with that half-fairy baby—"

Erris leaned forward. "Baby? Half-fairy baby?"

The driver stiffened and withdrew like a lumbering old tortoise pulling in his shell. "Who are you folks, anyway?" he said. "I'm sure you heard he isn't even home."

"We just want to look at the place," I said. "We heard he's a legendary sorcerer, and we're . . . curious."

"I'm a sorcery student," Erris added. I was glad he had offered a good explanation. Women were not permitted at sorcery schools in Lorinar, so I couldn't think of much reason I would seek out a famous sorcerer myself.

No response from the driver, but I didn't think he believed us. We made such a strange pair I doubted any explanation would legitimize our presence.

I was a little surprised no one recognized us from the papers, for that matter, which showed how far we had traveled. Just a month ago, the story had been on the front page of the *New Sweeling Times*: the lost prince of fairy, Erris Tanharrow, found trapped in the body of a clockwork man, thirty years after the war in which he had disappeared! Here, we were anonymous again, if not unnoticed.

The carriage jolted along the surprisingly well-maintained road, past trees just beginning to turn color. Autumn began early this far north. The cool sea breeze felt pleasant now, but I could tell winter would be long and bitter—already the air whispered a warning of things to come.

We drove through thick forest around the foot of the mountain, turned a corner, and there, visible in the distance where the land jetted toward the sea, was a formidable stone house with red trim around arched windows, giving it a surprisingly fanciful air. I knew it must belong to Mr. Valdana.

"There it is," the driver said.

"I didn't expect it to be so fetching," Erris said, which prompted a sharp grunt from the driver, as if he scolded Erris for appreciating the house of such a man.

There was barely a driveway carved through the trees. Some of the windows were open—a white curtain even fluttered outward from one—but there were no signs of life.

"Shall I wait here while you satisfy your curiosity?" the driver asked.

Erris was already climbing down. "No," he said. "We'll be here a while."

"Mr. Valdana isn't home!" the driver said, sounding almost angry that we would want to spend time there.

"But someone is," Erris said, offering me a hand again.

Curse the electricity of desire that shot from my fingertips to my heart at his touch! My body didn't seem to know that beneath his clothing, Erris was nothing but clockwork.

If that were ever to change, Mr. Valdana was our only hope.

Overgrown grasses brushed my skirts as we approached the door. I put a hand to my hat as a strong wind, scented of the ocean, swept over us, almost roaring as it stirred a million leaves. Erris stopped for a moment and looked around, a strange expression on his face—half wonder and half sadness.

I can't feel the trees anymore, he had said to me, the first day after he had been granted a kind of life again.

He knocked on the door.

We waited long enough that I took a turn knocking. Someone was home, but would they ever answer the door?

"Maybe we should try walking around the back," I was saying, just as the ancient hinges creaked and the great slab of carved wood swung open with a groan.

A girl looked out at us. I couldn't help but notice her scar before anything else—it spread across her cheek, leaving the skin red and mottled, suggesting an accident with a lantern or candle, perhaps.

Without it, she might have been lovely. She was almost as dark as me, with glossy hair the deep brown of pine bark and bold, round eyes. She was tall and slightly plump, in a simple blue dress and apron, no corset.

"Who are you?" she said. She was holding a broom, and I had a feeling she wouldn't hesitate to strike us with it if she felt the need.

"Erris Tanharrow. My sister was Melia Tanharrow." Erris cupped his hands in a fairy gesture I'd seen him make before. It seemed to indicate a plea.

Now the bold fire in the girl's eyes was replaced with something welcoming. The change was startling. She held the door open for us. "Oh, yes. Of course. We had hoped you'd come!"

There was a chill in the dusty room, which had a museum quality to it—the tapestries on the walls were faded; the chairs were ornate and obviously fine, but the fabric seats were frayed. A few newer needlepoint pillows were strewn about and looked quite out of place. There was a sheepskin rug in front of the fireplace and, above it, a painting of a lovely woman carrying a beacon in one hand and a sword in the other. Candles lined the mantel, unlit but dripping with wax.

"The Queen of the Longest Night," I said softly, gazing at the painting. She had been the one to grant Erris life. Necromancers sometimes worshipped her, for she led spirits into the next world.

"Er . . . yes," the girl said. "I'm sorry it's so dusty. I try and keep up with it during the summer while Mr. Valdana is here, but . . ." She shrugged.

I assumed she must be the housekeeper, then, and she appeared to have no help keeping up the house. She looked about my own age.

"Mr. Valdana told me you might come," she continued. "Maybe . . . maybe you can be of some help. I'm Celestina."

"What is it you need help with, Celestina?" Erris asked. "We are actually here to ask for Mr. Valdana's help ourselves."

"Oh, he won't come back until spring, I'm afraid," Celestina said.

"Is there any chance he might?" Erris persisted.

"Or maybe we could go to him," I suggested. "We can't wait until spring."

"I don't know where he's gone," Celestina said. "He travels the world. He might be overseas, he might have crossed the gate into fairy. The northern gate isn't far at all."

Erris frowned. We didn't dare go to the fairy lands just now. Although Erris was the direct heir to the throne, his cousin had ruled for the last thirty years and would not be happy to see Erris.

"You could wait for him to return," Celestina offered.

"All winter?" I already missed Karstor's apartment full of art and books, with fresh baked goods every day.

Celestina paused, wrestling a difficult question, before she said, "I'm taking care of Mr. Valdana's daughter, Violet. She's fifteen, but it's a wonder she's lived this long. She's very ill. Maybe . . . you could help. You're her uncle."

"Erris has a niece? But back in New Sweeling, the sorcerers said all the fairy royals died in the war except for Erris," I said. "If Violet is really his niece, why don't the sorcerers know about her?"

"Violet is protected by an enchantment," Celestina said. "If the two of you were to leave this house, you would forget she existed within hours. If I left, I'd forget her too, although it might take a few days since I spend so much time around her."

"Did Ordorio make that enchantment?" I asked.

"It was the Lady. The Queen of the Longest Night." Celestina shook her head. "I'll explain later, if you decide to stay. And if you don't, you mustn't speak of this anywhere, even if you do remember bits and pieces of it. I'm putting my trust in you because I'm rather at the end of my wits. Please, won't you look at her?"

"Of course," Erris said. "Of course I want to see her anyway. My sister's child . . ."

Celestina led us up a steep and narrow staircase and stopped just before an open door. Her voice dropped. "She's in here."

We followed her into the room. Here was the origin of the white curtains I had seen fluttering out of the open windows, matching the white curtains on the canopy bed. They were tied back, and within the airy cocoon, a girl lay sleeping on the pillows. The moment Erris laid eyes on her, his footsteps quickened to her side.

"Mel . . . ," he said breathlessly. "She's the very picture . . ."

She was like the ailing young women in romantic fiction, with just a thread tethering her to the mortal plane. Her cheeks were flushed, the rest of her pale as could be, long brown hair rippling across her pillows and nightgown. She barely looked fifteen.

Erris put a hand to her forehead. He looked so tender. My heart ached for him to see this girl who apparently looked like his sister and know his sister was gone. But I couldn't help my own heart's aching, thinking how lovely Erris was and how I had saved him, yet he remained elusive. I didn't want to need him. I didn't want to feel selfish and wish I were the one to capture all his attention.

"What is making her sick?" he asked.

"The doctors aren't sure." She looked weary. "She's as bad as I've ever seen her. I've hardly been sleeping for making poultices and giving her medicine and urging her to eat her bread and milk, but if something happened to her, I'd die myself. Mr. Valdana lives to bring her presents and tell her stories." The girl who had been so fierce at the door now slumped against the bedframe, as if she had been strong for a long time and our appearance had finally given her another shoulder to lean on.

I knew how that felt.

"I'm no healer," Erris said. "Even what little magic I had is gone."

Celestina looked at him a moment and then nodded. "Yes, I understand. . . . I just don't know what else to do."

As she spoke, the girl stirred. Her eyes blinked open to Erris standing over her. Suddenly she gasped, sitting bolt upright and coughing. "You—" she started.

Celestina rushed to her side. "Don't overexert yourself."

"Your face, I know it!" Violet said, regaining control. Her voice, though weak, sounded terribly excited. "You look like Mother!"

"I'm her brother," he said.

Violet, moving with unexpected speed, reached out to hug Erris. I could see his reaction before he even thought it through, shoving her down with a strength he still wasn't accustomed to. She fell back on the pillow, looking stunned.

"I'm—I'm sorry," he said. "I didn't mean to—I just don't want to be touched." He was looking at the floor. "I'm not . . . a fairy anymore."

"Don't be sorry!" The girl paused to cough, and then pushed back the covers, reaching for Erris again. He went rigid as she made a second attempt to embrace him. "I've been waiting for you," she said. "Father gets the papers from the city in the summer, so I know all about it, and I hoped you would come."

Just as Erris gingerly reached out to return her embrace, she jerked away, her whole body wracked with coughs. Her face flushed with exertion.

Celestina patted her back. She regained some control, breathing in a strange way, and sank back on the pillows.

Erris looked around the room. "Well, it's obvious what the trouble is. There should be plants here. And flowers. Fairies grow sick without exposure to nature. She should be outside. That will help her heal."

"Mr. Valdana knows she needs plants and trees around her," Celestina said. "But how can we take her outside when it's cold half the year? And what plants could live in her room?"

"When the snow comes, we'll cut boughs from the evergreens," Erris said. "That's what we did back home. And what is she eating? Bread and milk, you say?"

"Yes. Good food. Sausages. Fish stew. We don't have much fresh meat, but we have eggs sometimes."

"Meat should be sparing," Erris said. "She needs food from the forest. And no bread and milk."

"What will she eat, then?" Celestina said, a hint of skepticism creeping in. "What on earth is wrong with meat and bread?"

"Well, we have rules about meat, where I'm from," Erris said. "It has to be hunted in a certain manner that is respectful to the forest and the animal. When I was sick, my mother fed me fresh fruits and vegetables." He sighed. "Knowing Mel, I suppose it's no surprise she didn't think to tell him how to raise a fairy baby in case something happened to her. Planning never was her strong suit."

He suddenly reached for the girl, scooping her up as if she were a little child and gathering up her blankets around her. She wrapped her arms around his neck and settled her head against his chest, where I knew she would hear his clockwork innards ticking.

Celestina glanced at me and followed Erris out. Violet seemed to trust him instantly. She must've been deeply comforted by the familiarity in his face. Indeed, the two of them looked very much alike.

Maybe it would make Erris happy to nurse her back to health. Yet, even if Ordorio knew some way to restore Erris to a real body, where did that leave me? Would Erris be interested in me when his old life returned? If he was to be a fairy king, I was no fairy, and no queen. Just a dancing girl from halfway around the world, with nothing and no one to call my own.

No. I could not pity myself. We had too much to do first.

4

Celestina spread a blanket across the lawn, and Erris laid Violet down upon it. It seemed a very strange introduction to a new house, to have barely exchanged names and proceed to spreading oneself upon the grass, but perhaps fairies did much of their entertaining out-of-doors. Celestina pulled Violet's blankets closer around her body, nodded with satisfaction, and walked away.

"I'm so happy," Violet said breathlessly. "My uncle! You can tell me all about my mother. Father doesn't like to speak of her. She was awfully pretty. I'll be prettier when I'm well." She rattled all this off, oblivious to the increasingly pained look on Erris's face until he waved a hand at her.

"Oh . . . I've said something wrong, haven't I?" She glanced at me.

"We've had a long journey," I said. Even without the thin cheeks and sallow skin, her features reminded me of a little woodland animal's, like a sparrow's or a vole's—cute, perhaps, but not a great beauty.

"Violet, how long have you been sick?" Erris asked.

"Oh, always. Sometimes I feel better in the summer, and then I get sick again."

"Hmm," Erris said. "You must be outside more in the summer."

"I suppose everybody is," Violet said. She didn't sound especially interested in her sickness or the outdoors.

Celestina returned with a plate heaping with moist bread studded with blueberries, and two pillows, which she positioned beneath an oblivious Violet.

"But, Erris—*Uncle* Erris—I want to hear about your adventures. What was it like fighting those sorcerers? What was it like being trapped in clockwork?" Violet reached for a piece of bread, but Erris pulled the plate away.

He handed it back to Celestina. "This isn't good for her, I said. No bread at all."

"What!" Violet cried, her voice hoarse with coughing. "What's wrong with bread? I never heard such a stupid thing!" She started to get up, but Celestina pressed on her shoulder.

I was starting to think Violet was a girl quite used to having her way.

"It looks delicious," said Erris. "But I suppose my mother knew what she was doing, since she brought up ten children to adulthood. She would have said no to that if I was in your condition." He paused, lowering the plate again. "You remind me so much of Mel."

Violet stopped fighting Celestina's grasp at that. "Was Mother much like me at my age?"

"Very." He smiled at her. "She asked impertinent questions to our visitors at court, and my mother finally told her she was not allowed to say a word except 'please' and 'thank you.' "

Celestina started to go again, and I got up to follow her. "Do you need any help?" I asked, ignoring Erris calling after me, and my own horrible thoughts. I couldn't take another moment of him coddling Violet and talking of his sister, but if I told him that, I would seem quite the villain.

"There is always plenty to do, before the snow comes," Celestina said. "Besides, I think we should leave the two of them alone."

I tried not to stare at the scar on her cheek. She didn't seem at all self-conscious, which made it easier. "Yes," I said, trying to sound as if I was happy to leave them alone myself. "It's wonderful that Erris still has family."

Celestina marched along the path, where weeds sprung up between the stones. "Your arrival is all such a surprise." She stopped at a small door at the side of the house, handed me the plate of bread, and took keys from her pocket. But instead of unlocking the door, she met my eyes.

"Will you consider staying the winter?" she asked. "I know the place is a bit run-down, but we have abundant stores of jam and delicious pickles. I make really wonderful pickles. Erris could help Violet so much, I can tell. I hardly know what to do with her."

One would imagine that I was used to abrupt changes of residence. So many times had my life been pulled out from under me, only to be replaced by something vastly different—from my childhood in the royal court of Tiansher, to my uncle's farm, to a cheap dancing show in Lorinar, to Hollin Parry's fine mansion. Now I found myself invited by a stranger to spend a cold winter eating pickles in a lonely house. But it remained as strange a feeling as on the day my father had entered my room and started throwing my clothes into a traveling sack, spitting out three frustrated words: "We're leaving, Nim."

I wanted to tell her that we ought to go back to Karstor's

apartment in New Sweeling, where I could pretend Karstor would take care of everything. But, truthfully, I feared we were in his way. And I knew he couldn't take care of everything.

"We need to see Ordorio, one way or another," I told her. "If you don't know where he's gone, I suppose we will have to wait for him."

She nodded, the slightest smile crossing her lips. "I'll show you what I've put up," she said, unlocking the kitchen door.

When my father lost the family fortune to gambling debt, we had moved to the farm where my uncle grew fat root vegetables, along with a handful of fruit trees, and a few goats for milk and cheese. I had been surprised to see how poor and plain my cousins appeared compared to the children at court. Most of my fine things had been sold, but what was left still made their eyes bug, and I had shown it all proudly. They introduced me to their friends as "Nimira, from the royal palace," their voices full of wonder.

That had lasted less than a week. I was asked to do more and more chores, and I did a poor job of most of them. They laughed when I complained about my dirty hands. They teased me mercilessly when I was afraid to milk a goat. They told all their friends I was snooty and mean, and at night I would cry silently for the dancing and the food and the servants at the royal court, hating the farm, hating my cousins, hating my mother for dying and my father for getting us into this mess.

That was why, when I was thirteen, I jumped at the chance to come to Lorinar, where I thought my singing and dancing would bring me fame and fortune.

There was one matter I had not wanted to admit.

Perhaps I had been a little snooty and mean to scorn hard work. There are things I didn't see at twelve that I understood at seventeen.

I thought of these things, standing in the clean but lived-in kitchen, while Celestina took a match from a tin box and struck it, briefly releasing the stink of sulfur, and touched the match to a candle wick. I followed her down narrow steps to the dark cellar full of jars and crocks and boxes, with apples and pears neatly placed not to touch each other, all the fruits of her summer labors.

For a moment, she stood with a hand to her hip, directing the candlelight across glass jars that gleamed at the attention. "Blueberries, blackberries, raspberries," she said. "We still have more apples to put up, but they're almost there. Not many cherries this year, but peaches, and quince and crabapple jelly."

"Do you do all of this yourself and take care of Violet too?" I hadn't seen evidence of any other servants in the vast house.

She shrugged slightly. "There's Lean Joe. He chops the wood and tends the grounds, and people don't rob the place because he's here, but I don't see much of him. He's the sort of old man who keeps to himself. And we send out the laundry. But people don't want to work for Mr. Valdana. Hence the dust in the parlor."

Finally, I could ask the burning question while remaining prudent. "I noticed he isn't popular in town. Is it because he's a sorcerer?"

"It's not just that," she said. She glanced back at the cellar door and started walking toward the light, as if she did not wish to discuss these things in the darkness. "I was five or six when he came back. They thought, for a long time, that he had died in the fairy war. I remember the stories about how he came home with a baby girl and his wife's body, still looking half dead himself, and how his mother wept that he had come home. She died not long after his return, and that didn't help the rumors either."

My heart began to beat faster. The fairy war. That was where it had all began, where Erris had been turned from flesh and blood to clockwork.

She cut a slab of blueberry bread and offered it to me, then cut another for herself. "He was one of the sorcerers in the fairy war," she said.

"I guess that when he left he didn't trust fairies, like just about anyone else," she continued. "He was such a great sorcerer at such a young age, people thought he would take care of everything." She bit her lip. "That's what my mother used to say. And then, he didn't. He disappeared right in the middle of everything, because he had fallen in love with a fairy princess."

"Oh," I said. "That's very . . . romantic."

Celestina was slightly flushed. "It is, really. But no one around here thought so. I guess they were upset that their great hero fled the scene. They forgave him when they thought he was dead or kidnapped. But when he showed up again, the truth came out. At least a little. They thought he was a traitor."

I wondered how she had come to work here. "You must have been scared of him."

"I was, at first, just because that's how everyone talked! But not anymore. No, when I came to work for him I was very apprehensive, but he's a good man and he never avoided looking me in the face, but he never stared either." She touched the mottled skin. "It was an accident with a lantern when I was fourteen."

She made a little dismissive sniff as if to dispel the heavy mood. "So, it's hard work here, but I'm happy. I have the run of the place, and it's lovely. I'm glad he pays to send the laundry out, of course."

I smiled. "Me too, if I'm to stay until spring."

"So . . . Erris is . . . a clockwork man? What does it mean, exactly?"

"It means that his face and hands look real, but under his

clothes his body is just . . . metal armature." I could never explain without a horrified shiver sliding down my back. I couldn't imagine being in his position. I couldn't imagine what we would do if we couldn't fix it. "Every night the clockwork winds down. And every morning, he must be wound."

She was silent a moment. "The poor man. I don't know how Mr. Valdana could possibly help him, but I hope he can."

Celestina stood and took my empty plate. The bread had been delicious, giving me slight sympathy for Violet's chagrin. "Shall we see how Violet and Erris are doing?" she said, and turned to the kitchen door. The white paint on the doorframe was full of thin scratches, which I guessed came from the gray tomcat sitting contentedly at the window.

We retraced our steps to the lawn. Ahead, Erris stood up and approached us. "I should find food for Violet while the sun is high," he said. "Do you have a basket?"

Celestina ducked back into the kitchen and produced one.

"Violet should stay outside until I return," he said. "Violet, if you get cold, ask Celestina for another blanket. I'll be back."

He smiled at me, and then turned to the woods, without the invitation I was hoping for. He wanted to be alone. I understood that, but it hurt me deeply all the same.

Celestina didn't want to leave Violet outside by herself, and she sat down beside her. I didn't want to listen to the girl prattle about her mother and how pretty she was.

"Do you mind if I explore the grounds?" I asked.

"Not at all," Celestina said. "When Erris returns, I'll show you to the guest rooms."

The forest here felt very old, from the moment I stepped beneath the shade of the trees. The ground was carpeted in leaves and forest debris; I imagined it went down into the earth forever, centuries upon centuries of woods shedding their skin. But I didn't look closely. I was too weary and lonely to look for birds or berries. This ancient place felt indifferent to my pain, which was an odd comfort—as if everything I felt was inconsequential.

I did not roam too far or too deep. I was afraid I might get lost, and besides, I didn't know if there were wild animals here, or suspicious neighbors whose land I might stumble onto. I kept the great stone house in view.

I didn't mean to come upon Erris, but once I spotted him, it felt rude not to greet him. I hoped he didn't think I followed him, as if I needed his company. He was gathering nuts into a basket already full of greens and a few berries.

"I found some mushrooms back there, but they wouldn't tell me if they were poisonous."

I suppressed a smile. "Do mushrooms talk?"

"They don't really talk. You just know. It's very strange now. My connection to everything feels broken. Maybe it's just because I was trapped indoors for so long. Maybe it will come back."

"Yes," I said. But mushrooms never had and never would talk to me.

"Still, it's a good thing I came along," he continued. "Celestina seems nice, but she clearly doesn't know how to take care of a fairy. And Violet is so much like Mel."

"She isn't Mel, though," I pointed out. Perhaps I shouldn't point that out—perhaps he was trying his best to pretend she truly was his sister. But it seemed that thought could lead to nowhere favorable.

"We were all pretty spoiled," he continued, like I hadn't said any-thing. "I know I did a lot of ridiculous things. I was telling Violet how Mel was so fussy about her hair. She used to put it up in pins at night so the front part that fell over her ears would curl. That was how the human girls wore it, and I thought it made her look like one of those dogs with the floppy ears, but she insisted." He made a thoughtful sound, not quite a laugh.

"I wonder how she died," he said. "I didn't want to ask. I guess she made it through the war after all, but . . ."

"Maybe she just got sick," I said.

"Or she was heartbroken," he said. "Because she thought we were all dead."

"She had Ordorio."

"Yes, but . . ."

"But I guess that's not enough if her family was all dead," I said, losing my grip on my emotions. "I'm sure your family was wonderful . . . and you sound like you were all very close and happy . . . and I guess nothing will ever be enough now that they're gone. I can never . . ." *Be enough.* I couldn't finish. It was too hard to say. I could never be enough. I could never be enough.

"No, it's not that," he began, but I could tell he was only saying it because I was starting to cry. I bit my lip hard and shook my head quickly.

"I'm sorry, Nim," Erris said. "I don't mean to imply . . . It's just . . . I never even knew my family had died until I woke up as an autom-aton and all those years had passed. Well, maybe I knew in a deep-down way, the same way I knew time had passed, but . . . it's not the same. And thinking about Mel . . . going on without me . . . growing older than me . . . having a child, even . . ." He was getting that haunted look in his eyes again, the same one he so often had when I woke him.

"Never mind," I said. "It's all right. I understand. Please. Let's just let it go right now." My pride summoned a faint smile. "I'll meet you back at the house."

Erris returned with greens overflowing from his basket. Celestina showed him to the kitchen to help prepare Violet's dinner and took me upstairs to see the bedrooms.

She apologized that she had not aired them out. The room she offered did smell musty, but I assured her, quite honestly, that it was nice just to have a cozy room, with a canopy bed and clean linens. I didn't say it aloud, but it was also nice to be in a house that didn't feel so heavy with secrets and sorrow. There was a touch of it here, but nothing like Hollin Parry's mansion, where I had lived before Karstor's—where I had met Erris.

"Do you need anything else, Nimira?"

"Well . . . if you have pen and paper, I'd very much like to write letters to let our friends know we've safely arrived."

She nodded. "Just don't mention Violet. We try to avoid much in the way of paper records of her."

"Why is she such a secret?" I had little patience with secrets and vague excuses these days.

"Without the enchantment, Mr. Valdana says she would surely be killed by humans or fairies who fear the restoration of the house of Tanharrow. Or, on the other hand, taken by the fairies who want to restore the house of Tanharrow. He just wants a normal life for her, at least until she comes of age."

"Normal? But does she have any friends?"

Celestina looked solemn. "No, no friends. It would do her good, but circumstances just don't allow for it."

"No friends, no mother, and her father is gone from fall to spring?"

"He has to travel, to serve the Lady. In exchange for the powerful magic that protects Violet." Celestina raised her brows. "The long and short of it is, be very glad that you're not a fairy princess."

"Well, I promise not to mention her in my letters."

I wrote Karstor first. I missed him, although I didn't feel like I knew him well enough to admit it. I suspected it was really my father I missed, but my father felt so lost to me that it was easier to miss Karstor. And Karstor had always seemed so sad. During the day, he made little jokes and went to work for long hours as the new ambassador of magic, but sometimes I found him sitting in a dark room staring off into space, and once I had heard him weeping very softly, just for a moment, but long enough that I couldn't sleep for thinking about it. I had never imagined that powerful men shed tears. I thought of all this, but I kept the note short and friendly. I hoped it would bring a spot of cheer to his day.

Next I wrote Hollin's wife, Annalie, and her ladies' maid, Linza. Annalie was cursed, pained by the touch of light on her skin, but she seemed content enough to spend her days in a dimly lit room, speaking to spirits and writing. Her life should have been tragic, and yet she didn't seem to need anyone, as if she were halfway to dwelling in the spirit world herself. It was difficult to think what to say to a woman like that. Linza was easier to talk to in person, but her lack of education showed when it came to letters. Still, they should know we had safely arrived.

I wanted to write Hollin, but wasn't sure if he had moved on. Hopefully his travels abroad were all that he hoped for, even if the circumstances weren't quite what he wished.

Hollin. I didn't want to miss him. He had committed so many wrongs—from wooing me while he already had Annalie hidden away, to his inability to stand up to Smollings until the very last moment. It was Erris I loved—or tried to love, if he would have me—but it was Hollin whom I best understood. Hollin had told me once how he had been close to his mother and his uncle Simalt, who had traveled the world. Both had died, like my mother, and I don't think either of us had known what it was to be cared for ever since.

I had finished my letters and was sitting quietly, brooding upon unpleasant matters, when Celestina told me dinner was ready.

In Hollin's house, I had changed clothes for dinner like a lady, but no one seemed to expect it here. Celestina wore her stained apron, and my clothes bore the grime and scent of travel. A man sat at the table who I knew must be Lean Joe, not just through logic but because he was indeed very lean and weather-beaten, with a nick in his ear like a stray cat. He squinted at me, not with hostility, but curiosity. He had probably never seen a girl from Tiansher before. I was equally surprised to be eating with the help, but it seemed to be the way of things here. I suppose with Ordorio gone, they kept Violet company.

Violet sat at the head of the table, clad in a thick robe that must have belonged to her father, arms crossed around the turned-up sleeves, and wearing the pout that sat so comfortably on her lips.

Erris burst in from the kitchen with a plate of finely chopped greens, nuts, and apples, all raw and lightly dressed in vinegar.

Violet took one look at it and shoved the plate away from her so it crashed into the butter dish. "I won't eat that. It looks disgusting! It looks like food people would eat if they were lost in the forest and starving to death!"

"It's the kind of food we ate all day while we were out playing as children," Erris said, sounding almost delighted at her protests. "Your mother and me and all the rest of us. *We* didn't even have vinegar to make it exciting. And you will eat every bite of it before you have any sausage."

"No!" she cried. "I thought you were going to be nice! Father would never make me eat something I hated. How could anyone think vinegar was exciting? Celestina, this is unfair."

"Don't you want to get well?" Celestina said in a rather automatic tone.

"These plants are fresh from the forest," Erris said. "They are full of good things for animals and people."

"You're talking like I'm a child!"

"Well, I promise to stop if you give that poor salad a chance," Erris said. "I don't need to be a doctor to know that the human world is making you sick."

"It's not! And I'm half-human!" Violet obviously realized she wasn't going to win. She stood up, shoved her chair over so that it hit the floor with a bang, and stormed off, with one last shout at Lean Joe, who started laughing heartily.

Once she had left, we could hear her coughing all the way down the hall.

"I hope she doesn't hurt herself, with all this commotion," Celestina said, poking a sausage with her fork.

"She won't," Erris said. "Anyway, once she's calmed down, I'll bring her an apple." He looked at the salad hungrily. "If any of the rest of you would like some . . . I don't think it will keep long."

"It might keep through tomorrow," Celestina said. But she took a little, obviously out of guilt. Erris couldn't eat, and it was strange to eat piles of sausage and potatoes smothered with gravy while he had no plate or even a cup. The desire for food was constant in his eyes whenever I ate anything, even the stale roll I packed for the train.

"Why aren't you eating it?" Lean Joe asked.

"I'm not sure you'll want to know," Erris said. "I must apologize in advance for being so unnerving."

Lean Joe scoffed. "Unnerving? Why, I've been to prison. Not much you can say to unnerve me anymore, especially something that starts with eating rabbit food. There's men in there that would eat a lot worse."

"Like what?" Erris asked, but I kicked his leg.

Celestina started laughing. "Joe, at least give them a day before you tell those stories!"

"You can laugh, but there was a cannibal in that prison!"

"He never saw cannibals," Celestina said. "He was in prison for conning people out of their money selling fake medicine. They don't put murderers in the same place. And he's reformed now, aren't you?"

Joe nodded solemnly. "That's right, I've had my fun. I'm no fool. Best to shape up before you're dead."

"This house isn't much like Hollin's, that's for sure," I told Erris after dinner as we strolled the house. Celestina had encouraged us to explore while she attempted to coax Violet into eating the salad. I had shown Erris our guest rooms, and we roamed from there. I was happy to have him to myself again.

"I never did see Hollin's house, but I can imagine his gardener wasn't a con man."

"No. It was much more proper. Although, I think I like this place better."

Once, I might have called Ordorio's house gloomy. We poked our noses into portrait galleries lined with people frowning out from cracked paint and heavy wooden frames. And perhaps the tapestries had once been vibrant and beautiful, but now they were faded, slowly disintegrating on the walls. I suspected most of the furniture had been built by people wearing starched ruffs, who did not want their descendants to be any more comfortable than they were.

Nevertheless, there was a difference between a house full of mold and uncomfortable furniture and a beautiful house where sad secrets permeated the very walls. The absence of taxidermy was a comfort, and I saw very little evidence of sorcery. Ordorio probably had a library somewhere where he kept his books and artifacts, but it wasn't spilling all over the house like a warning that someone dangerous dwelt here.

"More paintings!" Erris said with dismay, pushing open the next door. "Were his parents art collectors?"

"With rather poor taste," I said. The men had beady black eyes and fiercely pointed beards, and the women fared no better; unnaturally rosy cheeks and huge bosoms seemed the fashion.

"They must have brought them over from the Old World," Erris said. "These are no doubt heirlooms, but nevertheless I feel sorry for him if these are his ancestors. And I'm not looking for paintings."

I would have been happy to stroll the moldy old portrait gallery with Erris, making jokes about the antique faces, laughing in the intimacy of shadows. "What are you looking for, then?"

"A piano, of course."

"Did you ask Celestina if there is one?"

"No, I like the hunt. I wonder what's up these stairs?"

I hoisted the lantern. "Let's see."

Erris followed, briefly grabbing my elbow with a steady hand when I stumbled on a crooked step. "I feel like a bandit, snooping around without anyone who lives here," he said.

"I'm glad we can snoop. Clearly, there's nothing to hide around here." In Hollin's house, I had found Annalie's hidden quarters on the third floor.

But most of the doors on the third floor here were locked. I rattled them all stubbornly, trying to force them open, until Erris pulled me away. "These are probably Ordorio's quarters. I'll bet he locks them to keep Violet from poking around with magic. I wouldn't worry about it. Although, if *his* wife is secretly alive up here . . . well, I could only wish." He motioned me back toward the staircase.

Not long after, we found the piano. It was not far from the dining room; we had just ventured in the wrong direction. Music has an uncanny ability to chase away misery, at least for a time.

"It's in tune too," Erris said. "Whoever Ordorio is, I could kiss him."

"That wouldn't be fair. You haven't even kissed me yet."

He smiled slightly, which wasn't really the response I yearned for, and left me feeling silly for attempting flirtation.

He played a few notes. "How about it, Nim? 'In Springtime Blooms the Rose'?"

I laughed. "Anything but that!" That had been one of the only songs he could play when he was stiff clockwork trapped at a piano, and it was hardly cheerful under any circumstance, about a man who goes to war, leaves his love behind, and never returns.

"I should learn to play the songs that you know from your home," Erris said.

"It seems we have all winter. I can teach some of them to you."

He played a soft little tune, his long fingers light across the keys. I sat on the edge of the piano bench, like I used to when he was trapped. I loved to watch his hands move freely.

We had fallen in love without being able to say much to each other. I think it was still hard for him to say the things in his heart. Jokes came easier. But he could speak through the piano, even now. His song remained slow, and it grew more melancholy. It could be that I ascribed things to the music that he didn't mean, but I didn't think so. I heard his regret that things had gone this way for him and for us. I heard him miss his family. I heard his desperation and his fear.

If he would share all of this with me, it couldn't be hopeless for us. Not quite.

He began to sing quietly in another language, the foreign syllables rolling soft from his tongue. The notes sounded like winter, beautiful but cold. And then he sang,

When winter comes, birds fly home
When winter comes, birds fly home
The soil sleeps
The spirit rests
When winter comes,
The birds go to their nests
And we fly home
To those who we love best.

He stopped. "I'm winding down," he said. "Time for bed."

We stood. "Good night."

He left without waiting for me, without lantern light. I did not go to bed right away, but sat at the piano for long moments, my mind full of equal parts waking dreams and nightmares.

I woke to a foggy morning, with the tops of evergreens just piercing the gray blanket out my window. It felt more cozy than gloomy. I exchanged my nightgown for a dress from my trunk and went to wake Erris, key in hand.

But when I walked into his room, Violet was there breathing raggedly over Erris's body. She snatched her hands to herself like I had just caught her at something.

"What are you doing here?" I demanded.

"I wanted to see you wind him." Violet pulled her oversize robe closer around her neck. The collar touched her cheeks. "He *is* my uncle. You don't have to snap."

"What makes you think he would want you to see him wound?" I said sternly. "He wishes no one had to wind him at all. The least you could do is ask him first!" I was ashamed for Erris, and perhaps in some way, ashamed for myself. I never forgot that I was the one who had done this to him. My anger overflowed, but a wave of sense rushed in behind and stayed my hand.

She seemed taken aback by my emotion. "I don't see what the trouble is," she said, sounding haughty but still hesitating.

"Because," I said, "how would you like it if you couldn't wake up in the morning until someone wound you? How would you like it if beneath your clothes, you weren't flesh and blood? Would you want people to know, and look at you? Would you feel like yourself?"

She glanced quickly at the keyhole in Erris's back, and her lips pinched in. She tossed her head and left the room at a hurried shuffle. She ought not to even be out of bed, I thought. But if she wanted to constantly endanger herself, well, I didn't care.

I frowned. It was true—no one would care if she endangered herself except her absent father. She likely never left this house, and never had visitors. Violet was as much a secret as Annalie had been, except she had no spirits to keep her company.

Well . . . that wasn't my affair either.

I found Celestina in the kitchens, wearing a linen shirt, men's trousers, and boots, which she nearly jumped out of when I said good morning.

"My goodness. You scared me. I'm not fit for company yet."

I smiled. "I don't care. Where I'm from, girls, even queens, wear trousers. Of course, they're more likely to be made from colorful silk than brown wool, but either way, I don't care if you dress like that all day."

"Really?" Celestina flipped her frying bacon. "Because, when Mr. Valdana's gone, this is exactly what I do wear all day. You know how long it took me to come to the door when you first knocked? It's because I was scrambling into a dress." She laughed.

I laughed too. "I wonder if fairy women ever wear trousers." I adored my fine clothes, the dresses made of silk and good wool Hollin had bought me, but sometimes I dearly missed having a good *lounge*. You couldn't lounge with a corset around your ribs and a collar around your neck, and it seemed that the lower the neckline of a Lorinarian gown dipped, the smaller the waistline became, so any comfort you may have gained was lost.

Erris walked in a moment later, moaning at the aroma. "Must you make things that smell all the way from my bedroom?"

"What do you think of trousers?" I said, changing the subject before Erris's teasing tone turned into melancholy.

"Trousers?"

"Did fairy women ever wear them?"

"Not often," Erris said. "Fairies are vain and prefer looking fancy, but we don't have such moral ideas about clothes as humans do, so I wouldn't be offended."

"In that case," Celestina said, "I will continue to practice shocking behaviors."

After breakfast, Erris went out for more foraging. Outside, the morning fog had vanished from the lawn, but it still swathed the bottom half of the trees, and I peered through the curtains as he vanished into it.

Celestina came back down from bringing Violet breakfast, scooping the cat up from the rag rug so his limbs dangled from her arm while she scratched his round cheeks. "Would you like me to measure you and make you some trousers?"

I laughed again. "Oh, I couldn't *really* . . ." I hesitated. There was no logical reason I shouldn't wear whatever I liked out here. The rules of Lorinarian society had clearly seeped into me almost unnoticed, like a disease.

"You might as well," Celestina said. "When winter comes, and there is work to do, it's so much easier."

I suppressed a bristle that she assumed I would do work during the winter. It stirred bad memories of the farm. But I was going to be more useful here. I wouldn't be complaining about every little thing like Violet.

Celestina motioned me from the kitchen. "Come on."

I followed her to a small room, feminine, but not overly so, with a sewing machine and a trunk spilling fabrics by the window. A bird perched on the branch of an apple tree outside the window but flew away when we drew near. Celestina whistled at it, almost absently, but it didn't come back. In the corner was a heavy wooden chair with plush green padding, facing a card game that seemed long abandoned—in fact, a few cards lay scattered on the floor now, and Celestina stooped to pick them up. A guitar leaned against the wall by the chair.

"Who plays the guitar?" I asked.

"Oh, I do, a little bit." She shuffled through a mess on the table by the sewing machine to find her measuring tape. "It belonged to my brother. And before that, my great-uncle. My brother left it behind when he went to the city, 'seeking his fortune,' which apparently meant a job at the slaughterhouse." She made a face, then unfurled a measuring tape between her hands and measured my inseam in a casual way, through my skirt. Precise measurements of these trousers didn't seem terribly important. "What's your waist measurement without your corset, would you say?"

"Twenty-two inches?"

"You tiny thing!" She scribbled down her numbers. "We'll make it twenty-three. You'll get fat with all the pie." She pulled some coarse brown wool from the middle of the pile of cloth spilling from the trunk.

Determined to be helpful, I asked if there was anything I could do while she started to measure fabric. I couldn't make clothes, but I could mend and sew buttons, and so she gave me one of Violet's dresses with a hole under the arm, followed by a shirt with two buttons gone.

"We should probably go into town soon," Celestina said, an unvoiced sigh hovering around her words. "I need some supplies anyway, but especially with two winter guests."

"I don't think the locals thought much of us," I said. An understatement.

"No, well, they don't think much of anyone who knows Mr. Valdana." She was facing the window, but I saw her shoulders tense. "I used to belong there, and now I don't like to go to market or anywhere. They really aren't bad people at heart . . . but they don't think beyond this village. Or at least the district."

"Are your parents still living?"

"Yes. My parents and two younger sisters and two younger brothers. And my older brother who works at the slaughterhouse. All still living. I don't see them much. They wish I had stayed home. I could care for them in their old age, I suppose." She snorted.

"Will you marry?" I was being more forward with her than I had been with another girl in a long time. But then, few girls were so immediately open with me. "Surely some young man would appreciate your pickles."

She laughed. "No, no, no. He must like me for more than my pickles! Oh, come to town with me and just see if there's a boy I would look twice at even if he would look twice at me. A lot of young men have been leaving, anyway, ever since they extended the train line. It became rather a highway to temptation, I suppose. The old men are forever grousing about it."

We both stopped at the sound of soft footsteps on the hall rug. Violet appeared, looking pale and peevish, swathed in a shawl atop her nightgown, skinny legs in whimsically striped socks.

"Get back in bed!" Celestina said. "You can't always be getting out of bed and wandering the house."

"Shouldn't I be out of doors like Erris said?"

"We'll wait until he gets back. It seems chilly to me, but we'll see. I can't go right now." Celestina talked to Violet like she was still a child.

And Violet responded accordingly. "Well, I want something to eat. I'm hungry. That nasty salad stuff isn't any good. I want blueberry bread."

"Erris said you can't have any."

"What does he know?"

"You must think he knows something if you want to go outside," Celestina said, with a tone of someone who has easily bested her opponent. "Anyway, he's a fairy and your mother's brother. Don't you think we should trust him? So go back to bed and when he returns, we'll see."

Violet's lips compressed and her pale face turned red rather abruptly. Her eyes cut to me, her rage plain, as if I had anything to do with it. I kept my face blank, and she turned with a toss of her hair. I felt I had been involved in some argument I did not clearly understand.

Neither of us spoke until the sound of Violet's footsteps had shrunk into nothing.

"I'm sorry about her manners," Celestina said.

Celestina didn't like Violet either, I realized. She had been so solicitous to her, I had assumed her to be the sort of person who lives to care for others, but it was an incorrect assumption. I could see now that Celestina loved something here, the house and maybe even the romance of working for a man the villagers regarded as dangerous, but whatever the appeal was, it wasn't Violet.

"Mr. Valdana is a wise sorcerer in many matters," Celestina said, "but he's blind to her. You should see the instructions he always leaves. 'Buy her oranges. Read to her at night. Help her wash up.' He seems to think her constant sicknesses have denied her so many things that he can't possibly deny her anything."

"But how can she grow up if he spoils her like a child?"

"I guess he thinks that will come when she is of age. *If* she comes of age."

"What does Ordorio intend for her, eventually? She's fifteen. I mean, most girls are beginning to be courted by then, aren't they?"

"He's mentioned that she might be able to return to the fairy kingdom and perhaps become queen, but not until she's grown."

"She can't be a good queen if she can't do anything for herself," I said.

"Maybe not a good queen," Celestina said. "But certainly she wouldn't be the first pampered and sheltered queen in the world. Perhaps it won't matter, now that Erris is here."

Yes. Erris might be the one to inherit the throne and all its troubles. I was not sure if this thought was especially comforting either. I changed the subject to music until the noise of the sewing machine forced us into silence.

By lunchtime, Celestina was handing me a simple pair of newly made trousers and one of her own shirts. I slipped up to my room to change, a flush on my cheeks, as if I were still in Hollin Parry's house and any moment he would turn the corner and say that I was a lady and should have fine things.

And I loved fine things, it was true. Since I was a girl, I had been attracted to a flash of gold or the shimmer of silk. Clothes do not change a person's appearance only, but their feelings as well. Now I changed from well-to-do girl of Lorinar in a fine full skirt and puffed sleeves, with my hair swept over my ears and demurely pinned, to a creature of the forest, camouflaged in cream and brown, rough and quick and ready. I looked ridiculous now with my hair neat and ladylike. I pulled out the pins and let it tumble down. The girl who looked out at me from the mirror was no longer a shadow of my mother or a foreign girl pretending to be a lady of Lorinar. She was wild. She was strange.

There was something about her I rather liked.

I plaited my hair, for the hair of a wild girl would quickly get knots and fall into her food, and went down for lunch.

7

After lunchtime, Erris still hadn't returned from foraging, so I set out to find him somewhere in what Celestina said was a hundred acres of forest and rocky shoreline.

The fog had vanished; the sun shone at last on trees just beginning their autumn transformation. It was not only that the day looked bright; it *felt* bright, sweeping into my lungs, scented by ocean, filling me with strange vigor. I started running just to feel my legs and heart pumping and my braids flying. I leaped over a fallen tree trunk, fleet as a deer, and then I stopped, gasping for breath. I wanted to feel like a child again, but my body seemed shocked by it; it had grown used to stately movement and stuffy rooms. Even dancing was something I rarely did anymore.

I recalled playing in the gardens as a girl, ducking under bushes, seeking hidden places. I remembered clambering up mountain paths and slipping off my shoes to cross the wide but shallow river near Shala, where the court went in summer. When had my limbs grown long and stiff and unable to slip under and over and through? My heart was pounding in my chest still. I didn't want to feel as tired and grown-up as I did.

My steps tugged me toward the shore. I crossed a plank thrown across a trickle of river and passed through a grassy patch that had been cleared of trees once, and where only bushes grew now. The trees turned to dwarves near the shore, and then the sky opened completely, a bowl of blue above the deeper shade of the sea.

Erris didn't hear me approach over the pounding waves. And for another moment, I let him be alone. I was alone too; we were alone together with the waves beating stronger than my heart. I had crossed the ocean, I realized, but I had never seen the shore. I had only come on and off of ships.

I made my way across sun-warmed rocks that separated the stubby trees from a slick world of tide pools and algae. Erris had a basket at his side, with seaweed and shells, but he was very still, looking out at the islands that rose from the water like giant turtles sunning themselves, carrying tiny forests on their backs.

"Erris?" I finally said.

He rose and turned in one motion. "Oh . . . it's you, Nim."

"Who else would it be?"

He shrugged a shoulder, then grinned. "I see Celestina dressed you up."

"Do I look terribly silly? Like a little boy?"

"Never like a little boy. No, not at all. You look naughty. Like a runaway." He walked near enough to touch me.

"I suppose I *am* a bit of a runaway," I said, looking at his hands. I wanted to touch them. I knew they would feel warm and alive. I didn't care if it was all an illusion. "I wouldn't be here if I hadn't run away from home."

"But you won't run away anymore?" he said casually, now look-ing at my hands. I wondered if it was something he truly worried about.

"You don't think I would abandon you, do you?" I answered.

"I wish I could abandon myself," he said, and suddenly we weren't casual at all. "Do you really think there could be a good outcome to any of this?"

"Well, yes. I mean, Annalie told us to come here."

"The spirits told her to tell us to come here. Who knows about spirits. What if that spirit was my sister? What if Annalie misunder-stood? Maybe I'm just supposed to help Violet."

"You don't think you're here to help yourself at all?" That was, admittedly, a bit of a horrifying thought.

"I have to be realistic. If I start hoping to have my real life back, I think I'll break down entirely. Hope is painful. I waited all those years to be freed from clockwork, and I don't think I can wait anymore. I can't imagine that my body is still alive some-where. This is it. This is all I've got, Nim. I've got to deal with that."

"So, you're just giving up?"

"I'm trying not to give up," he said. The cries of seagulls around us seemed to echo the desperation inching into his voice. "I'm try-ing to find some purpose, some rhyme or reason for what hap-pened to me. If I'm here to help my sister's child, then that is something I can do even as I am."

I wrapped my arms around myself. "Where does that leave me? I can't just . . . go back to dancing in penny music halls."

"I told you I love you," he said, putting his firm hand atop mine. "And I meant it." He started again. "But a clockwork man obviously can't marry. I know we'd prefer . . . I mean, in different circum-stances I would certainly court you, Nim." His eyes traveled along my boyish garb, the braids that draped across my chest, to my face, and then the back of his hand moved to my cheek. My hands fell away, and my breath came quick as he let his fingers slide down my neck, and now they hovered there, and I could hardly bear it. I wanted so much for him to be real flesh and blood. I wanted so much to pull him closer.

Abruptly, he shut his eyes, and his hand drew back a moment later. "I can't stand it. When I think about all the little flirtations and kisses with girls back home, and this is the first time I've felt like it actually meant something, and I can't do anything about it."

I put my hands over his now. "I still think you're giving up too soon on the idea that you might live again."

"Stop!" He was suddenly ferocious. "Please stop. Do you honestly think there is a chance the human sorcerers that enslaved me actually saved my body? That they've been keeping me preserved and no one knows about it? I've gone over every possible circumstance, and I can't imagine any in which that would be the case."

I was left briefly speechless. "But why did they save your soul at all? Do we understand any of this? Why make an assumption?"

"I told you. Hope is painful. I want to be myself again, or as close to myself as I can manage, and I can't do that if I'm thinking I might get my real self back. I have to be myself like this. I have to try. Otherwise I can't bear it. Does that . . . make any sense?"

I was afraid that everything he said both made sense and did not make sense at the same time. I could imagine his plight—and often did—but I would never have to live it. Maybe I could never understand the weight of it. Maybe I didn't want to.

"It does." The fresh sea air blowing across my face somehow helped keep away the tears.

He put his hands to my cheeks, cupping my face, looking

tender and sad. I wanted to return the touch, but of course, he didn't want to be touched. I closed my eyes and took a deep breath.

His hands lowered. My eyes opened. He smiled a bit.

"I'll walk back with you," he said.

Even now, I hoped he would take my hand, and when he didn't, I felt my empty hand as if it were missing a finger. But the day was lovely, and Erris pointed out the bright rowan berries and a whistling bluebird perched in a tree. He was trying so hard to cheer me, so I made an attempt to smile.

"I've been thinking about my magic," he said. "I wonder if it's gone only because I've been cooped up for so long."

"Do you think it could come back?"

"Well, does magic come from the body or the soul?"

"The soul, I would think," I said. "Only, the body must have something to do with it or fairies and humans would have the same magic, wouldn't they?"

"But are our souls fairy or human or . . . just spirit?"

I laughed. "Too philosophical. I don't know. But if you're asking whether or not your magic will come back, I say it will."

"You are an optimist," he said. "I didn't take you for one at first, but . . ."

"I would have had to be an optimist to have tried to free you in the first place, wouldn't I?"

He smiled. "I think I feel the magic stirring in me again."

"And we only arrived yesterday," I said. "You have all winter to get it back."

SOMEWHERE IN THE FAIRY KINGDOM

At first Ifra was timid as he traveled the fairy lands to find Erris. He peered in the windows of cottages at night, drawn by the warmth of hearth and life he could sense from miles away. He watched a mother nurse her baby, running her hand over the small head. He watched a father reading to his daughters. He saw a man sleeping by the faint glow of a banked fire, his arm slung affectionately over his dog.

Ifra had been raised by his tutor—a free jinn—along with five other jinn children whose parents were still enslaved. Free jinn always helped enslaved jinn, but his tutor was not affectionate. Like many free jinn, he believed the only way to truly find happiness was to maintain no worldly attachment to anyone or anything, and to prepare for a life of servitude. Ifra and the other children were sent many miles away during the growing season to work on neighboring farms, with no compensation besides food and shelter.

But the farmers Ifra boarded with were kind to him—so kind

that he had to hide it from his tutor, or Ifra knew he wouldn't be sent there again. Arkat and Hami had no children, and every year they looked forward to having him, treating him like a son. Hami told Ifra stories while her calloused hands ground seeds with her mortar and pestle. Arkat let Ifra name one of the horses and call it his own. He had learned to love and trust and miss them, just as he was *not* supposed to do. The growing season was a golden time; the colder months a shadow, where play was discouraged, and education only allowed to further one's spiritual growth and to cultivate one's sense of detachment. They lived in a rocky, barren valley surrounded by mountains on which nothing grew but scrub. Winters were harsh and food was meager, but jinn could go for a week without any food at all.

Ifra had never seen country like this—lush forest turning the colors of flame; lakes too wide to see across; deer and little striped rodents and sly-faced red foxes with slender black limbs. Ifra could feel the harmony of so much life packed together, and he longed to be a part of it and not just an observer, so he stopped peering in windows and began to knock on doors and ask for a place to sleep.

One late afternoon, he led his horse to a log house. A little girl sat in the doorway, shelling nuts, and he sensed two more inside. The girl called into the house as soon as she spotted him; a woman joined her, her dark red curls like a reflection of the autumn leaves all around them. Her mouth was set, her eyes staring, as she took in the sight of him and the horse. Luka had given Ifra one of the beautiful white fairy horses, so different from Ifra's stocky brown horse back home. But any horse Ifra rode could go for days without food or water.

Ifra lifted his empty hands in greeting. "Good evening. I'm passing by on a mission for King Luka, and—"

"We have no room. There's another house, down the road, three miles."

Ifra wondered if she was a supporter of Erris Tanharrow. Everyone else had freely opened their doors when he mentioned the king.

He was honest with her. She wouldn't remember him anyway. "Please. I'm a jinn. I'm merely a servant, not a supporter."

"A jinn? King Luka has a jinn?"

"That would be me. Yes."

"Come in," the woman said, looking grim. He slid off the horse and patted its side. *Don't stray far.*

The cabin had one room, warmed by a brick stove with a little opening like a mouth. Another woman, this one dark-haired and willowy, was slicing onions and tossing them into an iron pot, but she paused to look at Ifra with suspicion. The little girl went to her side wordlessly and left the shelled nuts on the table by the onions. Ifra looked around at the neatly made bed, the table and chairs, the kitchen tools, and the rafters painted with trees, birds, and snakes—not unlike the designs embroidered on the women's bodices—and felt like an intruder.

The red-haired woman spoke into the ear of the dark-haired one.

"How did he manage to find a jinn?" the dark-haired one said. "His circle must be more loyal than we supposed— Sery, don't touch those now, they're for the stew." The woman was cutting the shelled nuts in half as she spoke, staying the girl's hand when she reached for a potato.

"Remember how he sent his sons off to bring him gifts?"

"Oh . . . do you think . . . ?"

They spoke as if he were not even present, or as if he were not a person—the same way all people treated jinn, as he had quickly discovered with the handful of masters he had served thus far. A more experienced jinn would take no interest in the situation around him, would have no care for these women, or King Luka, or Erris Tanharrow. But Ifra hated to think he would become like that.

"You're correct," Ifra said. "The king's son Belin found my lamp."

The women turned their attention back to him, a little nervously. He supposed he must seem very foreign in their small cottage, with his gold cuffs and earrings, the woven sash belting his tunic and leather boots of home, the straight black hair that fell halfway down his back, caught with a leather tie.

"Can you tell me anything about King Luka?" Ifra asked. "And Erris Tanharrow? I must do the king's bidding, but nevertheless there are things I can do to shape circumstances . . . if I understood them better."

The women shared a glance, and the dark-haired one shrugged a little. "The Tanharrow family has ruled the fairy throne for centuries, through many wars with the humans. The city folk have always been different, with their glamours and feasts and fancy things, but they took care of us. If there was a long winter, we could go to the capital and ask for magic to help our patch of the forest survive, and if the humans came onto our territory, they'd send a patrol."

The red-haired women nodded. "We're supposed to trust our king. It's said that as long as trees grow in the Hall of Oak and Ash, all is well. The wisdom of the trees is supposed to reflect upon our ruler. But . . ."

"I don't understand what King Luka is trying to do with the humans," the dark-haired one said. "After the last war, he gave the humans far too much leeway. Any fool could have told him they'd take advantage, and now he wants to go to war with them again. Disaster all around, and he brought it upon himself."

"King Luka says there won't be peace until he's wiped the humans off the continent," Ifra said.

"Or they destroy us!" the red-haired woman cried out. "That's how it will go, if we pursue war!" The little girl's eyes widened. Alarm crossed the woman's flushed face. "I've said too much."

"I'm not going to report any of this back to him," Ifra said. *Unless he asks . . . I can't really lie to him.* But hopefully Luka would have no reason to ask. "I'm very grateful for your hospitality." He bowed to them. "My name is Ifra, by the way."

"Keyelle," said the red-haired woman.

"I'm Etana. And this is my little one, Sery. Keyelle's brother was my partner, but we had a dispute about this very thing. He supports King Luka."

She frowned and turned to the shelf that held the kitchen implements, wooden bowls, and plates, and began setting the table. She looked cross, probably at herself, for speaking freely to someone she didn't know.

"King Luka is ill, you know," Ifra said.

"Ill?" Keyelle looked skeptical. "I haven't heard."

Ifra knew he shouldn't speak freely with her either, but he wanted to gain her trust and as much information as he could. But more than that, he simply wanted someone to talk to. The isolation of a jinn's life was hard to bear. He told them everything he had seen in the capital—the way Luka looked beneath his glamour, his sons, Luka's coy answer about what he would do with Erris once he found him. The women listened, obviously rapt, but all the while they worked in silent harmony—cleaning, moving, arranging, stirring—preparing for dinner, answering a question Sery whispered in their ears.

Ifra soaked in the warmth of the place, hoping he could store the feeling. When the stew was done, Etana brought it to the table. Sery settled into her chair, holding on her lap a doll made of cloth scraps and buttons. Keyelle poured hot water into a teapot, stirring up a memory of Hami's coffeepot.

"You look sad, Ifra," Etana said, sitting across from him.

"I'm fine."

Etana smiled faintly. "That's what I say when I'm not fine at all." She hesitated. "If you don't mind me asking . . . I know jinn aren't supposed to age, but are you as young as you look?"

"We do age," he replied. "And yes. I am as young as I look. We only age while we're actively granting wishes. Our bodies might live a very long while, but we will only experience a normal life span."

"In captivity?"

"Well, we hope to die free. If we're lucky."

"I don't know much about jinn," Keyelle said. "Do you have parents?"

"Of course."

"And where do they live?"

"My mother is a servant in a wealthy man's house."

"Is she free?"

"No. The wealthy man is my father." He didn't talk about this much. "I wasn't raised by her, of course. Free jinn always take in young jinn whose parents aren't free. But she wrote me many letters." He realized how strange this must all sound to a family like this, where children never had to be taken from their parents. "There are a lot of myths about jinn. It's part of the magic—once people make wishes, they forget what they wished and how it worked. It would be chaos if people were too informed. Not that we're capable of some of the great feats we've been credited with in tales either. We can only manipulate the world as it is. We can't remake it."

"But you can find the missing fairy prince?"

"I can, although he does have a confusing spirit. King Luka told me his spirit is trapped in a clockwork body, and I can pick up the trail of that spirit, but it's weak."

Etana looked alarmed. "Weak? Why?"

"I don't really know. Maybe his tether on the world is weak. But then I sense a connection between him and King Luka. The king said it must be because he died there, and it wasn't a proper death, but . . . it's unusual."

Keyelle sat straighter in her chair, almost rising. "That would certainly fit the suspicions of the other Green Hoods. There have always been rumors that the king did something to Erris—that he didn't die properly."

"Green Hoods?"

Keyelle motioned to a pair of green capes hanging by the door. "That's what we call ourselves. Supporters of the Tanharrows."

"I saw lots of people wearing green capes in the capital," Ifra said. "Are they all Green Hoods?"

"No," Keyelle said. "Most people own a green cape, but that doesn't make them a Green Hood. Hundreds of years ago, in the troubled times in the old country when the human king's men were after us, a group called the Green Hoods used to protect the people. We've taken cues from those stories, using ballads for code and such. We see a parallel with those times and now, only it's our own king causing the trouble."

Ifra glanced at the green capes once more, intrigued by the idea of rebellion. If only his people had such a concrete enemy to rebel against. At the same time, he thought of King Luka and felt a curious sense of pity for the man who looked so frail beneath his glamour.

"I can't alert anyone of my mission," Ifra said. "It's part of the magic of the wish. I've been wiping the memories of everyone I pass. But I'm not going to wipe all of yours. You'll remember me, even if you don't remember exactly why I was here. I'll see what I can do."

Weeks passed, and we settled comfortably into our new lives. I helped Celestina pick apples and turn the uglier ones into pies and jars of apple butter. Erris couldn't bear the sweet comforting smell, but he was happier outside anyway, roaming the forest hour upon hour, or sitting with Violet on the lawn, telling her stories of the fairy kingdom. Sometimes I sat to listen, but mostly jealousy crawled up my spine within moments and I returned to my business. I knew I shouldn't be jealous, and I lay awake at night trying to reason myself out of it but never quite managed.

Autumn broke out in earnest, and it was no wonder Erris wanted to be outdoors, as the woods erupted in shades of furious red and cheerful gold, dotted with the permanent green-black fringe of fir and spruce.

Early one morning, Celestina and I laced each other into our corsets and donned our best dresses and hats and gloves so we could go to town for supplies.

Violet raged that she could not go. I stayed out of her way, but I heard her throwing things, and Celestina emerged flushed from the effort of calming her down.

"Usually she likes staying with Lean Joe," she said. "He's happy to take the day off and play games with her. I guess it's just been too much excitement."

"Maybe we should take her," Erris said.

Celestina's mouth opened. "But she's sick! And even with the enchantment as protection, we can't risk the townspeople seeing her."

Erris shrugged, apparently thinking it not worth arguing about. He fussed with his ponytail. "Do you think I should cut my hair? None of the men in town wear it long like this. I worry they'll recognize me as a fairy."

"I saw men with hair longer than yours in New Sweeling," I said.

"This is hardly New Sweeling," Celestina said.

But in the end, we decided it was better not to take the time to fuss with Erris's hair. Celestina loaned him a bowler of Ordorio's to make him look more respectable. Lean Joe readied the horses, and we rode to town piled into a rattling cart. Celestina became quite businesslike at the reins, her gloved hands capable, her back straight as a tree, with a fine little hat atop her head, but I knew going to town made her as nervous as it made me.

In fact, Erris seemed the most relaxed when he should have been the biggest oddity of all, a clockwork fairy with the hair of a city aesthete. He made most of the conversation on the trip, effusively complimenting Ordorio's fine brown pacers, although I was sure they must have been nothing compared to the royal fairy horses, which were known throughout the world. But then, I suppose he hadn't seen those horses in an awfully long time.

Cernan was a larger town than I had realized from the train station alone. To be sure, it was no city, but it was, as my old dancing troupe manager used to say, "worth a dime, not a penny." Two streets ran parallel with a plaza in the middle, where merchants set up booths of wares like fruit and even birds in tiny cages. I had often passed a similar plaza in New Sweeling, only it had a statue in the center instead of the gloomy obelisk Celestina told us was to commemorate the casualties of some shipwreck.

Celestina marched into a shop without any word for the craggy old men milling about in front, smoking pipes and muttering to one another in some unfamiliar language. Erris and I hurried after her.

Inside, the shop was lit by spacious windows but no gaslight. Two younger men lounged at the counter, almost identical in their worn hats and vests. When they stared at us, Erris adjusted his bowler to a jaunty angle. No one else in town seemed to be wearing bowlers. I nudged him to move along.

"Celestina," one of them said, leering, while the other one snickered. "Haven't seen you in a while. Still rattling around that old dungeon?"

She ignored them in a practiced way, consulting her list and picking up an empty basket from the counter to fill.

Naturally, their attention turned to us next. "Who's your company?"

The shopkeeper, a plump man with an impressive black mustache, ignored all of us to help another young woman select cloth.

"It's those people who came on the train a little while ago," the snickering one said. "What's your name, ponytail?"

Erris looked at them, not quite nervous, but gauging the situation.

"I don't give my name out to just anyone," he said after a

moment, and although he said it about as politely as he could, they were predictably displeased.

"Oh, why? Is your name special or something? You can't tell me your name? You think I'm going to cast a magic spell on you?" His snicker got louder. "I heard you're a student of magic, is that right?"

Celestina suddenly dumped a tin of baking powder in her basket and whirled on them. "Do you have nothing better to do? We're just here for our groceries and that's it."

"Hey, don't twist your petticoat, Little Scar. We're just curious." Her cheeks burned at the name.

"Watch out," the leering one said. "They might put a curse on us." There was a threatening note to his voice.

The young woman left with her cloth, looking all too eager to depart the scene, and the shopkeeper finally turned his attention on us. "All right, Celestina, find what you want and be done with it. And I don't want to hear any talk of curses."

"Celestina never said one word about curses!" I said, my indignance suddenly overflowing.

"I won't hesitate to ask you to leave my shop," the shopkeeper said slowly. I was used to a certain level of mistreatment, but it was rare to hear such pure vitriol pointed at me without cause. I felt a twist of fear in my stomach and had to force myself not to leave that moment. Ordorio's house suddenly felt very vulnerable, surrounded by these townspeople who didn't even know who we were and would only grow angrier if they found out.

A boy walked into the shop, clearly with the intention of finding his friends, and stopped short at the sight of Celestina. The family resemblance to her was immediately apparent. He dropped his eyes to the ground and edged over to the wall.

Celestina put down her basket. "Let's go," she said, sounding choked, and she walked out with a straight arm swinging and head high, but I could see it was an effort. Erris looked at me and reached for her basket.

"I'd listen to her if I were you," the leering fellow said.

I wasn't sure if we ought to give our money to the shop, but then, we needed our supplies from somewhere. Erris must've been thinking the same thing, because he put the basket on the counter and motioned for me to hand him the money that I carried in a purse at my wrist.

Thankfully, the boys did not challenge our right to buy groceries, but their eyes bored into the side of my head as the shopkeeper tallied our goods, and they bored into our backs as we departed.

Celestina was standing outside, head bowed, wiping at the remnants of tears.

"Are you all right?" I asked.

She nodded, but it was a lie.

"That boy who came in was your brother, wasn't he?"

She nodded again.

"He would side with those louts and not his own sister?" Erris said. He looked like he wanted to go back in the shop and give the boy a talking-to, but I put a hand to his arm.

"Don't make things worse," I said.

"Those boys grew up playing with my brothers," Celestina said. "Playing with me, even. Mr. Caldero, the shopkeeper . . . we would go in with our pennies for candy. Now they all do their best to make me feel like the dirt on their shoes. I can't . . . really blame my brother for . . ." She shrugged. I could tell she wasn't the sort of person who ever liked to cry, and it was easier not to explain too much.

"The townspeople ostracize you because you work for Ordorio?"

"Yes."

"Just for that?" Erris said.

"Well, I suppose our appearance doesn't help," I said wryly. I hadn't told Erris everything Celestina told me about Ordorio's history with the townspeople, and how Celestina's parents expected her to stay home with them instead. He wasn't around enough for such conversations to arise.

"Well, I will try not to think of it all," Celestina said, with a brisk shake of her head. "We have our groceries. Now we must get the coat and boots for Nimira and pick up the mail."

Luckily for all of our nerves, no one at the clothing shop paid us hostile attention. There were no young people here, just one old man discussing boots with another equally old man, both wearing battered caps and sweaters, and a tall, energetic woman who helped us select coats and boots. I had never seen a shop like this, selling only ready-to-wear clothes and nothing in the least pretty. There were knit caps and broad-brimmed hats and coats for rain and coats for snow, turtleneck sweaters in drab colors, and all sorts of sporting clothes like vests with numerous pockets, and snowshoes. I knew I would appreciate the coat in the cold, but I was deeply unenthused by the lack of, say, purple, which happened to be my favorite color.

Besides that, Erris would not be talked out of spending money on a silly brown hat that made him look like he ought to be wrangling cows.

"It'll keep the sun out of my eyes," he protested. "Anyway, I see other men wearing these, but I don't see any bowlers."

He put it on right away, although there was no need to block the sun on the narrow alley we took to the post office. The houses were built almost touching one another, with balconies overhanging the street, and casting shade on the sidewalks.

Celestina posted our latest batch of letters—I had exchanged a few friendly missives by now with Annalie and Karstor—and picked up those that had come in. I had one from Karstor, but also a fat letter plastered with unfamiliar blue and orange stamps.

"It's from Hollin," I said with surprise. I hadn't realized how quickly mail could travel across the ocean these days; just over three weeks for a reply.

"Hollin?" Erris scoffed. "You're corresponding with him? I thought he was quite out of the way in New Guinnell."

I opened my mouth to tease him about being jealous, but then I thought, *Might he really be jealous?* That could be a marvelous thing. Maybe he wouldn't take my company for granted if he was. I tucked the letter away with a secret little smile. "Well, of course I'm curious to know what he's up to there. I wrote everyone as soon as we arrived."

"New Guinnell," Celestina said. "Oh my. That is so exotic. I would love to hear your letter, if you are willing to share later."

"Well, I don't know, I'll have to see what it says," I said with a dismissive shrug.

"I should hope he doesn't write you letters full of secrets," Erris grumbled.

⚬○⚬

I was not actually sure what to expect from Hollin. When we arrived home, I went to my room and unfolded it, the paper releasing a sweet scent that stirred memories of home. Until then I had never realized paper had different smells. Hollin was hundreds of miles from Tiansher, but much closer than I was.

Dear Nimira,

I can't tell you how pleased I was to receive your letter. Everything here is so exotic, and I can't help but think of you. I can't imagine you coming to my country, at a younger age than I am now, without family or work to give you direction in such a strange place. I know New Guinnell is far from your home, and yet I am reminded of you at every turn. . . .

My heart was pounding fast. Even if he did think of me, it wasn't proper to say so.

I have only just got settled in to my work and my new quarters. My room is almost all white— white walls, white bed linens, white sun streaming in. Quite the difference from Vestenveld! This week I've been going around with a Mr. Quendley, checking on local schools to inquire about their curriculum. The government wants to know if they are teaching magic to children.

Mr. Quendley is very much like the usual sort of well-to-do sorcerer of Lorinar; he is also quite obese and continually holds a handkerchief to wipe sweat from his face, and he has little use for anyone who isn't from Lorinar or Dolland. But society is different here, there are not as many women, although many men have brought their wives, and there is something both arrogant and wild about my peers,

*as if they are afraid this country will seduce them
even as they are half-seduced already.*

My cheeks were hot, reading the word "seduce" from Hollin, even in this context. He went on about people he had met and parties he had been to, and commented rather guiltily that it didn't seem like much of a punishment at all. Then, suddenly, his tone changed.

*The people are so different here. They wear such
colors! I see women in the street, with bare arms
and half-bare legs, all wrapped in gold and emerald.
They are quick to laugh. People move differently
here too. They look somehow more alive. Some of the
women practice magic, even. All I can think of
is home, and how dark it is, and how dark I felt,
and how cold. We always behaved as if someone
was watching us, even if it wasn't true. Remember
how reluctant I was to dance with you, to sing
with you?*

*And yet I feel different here. I am trying to hide
it, and maybe everyone is. I keep my head down
and follow all the rules. But I do think of you, and
how I think you planted something in me that wants
to blossom under the sun. And if it did, I don't
know what anyone would think of me.*

*I must beg your forgiveness for being so candid.
I'm not sure if my letter will be at all welcome to
you. But right now you are an ocean away, and I
am sitting at my desk drinking in the heavy scent*

*of flowers outside my window, and you feel like the
only person I can safely be honest with. You and I,
I think, will always feel a little bit alone no matter
where our lives take us. I don't think you shall tell
anyone. My thoughts are a muddle and I need to
sort them. I beg your indulgence.*

Most sincerely,
Hollin Parry

I was not sure at all what to make of this letter. A part of me
liked it very much, and I knew I should not.

From the start, Hollin had appreciated me more than most
other men of Lorinar, but he had still not seen me for what I was. He
had seen a beautiful, exotic creature from some far-off land that
he dreamed of escaping to. It had always been escape with Hollin.

Yet, even while half of me despised him, he knew how to slip a
hand under my skin and twist at my heart, appealing to my own
sense of isolation. And, for all his many mistakes, I thought his
feelings were genuine.

I made three false starts before I finally began to craft my reply.
Of course, I still started with pleasantries, that I hoped the climate
agreed with him and so on, and I spoke of the attractive grounds
and my friendship with Celestina, as if we were all a happy family
without any troubles. I didn't want to sound like someone who
felt alone.

But I understood what he meant about being honest an ocean
away. He was so far from me now, and I would not see him for almost
a year, if then, which felt an eternity. I might as well have been
throwing letters into the fireplace, for all that he felt accessible. I

should have politely reminded him that he was a married man and left it at that, but I found myself spilling words onto the paper instead.

Hollin, I know you always wanted to travel. You finally have your chance. Make use of it. If you truly believe that all people are equal, and you truly are fascinated by foreign lands, don't be held back by men like Mr. Quendley.

But I also hope you realize that New Guinnell is not necessarily a balm to your problems. The country is not there to lull you any more than I was. The people there don't think they are different, they are going about their normal business, and sometimes I felt that, while you respected me more than other men, you romanticized me. Someone or someplace that is romanticized can't be real.

This is a lesson I myself learned. I came to this country thinking the streets were paved with gold. I was struck down time and time again, and I came to loathe it, and close myself off, but I still had another lesson to learn. Not all people here are cruel either. Fortunes and happiness alike come with work, wherever you are.

I was only sitting in a room with the nonthreatening objects of everyday life—pen and paper, candle, desk—and yet, my skin was burning. This was a bold way to speak to a man. Especially a prominent man like Hollin Parry.

I read the letter over, trying to think as he might think when he read it.

In the end, I decided I didn't care. It felt true. It even felt a bit wise, certainly more wise than anything I would say in person. Would I be happier sending him a frothy thing full of pleasantries?

No.

And so I sealed the letter away, readying it for an ocean journey.

When I came downstairs to put Hollin's letter in the basket where outgoing mail was kept, Erris was there to tease me.

"We're not going to hear what you wrote to him? What did his letter say? Don't make me guess! 'Dear Nimira, I am terribly sunburned and red as a lobster. If only you were here to do your traditional Slathering Cream on a Sunburned Man dance.'"

I slapped his hand with the letter and put it back in the basket. "Can you be serious for two minutes?"

"Two minutes? I can probably manage that. Are you going to tell me what he said?"

"No! Certainly not with that attitude. Anyway, it was a long letter full of nothing much."

"You just have an awfully serious look on your face."

"I don't have any look on my face. At least, I didn't. Now I'm cross. You shouldn't insult my dancing. And Hollin isn't like that."

"Hollin is a bigot. With dead animals in his house. And, besides all that, as interesting as tree bark."

"You hardly—" I stopped. If I defended Hollin, this would become a full-blown quarrel. I suddenly felt entirely irked at Erris, and quickly shook my head to free my thoughts. "I'm not going to discuss this further."

The trouble with being upset with Erris was that I was attracted to him at the same time. It made it difficult to have a proper argument. Nor was he the arguing sort. Everything was a joke to him.

He laughed now. "No one can look so indignant as you, Nim. Well, unfortunately I can't prowl around at night and search your room, so I will have to trust you'll tell me if Hollin says anything unseemly to you."

"It isn't as if you're my suitor, anyway," I said, hoping to provoke him.

"Well, I should hope that doesn't mean *he* is your suitor." Erris still sounded teasing, but there was nothing teasing about the sudden slant of his eyebrows.

"No, it means simply that if he does say something unseemly, I shall defend myself."

"I have no doubt of that," he said with a grin. Which only irked me further.

❦

Another couple of weeks passed. It rained frequently, and the evergreens flourished with clusters of cones. The maple, birch, and poplar began to shed their leaves of flame, and one morning I woke to the first snow, falling soft and sparse.

As the world began to tuck in for a long sleep, Violet began to wake up. Erris's simple treatment of fresh food and hours of fresh, brisk air didn't make her catch cold as Celestina feared but instead brought color to her pale cheeks, although she was still thin. But then, she didn't eat much. She had a hideous tantrum when he tried to feed her raw carrots for breakfast.

The trouble with Violet's feeling better was that she wanted to follow everyone everywhere. Whether we were cooking or all gathered around the piano, Violet was there chattering as if she had years of stored conversation to unload. She told us stories from books she was reading when we'd rather simply read the book ourselves, and she sulked when we didn't pay attention to her. She was a champion sulker, capable of keeping the same sullen face and pose for an hour straight until it was impossible to have fun in her presence, but her good moods were almost as irritating.

One afternoon I had just set out on a walk, and Violet came running after me like an excitable puppy. She panted dreadfully when she caught up to me. I thought for a moment she might pass out.

"Nimira—where are you—going? I want to—come."

"To the bluff."

"Oh—near—Mother's grave?"

"I don't know. I've never seen a grave there."

She paused to breathe a moment and then said, "You haven't seen it? I'll show you!" She sounded rather eager about a grave, I thought.

Along with color in her cheeks, Violet now wore proper clothes every day and not nightgowns and robes. Celestina had offered to make her trousers, but Violet had a wardrobe full of dresses and she wanted to wear them. They were the dresses of a girl, not a woman. Today it was a plaid affair with a square white collar. The ribbons in her hair matched the dress, and the whole thing was topped off by a double-breasted coat with puffed sleeves and white piping.

"When will you put your hair up and your skirts down?" I asked her as we trudged through fallen leaves. The last snow had melted, but the leaves were wet.

"Oh. Should I? What age do girls usually?"

"Fourteen?"

"I'm fifteen! Celestina never told me."

"Well, it's no use if you're in bed all the time anyway, but maybe now you should."

She nodded. "So I should have all new clothes. But it should have been last year. I wasn't sick all last year. Is it too late to go to town and get new clothes? We really should go to the city even. That's where these clothes came from. Papa took me to the city."

"It's certainly too late to get clothes now. And we can't take you to the city! Just ask your father when he gets back, I suppose."

She sighed heavily. "When will I ever get to do anything?"

"I don't have anything to do with it," I said. "I think it's ridiculous that you can't go anywhere and everyone forgets who you are. How are you supposed to get on in the world like that?"

"You came from some really faraway country, right, Nimira?"

"Yes."

"How old were you?"

"Thirteen. Well, almost fourteen."

"Were you scared?"

"Well, I was, but ... I don't know. Once you commit to something, you just manage through each moment. And nothing truly awful happened. The voyage over was uneventful. I found work right away, just not very good work. The worst thing wasn't something terrible, it was the lack of anything wonderful."

Violet sucked in her breath. "What about Erris?" she asked.

"Erris? I met him much later."

"Yes, I know, I just . . ." She tugged on one of her hair bows. "You fell in love with him, right?"

"I—I don't know," I said. "It's not polite to be so blunt, you know."

"I'm not trying to be polite," Violet said. "I want to know what it's like to be in love. I want a girl to talk to, and Celestina is no help. She says things like, 'Oh, you don't need to know about that, you can worry about that later.'" She mimicked a bossy tone.

Violet must be desperate if she wanted to confide in me. I hadn't even been nice to her, and she wanted to talk to me about love? But I wasn't sure how to talk to her about it. I wasn't even sure what I felt anymore. What had I ever felt? My feelings for Erris had been so intense when I was trying to save him, but they had been replaced as of late by more of a guilty desperation, and I wasn't about to tell Violet that.

We had reached the bluff, one of my favorite places on the grounds. A rocky promontory jetted into the sea, within distant view of the shore where we took walks and gathered seaweed and shells. From here, I could see dozens of islands and, on a clear day, which this was not, even the Cernan Light, striped like a black-and-white candy cane.

The bluff was marked by the burned husk of what might once have been a two- or three-room structure. Most of the chimney still stood, but otherwise it was just the foundation with some charred wood pieces jutting from it. Celestina had told me it was an old hunting lodge, but ruins held a certain fascination for me, even perfectly ordinary ones.

"Oh, I forgot about the haunted cabin!" Violet said, poking the ruins with her toe.

"Is it haunted? Celestina said it was nothing."

"No," Violet said, sounding rather displeased about it. "I just used to pretend it was. I didn't have anyone to play with, so I was always wishing things were haunted, and they never were. Well, there it is." She pointed to a rock formation that I had never paid much attention to, a large, somewhat flat rock stacked on two smaller rocks.

"That's your mother's grave? Those rocks?"

Violet nodded. She went to the rocks and leaned her head against them. "It's a fairy grave."

I shivered. "Let's not talk about it," I said. I didn't want to think of Erris's body buried under stones like these.

"Why not?" Violet said. "I'm not sad. I don't remember her." She spoke almost too emphatically to be believed.

"Aren't you sad you don't remember her?"

"Well . . . I do miss her. It's just that she feels like a story. Actually, worse. I think I know the mother in the Poppenpuffer Family books better than her. I guess everything would be different if she were still alive. Papa wouldn't have gone to work for the Queen of the Longest Night." She turned to me. "But don't feel sorry for me or anything."

"I don't," I said, although, of course, I did, a bit.

It was windy on the bluff, carrying sounds away from us, but we were both suddenly alert to hoof-falls, coming from the forest. Had something happened? I couldn't imagine Celestina would take a horse if she needed to find us, unless it was urgent.

Violet and I looked at each other, wide-eyed, silently asking the other if we should run. What if it was those nasty boys from the shop?

Violet grabbed my sleeve. "Let's hide behind Mother's grave."

The stones were big enough to conceal us from view of the forest, but terribly exposed on every other side. I knelt with her, but I was restless, my hands gathering small rocks I could throw at the face of an attacker. At least I was wearing my trousers.

I heard the horse step from the woods. It came closer, and closer, until it was sniffing the gravestones on the other side. Hiding became an almost unbearable tension, and it seemed unlikely the horse or rider would not find us at any moment, so I stood up, one hand full of rocks.

For a moment, I was speechless. Violet stood alongside me, equally speechless. The horse was unlike any I had seen—strong but delicate, like a stylized horse in a painting, with a pure white coat and curious, too-intelligent eyes.

But its rider was even more stunning, with skin like honey and eyes keen as a tiger, his straight black hair caught in a ponytail that stirred with the wind. He was not dressed like anyone from Lorinar; he wore a blue shirt that fastened with a sash, with an open neck and bare arms, and boots made from brown hide stitched with red thread.

And in his ears, gold hoops. And at his wrists, golden cuffs like a second skin.

It didn't seem possible, but ancient tales were stirring in my mind, tales that traveled the world like spices and cloth, tales of imprisoned people with great power, the power to dissolve into smoke, the power to grant a heart's desire, creatures recognizable by their golden cuffs of bondage.

A jinn.

Violet took hold of my sleeve again, and I met those golden eyes.

"Who are you?" I asked. My voice stayed steady.

"I was sent by the fairy king."

The fairy king. He had found us. Celestina said he couldn't harm Violet, and I prayed that was true, but Erris . . .

How quickly I had relaxed. I had started to delude myself that the fairy king wouldn't bother with us, and I didn't want to remember how this fear felt, knowing I must do and say just the right thing to save us. But here it was, like a fist inside me, squeezing on my lungs.

"The fairy king?" Violet asked. I squeezed her hand as a signal that she should let me do the talking. Clearly, the signal was missed. "Well, don't bother. You can't hurt me. You can't lay a finger on me."

"Who are you?" the jinn asked.

"It doesn't matter."

"Why would I want to hurt you?"

Violet shied back, apparently realizing rather belatedly that she'd said too much.

"I'm looking for Erris Tanharrow," the jinn said. "Do either of you know a gentleman by that name?" He spoke very calmly, as if he already knew we did.

"You're a jinn," I said. I wanted to be sure of this before I thought what to do, although even then, I was not at all sure if my knowledge of jinns was true or formed by the exaggerations that inevitably come from tales carried by trade routes.

Violet was breathless, staring at him as if hypnotized. "A jinn . . ."

Possibilities raced through my mind. Jinns were bound to their master until they granted three wishes. At least, that was what most of the stories agreed upon, although I had heard tales of one wish, five wishes, limitless wishes. I also had no idea how powerful these wishes were.

What if the fairy king had wished for this jinn to harm Erris? Would any force keep him away? Jinns in stories always granted their wishes; they never said, *Oh, I tried to grant your wish but a couple of young ladies prevented it.*

"Why do you want Mr. Tanharrow?" I asked.

"The fairy king wants him, and that's all I know. I won't harm him."

"But what of the fairy king?" I said. "Will he harm him?"

"I cannot vouch for him, but *I* will not harm him."

None of us here had magic. Erris had brute strength in his metallic body, but what was strength against magic? Especially without particular training. This jinn had unknown abilities.

For a split second, I pushed him from my mind. *If I get out of this, I swear I will never be caught helpless again,* I thought. But how could I get out of this? Would the Queen of the Longest Night help me now as she did when I gave Erris life? But I had time to summon her properly, then.

Perhaps I could lead the jinn in the wrong direction? But Erris would have no idea what I was doing, so he wouldn't know to hide.

I was in the middle of these thoughts when Violet made a sudden dash for the jinn. Maybe her knowledge of the protective spell on her made her foolishly brave. She grabbed the hem of his tunic. "Nimira, run away!" she shouted.

"Violet! What on earth are you doing?"

"The jinn can't hurt me, so you just go!" The jinn himself did look startled by this turn of events. If I was going to run away and warn Erris while the jinn was distracted, the moment was now. What would Celestina say if I returned alone and Violet was gone? But I didn't know what else to do. I turned and bolted back to the house.

Stupid, stupid girl! She really should know better than to test her magical protection against a jinn. If I had to choose between

Erris and Violet, of course I would choose Erris . . . yet, it nagged at me even as I ran. Violet seemed so innocent—if irritating—and truly living. Not to mention she was the precious daughter of the man who would hopefully save Erris.

Maybe Erris would have some idea, I thought wildly, without even a guess as to what that idea could be.

I burst through the kitchen door. Celestina was sweeping the floor.

"Is Erris here?" I cried.

"He's outside, just like you were. What's wrong? Where's Violet?"

"There's a jinn," I gasped. "At the bluff. Violet wouldn't come with me."

"A *jinn*? And Violet is still there?"

"It's Erris he's come for, but she ran up to him, and . . . I guess she's all right, if that protective magic holds, but— Well, I just don't know what to do!"

"I'd better go after her. If something happened to her . . ."

"And I need to find Erris. Hide him, or something. I don't know how strong a jinn's powers are. But you be careful."

"All right," Celestina said. "You go to the shore and I'll go after Violet. If I find Erris first, I'll tell him what's going on, and we'll meet back here. When we can."

I nodded, and took off again down the path to the shore. It slanted ever so slightly downhill as it wound its way through the apple orchards, forest, and meadow, making it a little easier to hurry. Still, my heart was leaping from my chest.

I was not surprised to find Erris at the shore. Watching the water was one of his favorite things.

I shouted a brief version of events to him as I scrambled over the rocks.

"Luka has a jinn?" His face drained of color.

"Yes. You have to hide."

"If a jinn wants to find me, where can I hide?"

"I don't know, but I'm not about to turn you over without a fight. Maybe we could hide you in one of those shut-up rooms in the house. Maybe . . . or maybe in the cellar? Behind crocks of pickles?"

Erris looked understandably skeptical. Supposing we even had time to get him back to the house without running into the jinn, surely he would search the house. There must be places to hide in the woods, but I couldn't think of any offhand, and did we have time to find one?

"You know," he said, "I don't actually have to breathe." He looked at the water.

"Underwater? But—will it damage your clockwork? Salt water?"

"I don't know, but if there's one place he won't think to look for me, I bet it's underwater. From all I've read, jinn have more natural power than any other being. But they are fire spirits. If anything will foil them, it's water."

"But . . . it's so cold," I said, looking at the waters that suddenly seemed too dark. The waves were gentle, but I didn't trust the water with Erris.

"Nim, do you want me to be carried off by a jinn or not? I'll hide behind that rock there." He pointed. "At least 'til the tide goes out. If I hear anyone coming too close, I'll duck underwater, so shout when the coast is clear."

I had no better plan, and I couldn't dither here forever, so I briefly squeezed his hands, praying the water would be kind to him, and nodded.

"I'll be all right," he said.

"You'll ruin your suit." I smiled a little, and he smiled a little back, but our eyes were sad. If his suit was the only thing to come out of this worse for wear, we would both be lucky.

He turned to the water and I turned to the trees. I couldn't watch the water lapping at him.

ORDORIO VALDANA'S MANSION

As the young woman with the dark braids ran away, Ifra stared at the girl holding his arm. She was small and pale, with her hair in bows. She looked afraid too, and the way she peered up at him made him feel sheepish. Her hands encircled the cuff at his wrist, but when he looked at her, she let go.

"Where are you going to take Erris?" she asked softly.

"To the fairy king."

"Can you take me instead?"

"Why? Who are you?" Ifra hadn't heard anything about a girl.

"I'm his niece."

"His niece? You are a Tanharrow too?"

"Yes. I'm Violet. My mother was a Tanharrow."

"Luka didn't mention you," he murmured, and he wondered why. Was it because she was a girl? But fairy society had not struck him as especially patriarchal.

"He doesn't know about me," Violet said, her voice flattening.

"No one does. My father asked the Queen of the Longest Night to put a spell on me so no one would remember me or know I exist. So the fairy king couldn't hurt me."

"Then why would you want me to take you to him?"

"Because . . . I want to know . . . where my mother comes from. She died when I was little. I don't know anything about fairies."

Ifra slid off the horse, but he wasn't sure what else to do. She looked so sad. "I understand," he said.

"*Do* you? Does anyone? I've never had a friend."

Neither have I, he might have told her.

"When you came out of the forest, I—I was really hoping you were just a lost traveler who'd have to stay the night, except nobody around here would look like you, not even Nimira. She's from some other country but she's boring. So I didn't know what you were, or where you could possibly come from. It was like . . . I dreamed you up." She didn't look as scared of him as she ought to be.

"I'm no dream." Despite the cold air, his palms sweated. He'd never had much chance to be around girls his age. "I'm here to take your uncle away."

"So take me. I wouldn't miss much. Celestina only scolds, and she never told me that I was too old to wear bows in my hair. How would I even know? I hardly ever go to town, I'm sick all winter, and Father is never home. Nimira and Uncle Erris don't like me either. Maybe Uncle Erris does, but only because I remind him of my mother. Whenever we talk, he just goes on and on about his sisters. Well, they're dead, aren't they?" She screeched the last bit, her eyes flashing anger.

"See," she snapped, "I don't even care if I scream at you because you won't remember me tomorrow."

"I might," he said.

"No one does."

"But I'm a jinn. And most people won't remember me either. I had to erase the memory of everyone I met along the way to find your uncle. And King Luka, when his wishes are granted, he'll forget me too. Masters forget their jinns. After a little while, they think good fortune came on its own."

"Maybe we'll both forget each other," she said.

"Possibly."

"Then we can say anything we want. It doesn't matter."

Ifra glanced over his shoulder, unnerved by the way she peered up at him through a fringe of lashes, suddenly wishing the girl with braids hadn't run off. But they were still alone. "I don't think . . . we have much to say to each other."

"I do. I think you're beautiful." She rushed through the words.

His cheeks warmed. "Don't say such a thing! I'm dangerous."

"Do you have to do whatever your master wishes, because you're a jinn?"

He nodded, averting his eyes from her.

"I wish . . ." She hesitated, and then she burst out, "That you'd kiss me."

"But you're not my master."

"I wish I was."

"I'm not sure I do." He smiled a little. He suspected it was rare anyone ever said no to this girl. Disciplined young women wouldn't demand a kiss from a strange magical person who walked out of the forest.

"You wouldn't prefer me as a master over the fairy king?" Violet asked.

"I would hope that if you are ever a jinn's master, you would set him free."

"I would if you'd kiss me. Would you, if I was your master? I'm beautiful, aren't I? Is it the hair bows?" She tugged one loose.

Ifra shook his head. The way her hair suddenly spilled over her shoulder seemed indecorous.

"What?" she asked.

"Where I'm from, you only kiss if you're married. And . . . you don't look like the girls from home." No, she wasn't lovely and bewitching like some of the girls in the bazaar, but she did seem much more real.

She scowled, her eyes dark in her pale face. "Celestina never told me how to talk to men. But of course I'm respectable. I'm a *princess.*"

Ifra leaned in and pecked her forehead.

That was definitely something a jinn should not do, unless they were trying to seduce their master into setting them free. But he would forget her anyway, possibly.

She looked at him a moment, then quickly touched her lips. "One more time," she said, reaching for his collar. "That didn't really count."

She aimed for his lips this time, but he was suddenly shaken at the idea that he might kiss this strange Tanharrow girl. Developing feelings for any Tanharrow was the worst thing he could do. He turned so she met his cheek.

Violet drew back, biting her lower lip.

Just then, something shifted in his senses. Erris disappeared. It was as if he'd vanished from the world—no, there was still a slight tug back in the direction of the fairy kingdom—but just moments ago, Erris had been *here*. Close. "Does Erris have magic?" he asked her.

"Why?" she said.

"I don't sense him here anymore. My magic . . . isn't calling me here. It's calling me back to Telmirra."

Violet looked confused. She shook her head.

I have to follow where the magic tugs me. If I sense Erris in Telmirra, even if he isn't there, I am still following orders. He could put off granting the wish even longer.

Ifra heard sudden footsteps—the wind had obscured the sound, but now they were close, and Violet stiffened.

"Someone's looking for me! You'd better hurry."

"You don't really want to come with me. Whoever I bring back, the fairy king will want to use for his own purposes. And surely your father will miss you when he does come home." He looked at her seriously. "It's painful to be torn from your home without knowing if you'll ever see it again."

She frowned, cheeks flushed, in a tight, almost childish way and reached upward. "At least take me back to the house on your horse and act like you *considered* kidnapping me. I don't want Nimira or Celestina to find me yet."

He couldn't help but smile and pulled her up onto the horse.

10

As I headed back to the house, the jinn and his mount were coming through the apple orchard. The white horse and the jinn with his gleaming gold seemed almost like an apparition haunting the winter-bare trees. Violet sat in front of him, clutching the saddle horn, looking pale. He whistled and the horse stopped, with a delicate snort.

I held up my hands, but I stopped short of saying anything. What would I say, "Give her back"?

He seemed to take note of my worried look. "Well. You should go," he said to Violet. She had a strange, lifeless look as the jinn hooked his hands under her arms and lifted her off the horse.

"I'm not interested in harming her," he said.

"What did you do to her?" I asked. "She looks like she's had the life sucked out of her."

Violet coughed. "I'm fine. Really. I'm sorry I worried you, Nimira. I just wanted to . . . help Erris." She walked over to me, but she kept looking back, as if the jinn had somehow bewitched her with those golden eyes of his.

"Where is Prince Erris?" the jinn said. He glanced at the sun, which was beginning its afternoon dive.

I shrugged, keeping my expression cool.

The jinn looked around him a long moment, while Violet looked at the ground. I wondered if jinn could track, but they were not forest creatures, and no recognition dawned on his face.

Good. Maybe Erris was right about water foiling his abilities.

He looked at me a moment, and at Violet another, and then he gave the reins a twitch, and his magnificent horse moved away with a fluid grace it seemed wrong for a horse to possess, like a woman so beautiful no other can compete with her. I think the horse knew it too, which made it all the worse.

I prayed that he would not find Erris in the water. I wanted to follow the jinn, but my presence would do no good; I might even give some accidental hint as to Erris's whereabouts.

"He didn't . . . say good-bye," Violet said. She coughed.

"Oh, I'm sure he'll stop by the house for tea when he's done looking for someone else to kidnap," I muttered. "Let's get you to the house, you look peaked."

I put my arm around Violet's shoulder. I was still feeling kindly toward her because she had looked so small on the jinn's horse, even though she had acted foolishly. She let me lead her along.

"What happened back there with you and the jinn?"

"Nothing."

I recalled a time on my uncle's farm when I had eaten a sweet yam bun I wasn't supposed to have. My response when my uncle asked me where it had gone was much the same. But I didn't want to demand an answer. That tactic had not exactly endeared my uncle to me. "You seemed awfully eager to sacrifice yourself on Erris's behalf."

She made a little grunt. I doubted there was anything more I could say, so I let her be.

As we neared the house, Celestina came running toward us. "Did you find him?"

"The jinn is searching the grounds, but Erris is hiding ... in the ocean. I think it's out of our hands now ..." I took a deep breath.

Celestina startled me with an embrace. "It will be all right," she said. "I only hope he doesn't burn down the house if he can't find Erris. Or take us hostage. Or some awful thing."

"I don't think ... he's really cruel," Violet said. "When I was crying, he was rather nice."

"What? When was this?"

Violet looked a little flushed. "I didn't mean to cry, but for some reason, I got so upset about ... trying to protect Uncle Erris, so I started crying."

"What did he say to you?" I asked. I wanted to know as much as I could about this perplexing creature.

"I don't know. We talked a bit. And then he helped me onto his horse. And that was when we saw you, Nimira."

Celestina took a deep breath. "Well, I'm glad to hear you're all right, but it certainly gave me a scare. And where is your other hair bow?"

"I guess I lost one."

We had just entered the warm, cozy kitchen. Violet took an apple from the counter and sat down heavily. Celestina had just baked apple pies yesterday, and now she took one from the pantry and cut a huge slice from it. "Do you want any?" she asked me.

I shook my head. I moved to the window, and stared out even

though there was no sign of the jinn. The loudest sound in the room was Violet's slow crunching of the apple.

After a bit, Celestina said, "Come away from the window, Nim. There's nothing we can do now."

"I'm all right here."

My thoughts were racing. I wondered what I would do if the jinn found Erris. Would I go to the fairy kingdom and try to save him? That seemed too impossible to even consider. But where would I go instead? Celestina liked me, she would surely let me stay the winter, but what about when Ordorio returned? Maybe he would agree to help rescue Erris and I could accompany him, although I wasn't especially useful. Ordorio was Violet's family, not mine, and I wasn't Karstor's concern either. I wondered if everyone would shut their doors to me if Erris disappeared. He was really the person who mattered.

Then it came back again to what I would do with Erris, anyway. If he remained an exiled automaton, we could never marry. Would I just remain the keeper of his key? And if he became the fairy king...?

The more thinking I did, the more hopeless I felt. It was best not to think at all, ever, but that was impossible to maintain.

I needed to make myself useful.

"I want to learn magic," I said suddenly. "We can't let this happen again."

"It's dangerous without proper instruction," Celestina said. "And no one gives proper instruction in magic to women."

"Oh, come now," I said. "Don't say that." It was true, magic was something women simply didn't do in this country, beyond perhaps a little healing or birthing magic. But I hadn't taken Celestina for the type to follow all the rules. "My life is clearly dangerous whether I like it or not. We should be prepared."

"Yes," Violet said. "We should learn magic! Won't Papa have some good books on it somewhere?"

"No," Celestina said. "I'm not going to have your father coming back to find the house burned down!"

"If we're careful, I doubt we'll burn the house down," I said. Magic could be dangerous—I knew it well—but I imagined it would be less dangerous if we had time to practice. "Celestina, we can't just let the jinn come back and take Erris. Or Violet!"

"Maybe Erris could teach me fairy magic," Violet said.

"That won't help the rest of us!" I said. Goodness, if Erris started teaching Violet how to talk to the forest while I sat around uselessly, I would scream.

"No one is learning magic until Mr. Valdana comes back!" Celestina shouted, shoving back the empty plate she had been eating pie from moments ago. "He left me in charge and I must *insist*."

"Why?" Violet asked.

"Because it's dangerous, as I *just* said."

I had never seen Celestina be short about anything. I raised my brows.

"I hear the horse," she said. I thought she was only looking for a diversion, but when I pushed aside the curtain, sure enough, the jinn had ridden his horse to the door and slid off as easy as I might climb out of bed. He knocked on the door.

Celestina shot me an apprehensive glance, then opened it. "Yes?"

"Where is he?" the jinn said.

We were quiet, although Violet stood from her chair.

"You've foiled my magic." He put his hand to his heart and dipped his head, an acknowledgment. When his head came back up, his eyes met mine. "He was the first thing King Luka asked of me."

His voice was soft, and yet, I could feel his power like the electricity in the air before a storm, and I wondered how we would ever foil him twice.

His eyes lingered briefly on each of us, and then he turned back to his horse. Celestina shut the door, and Violet moved to the window. We all watched him go.

"I'm going to study magic," I said firmly. "But first, I must get Erris."

I waited awhile and approached the shore warily, still looking and listening for the jinn in case of trickery. And when the sea came in view, it looked empty, like it had surely swept Erris away without a trace.

I screamed his name. The sea winds roared in my ears. I cupped my hands around my mouth and called even louder.

He stood up from behind the rock, just where he'd said he'd be. I tried to hide how scared I had felt. He straggled up to me, clothes soaking wet. His hair was still dry. He never had to submerge himself completely, but he'd still been in the water over an hour.

"Are you all right?" I touched his wet shoulder.

"I think so." He clutched his chest. He looked quite pale. After a moment he said, "I feel cold and clammy all over. Not right at all."

"You'll probably feel better as you dry out," I said hopefully. What would it be like to feel the cold sea rush not just over your skin, but all through your insides?

"Yes . . ."

"Well, let's get you back to the house."

"You go on without me," he said.

"But—"

"I want to be alone," he said, with the slightest hint of desperation.

I regarded him a moment, reluctant, and he nodded toward the line of trees, urging me on.

"You always want to be alone," I said softly. I turned from him, sniffing back the tears, and started to walk away.

"I'm sorry," he called.

I couldn't take that. Like he could just yell out that he was sorry and everything would be all right. "I was so worried about you," I said, my hands trembling as I turned back around. "I know you want to be alone, but—but can't you ever let me care for you anymore? I was so afraid I was going to lose you today, and now you're safe, but you're pushing me away."

"I can't be good company right now," Erris said. "I feel all . . . all wrong. Usually I sort of feel like I'm made of flesh and bone, even if I'm not, but right now I feel . . . all wrong." Indeed, he seemed very shaken. He sat down on a nearby rock and clutched his hands together.

I went to his side. "I don't care whether you're good company or not. I care about you. And as hard as this is to deal with, is it really easier to deal with it alone?"

"Maybe." He didn't look at me.

"When you were trapped at a piano and you couldn't even speak, wasn't that worse? But you wanted me around then."

"It was worse. But . . . I felt like a ghost then. A ghost tethered to an object. Now I feel . . . alive. But all wrong. When I'm around other people, even you and Celestina and Violet . . ."

He didn't finish, but I knew what he was getting at. "Erris, don't you think I feel horrible about all this? I lay awake at night wondering if I was right to try and save you, because ... I gave you this. I gave you the best I could. I loved you, and ..." My voice was starting to break up now. "I couldn't give you enough, and now I can never really have you. I didn't save you after all."

I started to cry. I felt awful about it. He was the one with his insides full of seawater and I was the one sobbing. "I'm sorry," I said. My turn for those feeble words.

"Please don't cry," he said softly. He took my right hand, even as I covered my face with the left, and separated my fingers in a way that made me shiver. When the only place we ever touched was our hands, it was astonishing how sensitive they became to the slightest of caresses.

"Nimira," he continued. "I thought we were fine friends. I tease you, and you laugh, and we make music together. What else can I do?"

"No!" I shouted. "Enough about 'fine friends'! I can't stand it. All this teasing and laughing seems like a charade! I can tell you're in despair, and you never tell me about that. If you meant what you said when you told me you loved me—and *I* meant it—then let us be open with our hearts and minds!"

"Look at me," he suddenly said fiercely. And when I did, he pulled open his shirt so I could see gears ticking and their rhythm like a heartbeat. "You can't really love this."

I'll admit it was always an unnerving sight, the contrast of Erris's deeply living face and the clockwork under his clothes. I could pretend it didn't disturb me, but I think he could sense even the slightest hint of horror from me. And in fact, I was fighting deep in my core not to cry again, because I had done this to him.

"You can't tell me what I love," I said.

"You love a fiction," he said. "A romantic story of a fairy prince. But fair maidens don't fall for beasts. I know how the story goes." There was disdain in his voice. Disdain, for me, as if I were too stupid not to think beyond myths and fables!

I picked up a rock and dashed it on the stones in front of him, and then I stormed off to learn magic, whether anyone liked it or not.

When I returned to the house, Violet was sitting in the kitchen by the woodstove, arms crossed and feet splayed out. Her face was dry, but it looked like she'd been a bit weepy herself. She looked up at me with the very same doleful expression Erris gave when things weren't going well—eyelids slightly lowered, brown eyes soulful. The family resemblance had never been so clear.

"Are you all right?" I asked. "Where's Celestina?"

"She had things to do outside, she said."

"Well, all right." I didn't know what else to say, so I started to go.

"Are you really going to learn magic?" Violet asked.

"Yes. I am. Someone must do something."

"Can I learn with you?"

I didn't really want to include her. It was her house, however, and her father's books I'd be searching for information, so it felt wrong to tell her no. "I don't know how far I'll really get," I said.

"We should ask Erris for help," Violet suggested.

"Erris is in no mood to help anyone. He just wants to be alone every waking second. And even if he says yes, it won't do me one bit of good, will it, because I am not a fairy." I knew I was being snappish, but I just didn't care to be nice at the moment.

Violet's eyes widened at my tone. She coughed, and she was rarely capable of coughing just once or twice. It was as if she had to reach down and give her lungs a good resettling before she was done. Sometimes I think she only coughed when she felt like it, to remind us all she was sick and fragile.

"It's no wonder he wants to be alone," she said. "You're so sour."

"I'm not sour!"

"You didn't like me from the start."

"Because you're spoiled, and you act like a child."

"Then tell me how to act like a woman!" Violet suddenly tore from her chair and ran up the stairs, coughing and crying at once.

I wished I weren't wearing trousers. I didn't feel prepared for womanly instruction in them. Well, I'd be a poor choice to help her anyway. I wasn't even a woman from this continent, and I certainly knew little about fairies. I sat down by the woodstove in the chair Violet had just vacated, yet I felt unsettled. Should I go after her?

Celestina, with her trousers and pickles and apple pie, was obviously growing into the sort of woman who would probably make a good rustic wife and mother, but I wasn't that sort of woman, and I doubted Violet was either. Was it possible she had said those things because she truly wished I would talk to her? Was that why she'd asked me about falling in love?

I went upstairs. I found her flung onto her bed, face buried in the pillow, but door open, the classic pose of the young woman who hopes someone will notice her despair.

"Violet," I said.

"I wish Ifra *had* been able to kidnap me!"

"Ifra? You know his name?"

"I asked his name before he left. Maybe he would have tried harder to kidnap me if I hadn't been wearing hair bows. He probably doesn't think I'm anybody."

"Violet, you really don't want him to think you're anybody, and I don't think you want to be delivered to King Luka. He doesn't sound like a very pleasant sort of person."

"I almost wish Erris hadn't come to help me get well," she said. "When I'm sick it doesn't feel possible to leave the house, so I mostly don't think of it, but I can't stand it now. I feel like I could go mad. I don't want to wait forever, especially if fourteen-year-olds are more grown up than I am!"

"Well, I'm not sure if I really know how to be a woman, myself. I'm only a few years older than you."

"You aren't wearing hair bows," Violet said scathingly, yanking at the one still in her hair. The knot refused to release entirely, leaving her with ribbons dangling on her shoulder.

"But do we want to be proper women? Women in Lorinar don't learn magic, and that's what I think we should do."

"Yes. All right." She still looked sulky, but it seemed to cheer her up enough to slide off the bedspread.

We went upstairs to look for Ordorio's magic books. There was still the locked door, which Violet rattled irritably, but I pointed to the next room. "I saw some books here. We can find the key for this door later."

The books in the other room, alas, proved to be things like histories of Lorinar and encyclopedias of herb usage—perhaps useful at another time, but not for learning magic.

We went downstairs. Celestina was back and kneading dough in a bowl.

"Where were you two?" she asked. She sounded a little cross, like she knew perfectly well.

"Nimira was just talking to me about things," Violet said. "I was upset."

Celestina nodded. This seemed to appease her a bit. Maybe she was relieved I had talked to Violet.

I hadn't realized how cold the upstairs had been until I was near the heavenly warmth of the woodstove again. Erris really should be by the woodstove, drying out. I stared out the window for a long moment, willing him to return.

"Where is Erris?" Celestina said, apparently reading my mind. "It's cold out there."

I had a sudden image of Erris's wet gears clogging with ice, trapping him in a cold prison, and I shuddered.

"I don't know," I said. My throat was tight. "He wants to be alone."

"I wonder if he wants to be alone as much as he thinks he does," Celestina said. "When I burned myself, I said I wanted to be alone, but I didn't. I just didn't want people to look at me the way they did. He must feel kind of burned all over."

I nodded slowly. "I just don't know how to . . . I mean . . . I feel like he already hates me sometimes."

"He doesn't hate you," Violet said. "He talks about you. He says you're such a good singer."

That was almost worse. I didn't want to be just a "good singer." "I mean in some deep down way," I said.

I couldn't tell them how Erris and I had argued, how I felt or how I thought he felt. My pride was like a web of knots encasing me, holding everything in, and while the tension could be uncomfortable, it was more terrifying to think of everything spilling out.

"I know he doesn't hate you," Celestina said. "I see how he looks at you."

"How does he look at me?"

"I don't know. He just looks happy."

I shrugged a little. "These are not the most convincing statements."

"I think you should go find him and tell him to come sit where it's warm."

It was getting colder, and the sun was setting. She was right; he shouldn't stay out, however comforting he found the outdoors to be at a time like this. I put on my coat and boots and headed for the shore again, pausing at the apple tree to regard the hoofprints of the fairy horse.

Past the apple trees, the forest started to thicken, and it already seemed dark here, with the bare limbs of trees casting complicated skeleton shadows, and the sun at my back to the west. A branch cracked beneath my sturdy shoe, and I heard Erris call distantly, "Nim?"

"It's me," I called back, stopping in my tracks.

"Can you come here? I've hurt my foot."

There was nothing more he needed to say to set me running, terrified that he would be broken but just a little glad to be wanted and needed too.

I had once wondered if Erris had feet beneath his fairy shoes, back when he was a doll trapped at a piano. Now I came across him sitting on a fallen log, inspecting what appeared to be half of a foot. My heart sped up quite alarmingly.

"Don't panic," he said. "I think it can be fixed. Maybe the water weakened the wood, I don't know."

"Your feet . . ." They looked so unnatural that between his feet and the earlier glimpse of his insides, I was beginning to feel sick with what an alien thing he'd become—what an alien thing I'd turned him into.

He cringed with almost a hint of amusement, as if the situation were so unpleasant that he found it almost humorous. But I couldn't find any humor in this. He held up the front half of his foot. It had a sharp piece of metal, like some sort of screw, jutting from it.

"What happened?" I said, walking over to sit beside him.

"Well, I haven't felt quite right since I went in the water. My joints are a little sluggish. I guess I should have been more careful, but I was very upset and . . . a little desperate to feel alive. So I was running, like maybe I could shake off the stiffness, and I jumped off this tree trunk—and felt the snap."

His feet were much like a cobbler's form for making shoes, only with a joint that allowed a natural bend where toes would be. It appeared that the heel had cracked and the joint had broken off. I barely smothered my panic as he showed me the damage. I was always worried about him breaking down. In an ordinary person, the correlation between health and life was obvious, but I didn't know if Erris could die if something happened to him, or if he would remain trapped in the body even if it broke. I could presume, however, that he couldn't wake up if his mechanism failed and I couldn't wind him. This was just a foot, but what if it had been something worse?

"I think it could probably be glued, or maybe I could get Lean

Joe to help me fashion a new foot," Erris said. "But . . . I'll need help walking back to the house."

I regarded him a moment. It was obvious I would have to touch him in order to help him.

"It's all right," he said, but he sounded distant. He held out an arm, and I helped him up.

He was still strong, and needed me mostly for balance as he hobbled along on one and a half feet. Still, his body was quite heavy, and his movements weren't as smooth as before he went in the ocean. The house seemed very far away.

"Maybe you should wait here, and I'll get Celestina," I suggested, when I saw how slow our pace would be.

"I don't want Celestina. Please. Just you. And let's never mention this again."

"All right. I certainly won't."

We were silent with concentration a moment, maneuvering past a space where the ground dipped and the depression was full of wet leaves.

"I think it will snow again tomorrow," Erris said. In the morning, the sky had been a surprising blue, but now the clouds were back and the air smelled crisp. Wind rattled the bare branches of the trees.

I nodded. "Just stay by the woodstove tonight and get warm."

"I will."

We were quiet then, each of us no doubt with different but overlapping unpleasant thoughts.

Just before we got to the house, he said, "I am thankful for you, Nim."

That was about the nicest thing he could've said to me just then. It made me strangely shy.

Erris, with the assistance of Lean Joe, mended his foot and sat down by the woodstove with a book. I was helping Celestina with the dinner, putting together a fish stew with salt cod, jarred tomatoes, and some rather withered-looking garlic, while she finished the biscuits.

Violet sat near Erris's feet and scooped the cat onto her lap. "Uncle Erris?"

He lowered the book. "Hmm?"

"I want to learn magic. Fairy magic."

Celestina looked sharply their way. "I really don't think it's a good idea to learn any magic until Mr. Valdana comes home."

"I don't think we can wait until he comes home," I said. "What will you do if the jinn remembers Violet? If he tries to take her? We can't hide her in the ocean."

"She—I don't think—" Celestina stopped and brushed flour from her hands onto her apron. "I suppose I should tell you this. I didn't burn my face on a lantern. I burned it trying to do magic."

"How?"

"I had some idea of how spells worked from reading novels about sorcerers, and I started trying to do magic on my own, without any training. It took forever to learn how to make fire, and I thought it would just be a little candle flame, but it wasn't. It broke through my hand like a torch. For a terrifying moment I couldn't get the fire to stop. I caught my hair on fire. My father was so upset I thought his eyeballs might fly right out of his head." She winced. "They told everyone else it was a lantern, but Mr. Valdana knew it wasn't. A lot of people guessed it wasn't."

"Why didn't you ask him to teach you magic properly when he hired you?" Violet asked.

"Oh, he told me when he took me on that he had no time to

teach magic," Celestina said. "But he could offer me a home where my parents wouldn't frown at me and neighbors wouldn't preach to me, and a fair wage."

"I understand your fear," I said. "But I have to learn. Even if it's dangerous. I am not going to sit by helplessly while some magical villain hauls off the people I love."

"I think we could be very careful," Erris said, almost absently. He seemed to be considering the idea. "Fairy magic is very intuitive, and largely safe. Violet could start there. Human magic tends to be more agressive, but . . . Celestina, I understand that you are sort of the lady of the house in Ordorio's absence."

Celestina shrugged.

"I don't want to usurp your position, but if we all had some magic, and time to plan, maybe we can thwart the jinn next time."

She sighed. "I wish I knew what Mr. Valdana would say. But I won't stop you. You *are* Violet's uncle. I would just hate to see anything happen to any of you."

I wondered if that was a fate we could escape, no matter which course we chose.

❧ 12 ❧

The next day, Celestina handed over the key to the upstairs room in the hopes that I would find a book of magical instruction. Unlocking the door revealed a rather intimidating mess: stacks of books, unmarked crates, desks cluttered with tools and papers and writing implements and candles, things draped with sheets, and everything covered with dust. The walking space would have been almost entirely unnegotiable had I been wearing the standard array of skirts and petticoats.

"I see why the door was locked," I said, stepping over a globe to get to some of the books. There was a shelf in the corner that looked like it had been arranged in some tidier era; it was all books of magic grouped by subject. There were books about magical species, advanced necromancy, astrology and divination, life after death. I started opening ones with promising titles, but many of them looked too difficult, while others seemed useless, and a great deal of them were written with the air that understanding magic was indeed a sort of gentleman's club, not something useful so much as something with which to show off.

Erris started going through the books on the desk. While we searched—making feeble attempts to tidy up as we went—Violet opened one of the boxes on the floor. "Doesn't this look like parts for clockwork?" she said, and then sneezed.

"Clockwork?" Erris turned.

Indeed, Violet was peering into a box full of cogs and gears nestled in hay. The parts were still attached to each other, for the most part, and when Erris lifted them from the box, they formed a small four-legged figure with a tail, like a cat. He set that aside and took out a crudely carved wooden head. It looked like the clockwork would move the eyes and mouth, but some of the pieces had broken apart.

Violet gasped. "A clockwork cat! I don't remember anything like this!"

Erris was still digging past the hay. "Look at this, Nim."

I stepped over another box to see an array of crude little clockwork rodents, nestled in the straw with their keys.

"How cunning!" Violet shrieked with delight. "Do they still work?" She grabbed one and began to wind it, but when she released it, it made a rather regretful clicking sound and went silent again without moving. She tested one after another, and some of them didn't work at all, while others simply didn't work properly: their gears didn't catch or a broken foot made them wobble. Erris looked at them with a concerned expression.

"Violet, did your father ever talk about constructing things from clockwork?" he asked.

"No," Violet said. "I don't think he built them, or surely he would have made me some dear little clockwork mice."

I knew Erris didn't believe for a moment that these crates of clockwork animals were a coincidence. He started opening all the boxes within reach.

"I had no idea he had so many interesting—" Violet's words cut off abruptly, replaced by a strangled gasp. Erris had thrown back one of the sheets and found a face beneath it.

The wooden face had no hair and was only half painted, yet it was well done, and the staring glass eyes made it look lifelike—or rather, corpselike. In the dim light of the workroom, I could see why it made Violet gasp.

Erris looked at it intently for a moment, and then he started wrestling off the rest of the sheet. It was not easy, for a number of boxes stood in the way of the table on which the clockwork rested. He had to bend and reach, his body tilted awkwardly to favor his good foot, kicking up a great deal of dust in the process.

"What is it?" I said. Her inner workings looked very much like Erris's. I wondered if the same maker's mark was stamped on her back.

"It looks like it was meant to be a clockwork version of my—my sister."

"Your sister? Do you think she was ever— Do you think she—?"

"I don't think her spirit is here, no," Erris said. "Besides the obvious question of why Ordorio would have trapped her in such a way, we would know. You sensed there was something strange about me from the start, didn't you?"

Violet seemed torn between stepping closer to the clockwork woman or farther away. "But why would he make my mother out of clockwork?"

"*That* is still a mystery to me," Erris said. He lifted her arm and then carefully turned her over. The plate on her back with the keyhole had no mark at all. "And I think she's broken, besides."

"Yes," I murmured. I was no expert on clockwork, to be certain, despite how often I wound Erris, but the clockwork woman was dusty and neglected, and moreover, appeared unfinished. Her armature looked prone and fragile laid out on the table, and it was hard to imagine her making any movement on her own power.

We resumed our search of the room, but now we were more interested in clues than magic books, although I set aside a few prospects in that regard as I went along.

I tried to hide my excitement at our discovery. If Ordorio had been experimenting with clockwork, maybe he did know how to free Erris. Maybe we hadn't been sent here only to help Violet.

It was Erris who found the battered leather-bound notebook, full of Ordorio's small handwriting and sketches of clockwork parts and mice.

"'Three mice have been put into the death sleep,'" he read. "'Three other mice were killed. The mice placed into death sleep could be coaxed into inhabiting clockwork bodies, but the dead mice have thus far been unsuccessful. Is it possible that a spirit is unwilling to inhabit a contrived body without retaining some tether to its true form?'"

Erris looked at me, briefly, then back at the book.

"'Experimented with cat,'" he continued. "'The cat has been sick and listless as of late, yet attempts to persuade it to inhabit a clockwork form were unsuccessful until the cat was placed into a death sleep. There seems to be a natural resistance in living beings to inhabit these artificial houses, unless they are placed in death sleep, in which case . . . ? Thus far, I am still unable to raise the dead without a body, but I am excited by the prospect that death may be preempted by death sleep. How long will the cat continue to live in its clockwork body?'"

Violet chewed a fingernail. "Papa was trying to raise the dead without a body?"

"I suppose it would be a great goal for a necromancer," I said, thinking of Karstor telling me how such a thing was impossible.

"He managed to revive mice and cats into clockwork bodies from a death sleep," Erris said softly.

"What is a death sleep?" I asked.

"It's like being frozen. You don't need food. You don't age. But typically, it doesn't last forever. People tend to wake from it at some point, so you can't just keep them comatose for decades. Another spell commonly used by human necromancers." Erris was still flipping through the book, but he briefly glanced at the clockwork woman. "And clearly, he had hoped to revive my sister, but I think he failed."

"That's disturbing," I murmured. "Why wouldn't he simply let the dead stay dead? I don't really like necromancy one bit. But what about you? Do you think he's the one who did this to you?"

Erris slowly nodded. "Maybe you were right, Nim."

Our situation was still precarious, but if Erris would share my hope . . .

"But why would he do that?" Violet asked in a panicked voice. "Uncle Erris, you told me human sorcerers cursed you! Would my father do something like that to you?"

"Sure he might," Erris said. "He left to fight the fairies. He cursed me, but then he fell in love with my sister and defected. I guess only he can tell us for sure, but either way . . ." He didn't finish the sentence, but he met my eyes, and there was a spark there I hadn't seen since I had first freed him from the depths of the curse.

~13~

We had a good snowfall that night. Erris played the piano, and Celestina the guitar, and I showed Violet a folk dance of Tiansher. We were a mess of cultures, and nothing matched, but I found it all the more fun for that.

In the evening, I wrote a letter to Karstor explaining our situation, asking for his advice—perhaps he had some elementary books on magic or information about jinn. Karstor would want to protect Erris just as I would, and I was fairly sure he wouldn't disapprove of a woman learning magic, although I hoped he wouldn't ask us to return. I had come to like having the woods around me, and the space to breathe, and I didn't want to leave Celestina and Violet vulnerable.

The next morning, Erris went out to gather firewood, and when he asked if I wanted to accompany him, I happily agreed. This, more than anything, seemed proof that his mood had changed.

The air made my lungs feel scrubbed clean on the inside. There was snow on the ground now, a few inches deep in most places and pocked with animal tracks.

"Snow hare," Erris said with a smile, pointing at the soft Y-shapes, the big hind feet splayed forward and the small front feet behind.

"Oh, I wish we'd see one. They must be cute."

"But shy."

The light was beautiful in the morning, full of golden patches where the sun struck, and blue shadows. The snow squeaked under our feet. Erris carried a basket in one hand and with the other, a walking stick he had found with the umbrellas by the door. His foot was obviously still troubling him, and he limped.

"Does it hurt?" I asked. It might be a difficult subject, but I was too concerned not to ask.

"No. I've just lost feeling in the part that broke off."

"Even after you fixed it?"

"Well, we glued it in place, but it's not the same. I'm wondering if it damaged the enchantment somehow." He stopped walking. "Nim, this morning after you wound me, I sat and reread every word of Ordorio's notes. I think those were studies he did while in school." There was an ominous tone in his voice.

"Oh?"

"He talks about the clockwork mice, and the cat. Their bodies broke down quickly, strained by the magic, he guessed. He was always mending them and renewing the enchantment, but finally he let it go and put them back to their bodies and lifted the death sleep. The sick cat died. The mice were fine."

His brown eyes met mine briefly, and then he looked out into the snow-dusted tangle of bare branches beyond us. "The good news is, I am starting to believe you're right. Annalie sent us here because Ordorio is either the person who cursed me, or he knows who did. Maybe he even knows where my body is. The bad news is, I don't think the feeling in my foot is coming back. My whole body has felt a little sluggish since I was in the water. This body isn't going to last forever."

"Maybe you shouldn't be gathering firewood," I said nervously.

"No, I want to," he said. "I need to be out here. My magic is stirring. I need to teach it to Violet." He started to walk again.

"I was reading about human magic last night from one of Ordorio's books," I said. "It all sounds so . . . destructive."

"You know, back home we had a magic tutor," Erris said. "He said a lot of wise things I barely paid attention to at the time, but I find now make a lot of sense. He talked about magic of all the races, and he said that human magic is often thought of as destructive, because a lot of humans don't value their connection to the natural world. They kill birds for sport, they hunt whales for oil, they cut down trees and don't plant new ones. Their magic is thought of similarly—potent, but lethal."

"I'm not like that!" I said. "And I don't want to be. And why do fairies get such *nice* magic? Talking to mushrooms? Surely you're not all benevolent. Your cousin doesn't seem to be."

"No, we're not," he agreed. "Nature can be violent and heartless, and humans can be as selfless and good and heroic as anyone else. That's the kind of sorceress I imagine you would be."

My cheeks warmed despite the cold. I had never thought of myself as becoming a sorceress, but that was what I was after, wasn't it?

"Our tutor was always saying how everything has a spirit. Magic just taps into that. So it's all about how you use the connection, isn't it?" He grinned. "I really sound like I know what I'm talking about."

"Don't you?" I laughed. "Please tell me you're not making this up so I'll feel better."

"No. Though I was just thinking how much I've grown up." He sounded sober at the thought. He gathered a few sticks from the ground, his first concession to the original purpose of our outing. "We all learned some things about magic, politics, other races, propriety . . . things royal children should know. But it isn't until just now that I realized how much I know."

"That's good, isn't it?"

"If I'm ever going to be a king, it is." His brow furrowed, and he said nothing for a moment. We had come to a thin creek that ran through the woods. He wordlessly handed me his basket while he stepped across the frozen water, putting his bad foot forward first with the walking stick for stability, his other arm out for balance. I leaped across after him, and he took the basket back.

"A part of me was hoping my body really was lost forever," he said. "I'm terrified of ruling the fairy kingdom. I was never meant for something like that. But it's true what you say. I hated Luka when we were children. And from all I've heard of Luka as king, he hasn't improved much."

"You'd be a good ruler," I said.

"Would I?" he cried. "I've lived just seventeen years—maybe eighteen by now—but I come from a prior generation. I hardly know what's been going on. And when I was last alive, I wasn't interested in anything that wasn't fun. Is a kind but unwilling king any better than a cruel but competent one? I'm not so sure."

Once again, we stopped walking. The air was still, just as we were, but the high, thin sunshine of winter was shining on the white world. I touched his sleeve. "But are you unwilling? What do you really want? To die now? To be king? To melt away unnoticed?"

He made a face. "The last option is tempting." He paused. "I don't really want to die."

"I feel sure you would make a better king than someone cruel," I said. "I think it would be very hard at first, and then get easier." Part of me wondered why I was encouraging him to be king. I felt I was pushing him farther from my own life, and yet, I could see that future for him. "You're a brave person. And you take care of other people. Very good qualities for a king."

"Do you really see that in me?" He looked at me carefully, as if searching for a reflection of himself he had never before seen.

"I do."

"I think you're speaking of yourself," he said softly. "I think it's you who would make a good queen."

My chin briefly trembled. I could imagine myself a sorceress more readily than a queen, and neither would be easy. I had been raised into singing and dancing at a royal court, but it was another thing altogether to envision myself on a raised platform where the king and queen sat, garbed in jewel-colored silks, surrounded by gold platters of food and scores of willing servants. Of course, the fairy kingdom would not look the same, but the feel of it must be similar.

"Well, I'm not royalty, I'm afraid," I said. Not to mention, I was human.

"You can be an optimist about my fate, but not about your own?" Erris said.

"It's always easier to be optimistic about someone else."

"If the job was offered, though, would you take it?" he asked, looking at me.

"Can a human be the fairy queen?"

"Oh, yes. In fact, there were times in which it was preferred. Fairies believe that a little diversity is a good thing."

"Well, then, of course I would take it. Without hesitation," I said, my heart beating fast. Which was not exactly true—I might hesitate, but the end result would be the same. I had come this far. If Erris asked me to be his queen, I would say yes and manage it somehow.

~14~

It was only later that I had time to consider what the conversation really meant. Erris truly had shifted his focus toward the hope that he might live to become king. It made me tremble a bit. Still, we owed it to both Lorinar and the fairy kingdom to prepare.

A week or so later, I was in the kitchen—we did nearly everything in the kitchen—reading some of Ordorio's books when Lean Joe came back from town with the mail. "You have a package, miss," Lean Joe said, gathering everyone's attention as he dropped a small parcel in front of me.

"Oh! I asked if Karstor would send something to help with the jinn."

"No, it's from overseas. Mr. Parry."

"He's sending you packages now?" Erris said. "What is it?"

I chewed my lip. I wanted to open it alone, but that would only arouse Erris's suspicions further, and I didn't feel like making him jealous now when he was talking to me about being a queen. Celestina handed me a knife and I slit the brown paper open.

A silver bracelet slid out. Each end of the bangle depicted the head of a stylized elephant, and the trunks formed the clasp. It was clever and lovely and I wished for all the world Hollin had not been the one giving it to me.

"Oh, can I see?" Violet said. "That's wonderful!"

"He probably got it cheaply," I said, knowing it wasn't true.

"He does remember that he's married, doesn't he?" Erris said.

I let Violet and Celestina admire the bracelet for a moment, and then I slipped it back in the envelope. "Maybe he just wanted to give me a token of friendship," I said. "He knows I like elephants."

"Elephants aren't really *romantic*," Violet pointed out.

"I guess he can send you whatever he likes," Erris said. "But I hope you don't encourage him."

"It's nothing!" I said, perhaps protesting too loudly. "Annalie is my friend, and Hollin and I went through a lot together."

"Oh, 'together,' did you? What exactly did you go through together?"

"We—" I made a face. "He's one of the only people I have to write to."

Erris gave a dark look down at the surface of the table. Of course, he had even fewer people to write than I did.

I wasn't about to open Hollin's letters in front of everyone, but I felt almost as if I were sneaking off into a liaison when I took them to my bedroom. My heart pounded as if I were, especially recalling what I had written to him last. I could no longer remember the exact words, I just recalled it had made me nervous.

Dear Nimira,

I was so pleased to receive your letter. I suppose
the mail travels relatively swiftly in these modern
times, but things change so quickly in my life that it
seems an age passes between letters.

I hope you enjoy the gift. I remembered us
talking of elephants back at Vestenveld, so when
I saw this bracelet in the market, I had to get it
for you. Many of the women here wear silver bangles
of similar design.

I've been continuing my work with the schools,
but I no longer work under Mr. Quendley. I have a
usual round of twelve schools in a fifty-mile radius
that I'm supposed to check on each month. I then send
a report back to my superiors, about what kind of magic
the schools are teaching. I do believe the Lorinarians
would rather the natives abandon magic altogether,
but they realize magic helps prevent epidemics
and famine, and the people would rebel without
it, so they only try to suppress martial magic.

I do see, now, why this was considered a suitable
punishment for my mistakes back home. I'm traveling
twenty-seven days out of thirty each month, and the
conditions can be grueling. The roads are poorly kept,
the weather is unpredictable, and I'm always
dirty and exhausted. My lodgings vary greatly in
quality. I never thought I would be eating with my
hands, crouching on the dirt at an open fire, with a
woman offering me fermented milk of some unknown

animal. I've learned some of the language, but there
are so many dialects that half the time it does me
no good.

This is not travel as I imagined it. There is no
leisurely sightseeing, no servants, no hotels catering
to Lorinarian travelers. I don't know when in the
history of the Parry family anyone has worked this
hard.

Yet, it is so different from anything I've ever
known. None of the social mores of home apply.
It makes me wonder what is real.

I think you must know how it feels.

He went on for a while, in similar vein to the last letter—
musing how I must have felt coming to Lorinar and talking of how
different the people were. His tone had changed. It was more sub-
dued and thoughtful. The pages held less romance and more grit.

I had an odd, fleeting yearning to be there with him, to see
him change, to see his eyes open in a country where women wore
bright colors and bare arms again.

But I had never really been in New Guinnell and quite likely I
was romanticizing it myself. I didn't think I'd care much for fermented milk.

He didn't precisely acknowledge how I had scolded him in my
last letter, but he did speak of Annalie:

Nimira, I know you are a girl of good moral
character—better than my own—and I hope my
letters don't make you uncomfortable. I know you
are friendly with my wife, and I know I shouldn't

write any other woman but her, especially you, considering how I once offered to run away with you.

I'm not trying to woo you anymore, Nim, I swear to that. It was the biggest mistake of my life to even consider it, and I know I am the villain in this piece. You know the facts of what happened between us: I cursed her in an attempt to save her while she was sick. I left her touched by the dead, trapped in the dark, haunted by spirits.

But do you know how it feels to harm someone you love? To see them changing, to know you caused it, to be helpless to stop it? You do know how it feels, I think. And at first, for Annalie there was only pity and regret and thoughts of trying to lift the curse, to put things back to how they were.

At some point, I was forced to admit that lifting the curse was beyond my power, and at the time I felt like the cursed one. Annalie didn't want to see me. She wasn't girlish and playful anymore, but she also wasn't depressed and miserable. She was turning into that person she has become—strange and wiser than her years. . . .

I admit I am slightly frightened of her. After all that's happened, a part of me still longs to see that bright young girl who couldn't dance well, and I have such trouble knowing how to relate to her anymore.

I am not sure, in saying all this, if I am looking for your sympathy or advice, or if I am merely trying to warn you that Erris might be changing

with all he's been through, and I hope you can
weather it better than I could.

Strangely, I almost wanted to cry when I read this, and I wasn't sure why. Was I terrified that Erris was changing into someone I couldn't understand, or was I merely relieved to know that someone else shared my pain? I took a deep suppressing breath.

Now I picked up the letters from Karstor and Annalie, noticing suddenly the postmarks. They were the same.

Sure enough, Annalie wrote:

Linza and I have moved into Dr. Greinfern's
apartment. Vestenveld is rather isolated and he was
concerned for my safety there. Several people have
come nosing around since the public learned about
me. I'm not worried, but Dr. Greinfern's concern is
reasonable, and the house has always been too
large, especially with Hollin away.

Of course I don't want you to worry. Dr. Greinfern
has made things very comfortable for me. Moreover,
I must say I'm fascinated to learn more about his
work and how matters unfold with the fairies. He's a
very intelligent man. Hollin would never have talked
to me about magic and politics, but Dr. Greinfern sits
and talks to me and explains things very thoroughly.
I think he's lonely himself, poor man.

Karstor barely referred to the arrangement, merely saying he thought it better if Annalie stayed with him, but he did call her Annalie, not Mrs. Parry. He wrote me a very long explanation of jinn.

It's hard to get much concrete information about jinn, because they are surrounded by a certain magic that makes people forget them and what they're capable of. Besides that, their history belongs to antiquity, and surely is as much myth as fact. It's commonly believed that they are humans with a streak of demon blood. I am never inclined to trust anything that brings up demons. Writers love to bandy about the notion of demons because they're very sensational. I suspect story-tellers have done the same for thousands of years. But whether or not they have demon blood, jinn are certainly powerful—and pitiable, really, it seems to me.

Thousands of years ago, it is said the jinn did something or another to infuriate a king who was, in turn, favored by the angels. The king cursed the race of jinn to serve his kingdom of men forevermore. Even after the king died, even after his descendants died, even after his palace fell into ruins, the jinn would be trapped forever in the king's collection of vessels—oil lamps and decanters and such. To this day, any man who finds one of the vessels can expect the jinn to serve him.

This matched the myths I had heard. Sometimes my father even used to say, if I wished for something impossible, "Travel west for thirty days and your wishes will be answered"—a reference to that palace in ruins. I was never sure it was actually real. Travelers spoke of it, but no one I knew ever actually found a jinn. Then again, maybe they would forget about it if they had. It made my brain hurt to think of it.

Karstor continued with a list of things jinn were rumored to be capable of and not capable of. Nearly everything one could imagine appeared on the first list. If the myths were true, we were most definitely out of luck.

"I believe the best defense is likely spirit protection," Karstor concluded. "Unfortunately spirit magic is not so common. I'll try to find Ordorio and send him home, wherever in God's name the man might be, and in the meantime, I'll see what help I can provide. Don't worry."

Don't worry? This hardly seemed a time not to worry. I sat for a long time, chin in hand, the other hand tapping the folded letter against my leg, pondering all these troubling letters—Hollin growing tanned and strong somewhere while Karstor and Annalie shared an apartment and a jinn of unknown power looked for Erris.

Of course, I shouldn't be disturbed by Annalie moving in with Karstor. The logic was sound, the arrangement likely very proper—Karstor was old enough to be Annalie's father, and while kind, he had always struck me as a private, withdrawn person. But was it really the only safe place she could go?

I suppose I wanted Hollin and Annalie to have a happy ending, just as I wanted a happy ending for Erris and myself. What would Hollin do if he came back? If Annalie was lost to him, and Erris lost to me?

Was I worried Hollin would continue to express interest in me?

Was I even worried I might be tempted to reciprocate?

Hollin was fully alive. Safe. Handsome. I didn't love him—no, of course I didn't, but ... what if he changed enough that I could?

I almost could. I hated to think I would entertain the idea, even for a moment.

I love Erris, I told myself. Insisted.

But Erris didn't show me passion. Not like Hollin had. I had a flash of memory—when Hollin and I had fought the dark spirits off together, and he had pulled me close to him and said, "Thank God," fiercely and earnestly.

Then I would remember all the awful things about Hollin— the uncomfortable moments, the cowardice, the fact that he was married—and hated myself for ever thinking of him fondly.

Sometimes I wished he would never write me again. It always left me confused, and the last thing I needed was more confusion.

～15～

The magic that came most easily to humans was fire. I didn't need spell books to tell me that. Everyone knew it. Some people even suggested that humans were born of the fire element, just as they said fairies were born of the earth, mermaids of the sea, and winged folk of the sky.

Erris had told me everything has a spirit to be tapped into. Therefore, I needed to tap into the spirit of fire.

The sun set early now, so that by five o'clock we were lighting a candle to eat and work by, but on one particular afternoon, I decided to build an outdoor fire. Celestina was still wary of dabbling in magic, especially fire magic, but Erris and Violet agreed to help. Erris insisted on hauling the logs into place. He was the only one of us who had ever built a fire outdoors, and he seemed invigorated by the task, so I kept my fears about his fragility to myself.

Violet was so bundled up she probably could have survived a fall from a cliff. The snow from earlier in the week had melted, and the forest around us was a blue-tinged black in the dusk. We sat together on an old wooden bench and watched Erris get the fire going with a scrap of paper to catch the kindling.

I watched the small red sparks dance. Memories of my childhood stirred, but I couldn't recall exactly when I'd been around an outdoor fire. It must have been a long time ago.

Erris had on the hat he'd bought in Cernan and leather work gloves, and he walked back and forth with a pitchfork, fussing with the logs. He looked very absorbed, rugged and content, nothing like a prince, but very much alive. The fire popped and the dark logs shifted.

"Do you feel anything?" Violet whispered.

"Like . . . magic?"

"Yes."

"Well, no," I admitted. "But I imagine it must take time. Magic can't just happen in a moment, or everyone would be a sorcerer."

Fairy magic, I thought, may have begun with the earth, but it didn't end there. Fairies could heal and cast illusions and any number of things. Human magic was the same. I only needed to find some way to tap into the spirit of things, as Erris said. What did fire mean? Heat. Light. Warmth. In the winter night, the fire didn't feel destructive, but life-giving.

Still, it could burn. I didn't want to hurt myself like Celestina. I didn't try to cast magic at first yet. I just watched the flames lap at the logs, and I watched Erris, and I allowed my thoughts to wander to different futures. What it would mean if Erris became flesh and blood, what would happen when Hollin came home, what the fairy kingdom was like . . .

After a time, Violet went inside with a complaint about her

face being too hot and her back too cold, and left us alone. I knew what she meant—I felt a bit like a half-cooked roast myself.

I wonder if I could move the heat. Surely that couldn't be too difficult.

I reached into myself, becoming acutely aware of the warmth on my face and chest. I took a deep breath through my lips, pulling the heat into my lungs, and held it there a moment. Then I exhaled, concentrating on moving the warmth back to my spine, up through my neck and down to my feet.

Briefly, I felt it—stronger than I expected, even—energy moving through me and dissipating. I repeated the action, and that time, I held the heat in my spine a moment longer.

I laughed. I was shocked by what I'd done, but just as pleased.

"Everything all right?" Erris walked over to me, using his pitchfork as a walking stick.

I was still grinning. "I think . . . I just felt a bit of magic."

"Just now? What did you do?"

"The heat that's coming off the fire? I think I moved it. Inside me." I explained exactly what I had done.

"That's wonderful. See? You're a natural talent."

"Oh, I don't know about that."

"No, I'm serious." He sat down next to me. "Maybe it's just a small spell, but what strikes me is the way you did it. You didn't try to move mountains right off. And you used your breath. They always tell you to use your breath."

Now I felt sheepish. "Still. Don't flatter me. I don't want to start thinking myself a 'natural talent' or I'll get frustrated later."

"Pah." He grinned at me, then looked away, poking the ground with the pitchfork. "Well, I'm impressed. Clearly, I'm no natural talent myself, but I'm making progress."

"With your magic?"

He nodded. "Things are starting to wake up for me. Not that the plants have as much to say when they're going to sleep for the winter. It took me a while to figure it out. I don't have . . . breath and heat and . . . well, it's easier to connect with things when you're alive. All I've got is my soul. I guess . . . maybe what I can do now isn't fairy magic, it's spirit magic."

I shivered and covered his hand with mine. "Don't talk about it."

"Why?"

"Just let me think of you as alive right now." Then I had an idea and I took his other hand. "Let me try something."

I drew back my hands and pulled off my gloves. He took his off too. Maybe it would help. As always, his skin felt like a living man's, but beneath his clothes, the illusion ended, and cold metal and wood began. I thought he would yank his hands away as I slid my hands underneath his sleeves, but he didn't. I wasn't entirely sure what possessed me, but I kept thinking of the day he had come out from the water and told me he felt cold and wrong all over.

I wanted to know if I could make him feel warm.

I drew in a very slow breath, and as I released it, I tried to direct the heat from the fire and from my own heart into him. As long as I let the magic move very slowly, I felt I could guide it, and sure enough, the cold armature warmed under my touch. I slid my hands back to his fingers, and clasped them tightly a moment, keeping the heat close and contained.

I felt Erris tremble, but I knew it wasn't from cold. For a moment, we shared the same warmth, our eyes locked, until I started to lose my grasp on it. It slipped from me, dissipating into the air.

Erris kept staring at me for what felt like an age.

"Did it work?" I asked.

"I know I felt something."

He put a hand to my shoulder, and then his arms were around me, pulling me against him, and my lips parted, inviting him.

He kissed me, still trembling, his lips tasting like life—perhaps all illusions, but I didn't care. I didn't want to be mere friends. I wanted this. I wanted to know he desired me like I desired him even if he couldn't have me—yet.

"Nim." He spoke in my ear now. "Why did you let me kiss you?"

"You chose to kiss me."

"Yes, but— That magic you just did . . ."

I drew back a bit, suddenly feeling as if it had been very illicit. "I just thought you'd want to feel warm. I don't really know what I'm doing yet."

"No, it's not . . ." He sighed. "You did nothing wrong. I felt like my old self for a moment, is all, and— You looked so beautiful, doing magic. I can't explain it. There was something so confident about the way you took my hands, and . . ."

He sounded so anguished. Suddenly I felt awful. My own body was so warm, tingling with a desire I couldn't help, but my lips were dry as if he had never kissed me at all. The glamour left nothing behind. It was cruel to make him feel like his old self.

"I'm just so tired of pretending I don't want you that way!" I covered my face, taking a deep breath to keep back the tears. "Ever since I was fourteen, I've had all these *men* looking at me, while I danced. Ogling me. It made me feel like I didn't want to see men. Or boys. It made me feel like love was just a lie, no one around me seemed to really feel anything for each other. Even friendships meant next to nothing—I was just so alone. But here, with you . . . Even if you can't hold me and I can't touch you like we wish, it's still better than trying to act like we don't care. Or maybe you don't care. Maybe you hate me because I have to wind you every morning and it's all my fault. I never know what you really feel. First it's this and then it's that!"

"Nim, I . . ." He sounded choked. "Please don't cry."

"I'm not! I'm making a great effort about it too!"

"All right. *I'm* trying not to cry." He pressed his palms to his temples. "Seventeen is far too old to cry, but it's also far too young for . . . for this. I just—I need . . ." He swallowed. "Maybe you're right. I don't know what to do. I crave someone to hold me and . . . and *help* me with this. So badly. No one can really give me those things." His voice broke as he said, "I miss my family, Nim."

I pulled a wrinkled handkerchief from my pocket and wiped my nose. "I will hold you and help you, as much as I can. You just have to let me."

He nodded, fidgeting with the edge of his coat.

I stood up and moved in front of him and put my hands on his shoulders. Moving slowly, acknowledging each other with the slightest of gestures and expressions, I settled onto his lap, and put my arms around him, and drew his head to rest on my shoulder. I think it helped that we were so far away from anyone who would care. We could form our own ideas of what reality ought to look like.

"I truly do believe that your real body is alive somewhere," I said. "I'm not going to lose you."

He put his hand to the back of my head and held me close, so close, and then I did start to cry, but my magic warmed my tears.

16

Even if Erris and I had tried to pretend the kiss had never happened, I don't think we could have. Some things simply can't be
ignored.

Sometimes I was jealous of Erris winding down and sinking
into automatic sleep, because he didn't have to lie awake at night
and think about it all.

The snow came more regularly now, and every morning I woke
to windows furred with frost and loathed the thought of leaving
the cocoon of my bed, but I used these mornings to work on magic.
I would light a candle and draw a thread of warmth from it. Every
day I seemed a little better at making heat from almost nothing,
and one day I found I no longer needed the candle.

I didn't want to stop pushing the magic farther by inches. One
morning, I tried warming Erris's key first and using it as a channel
for magic when I wound him.

He didn't let me slip out of his room that day. He caught my hand and smiled. "Look at you, Nim! What've you been up to? Pretty soon we can use you to cook toast."

"I've been practicing. It's easy to want to practice when it's so cold." I hesitated. "But I can't *make* fire. I haven't even tried. With what happened to Celestina . . . I wish I had someone to guide me."

"You've been very cautious so far. You started by moving heat and now you're learning to make heat, so maybe you can do the same with fire. Move it first."

"Maybe you're right. I just don't want to burn the house down. Celestina will have a fit if I start practicing magic indoors."

It was snowing that morning, but when it stopped after lunch, I took a lantern out and teased the flame with my gloved hand, trying to connect with its spirit. At first I could still only move the warmth around, and then I realized the fire itself felt a little more fickle. Shy, even. Maybe because I was starting with a mere lantern flame, whereas I'd tried moving the heat with a steady bonfire. Or maybe kerosene fires were simply more difficult to connect with than wood fires. Soon I could "catch" the fire with my mind, but it slipped away if I tried to manipulate it. I must have tried to hold on to it a hundred times before I made any progress. Just as I finally managed to make the accursed thing grow and shrink in some small measure, the snow started again.

I came inside and slammed the lantern down on the counter by the kitchen door and started unraveling myself from my scarf. Violet was at the kitchen table, reading, one stockinged foot tucked under her and the other scratching the cat's back with agile toes.

"Are you mad?" she asked.

"No, just—I can't get it right. Well, I can move a candle flame. After hours of trying, I can *move* a candle flame."

"If it helps at all, I don't think you were actually outside for multiple hours," Violet said in a bored tone, still staring at her book.

"This is serious. I mean, I've been working on magic for weeks and I can move heat and I can barely move fire, which is all well and good, but it's not going to help me fight off a jinn! I don't know how stupid I must have been, to think I could learn anything useful in one winter. I guess I'll make the jinn nice and warm, and Erris can talk to some mushrooms—"

Erris wandered in, eyebrows raised, obviously lured by my shouting. "Are you all right, Nim? You're being way too hard on yourself."

"It's just . . . Well, you've been having magic lessons with Violet; is she learning anything?"

"*I* can talk to mushrooms now," Violet said, rather sarcastically.

Erris nodded. "I was thinking of a poisonous mushroom army."

"Are there even any mushrooms growing in the snow or are you two just toying with me? Because I'm in no mood. I just spent hours—or at least, *an* hour—trying to catch a candle flame, and as soon as I did, it started snowing and I had to come inside."

"I think you've done enough for today anyway," Erris said, pulling out a chair for me. "Sit down. Have an apple."

I kneaded my aching head. "I'm tired of apples." I took a deep breath, knowing I was verging on a tantrum. "I'm sorry, it's just—I had so much success with the heat magic at first, but moving the candle flame took forever. It's made me realize how silly this is. I can't become a sorceress in a few months, no one can."

"At least it's something you can do to feel in control," Erris said.

"Like giving a baby something to suck on," I muttered. "What will happen when the jinn returns? What if he takes you away from me? You can't hide in the sea now; it's freezing out there."

"I don't know," Erris said. "Maybe he won't come back."

"I bet he will," Violet said.

"Violet, one would almost think you fancy the jinn, the way you talk."

Violet finally put her book down and glared at me. "The jinn *was* nice to me. He is a person, you know. Jinns have to do what their master tells them, they can't help it. They'd rather be free."

I frowned. Jinns in stories were always trying to get free, but they weren't especially nice about it, and our jinn hadn't struck me as especially nice either. "Well, whatever his sweet and angelic intentions may be, we still have to consider it a serious threat, because he can't help it, and I'm sure he will come back, so we can't be complacent."

"We're doing our best," Erris said. "And you're beating yourself up over it. I doubt he'll come back in the dead of winter and risk getting caught in a blizzard. We'll all work on our magic and see how far we can get."

TELMIRRA

Sometimes Ifra forgot all about Violet, but every time he pulled the plaid hair ribbon from his pocket, the memories rushed back like a sweet surprise—the kiss, the haughty way she spoke, the fire in her eyes despite her fragile body, and the small hand pulling off the ribbon and thrusting it into his palm. "I don't want you to forget me," she had said.

He understood that so well.

His tutor, of course, had warned him a thousand times not to develop feelings for anyone. Procreation was important to further the race of jinn; affection, on the other had, was dangerous.

Yet Ifra wondered how affection could be helped if one was to take things as far as procreation. His tutor could speak of these things so coldly, but much of his advice seemed impractical in the real world, when everyone around Ifra was full of life and love and hate instead of calm meditation.

When Ifra returned to Telmirra, a girl approached and took

his horse to the stables. Ifra hoped he would ride the horse again. It had a lively, pleasing nature, and he had to stifle his emotion at seeing it led away. Belin met him in the main hall.

"You came back empty-handed?" he said.

"Well, for now, but—"

"Follow me. We'll talk in my quarters."

"Where is the king?"

"He's not feeling well today. He asked if I would speak for him."

Ifra followed Belin to the gardens, and then through a little gate in the wall, and down a path through the woods. It wasn't really a long walk, but Ifra felt more and more apprehensive as they approached a smaller wooden building, the size of a large house, constructed in the same style as the palace. A fire crackled on the hearth, and an array of carved wooden animals pranced and lumbered and scampered across the mantel. Whoever carved them had skillfully captured motion from static wood. Evergreen boughs were hung on the walls, and the rafters were painted with bright patterns of knots, vines, and trees.

Belin didn't bother to sit. As soon as the door was shut behind them, he said, "You don't have Erris. What happened?"

"Erris has some sort of ability to disappear when I'm near," Ifra said. "The strange thing is, I sense him in two places—in the northeast edge of Lorinar, and . . . well, right near here. Very near."

"Here? It must be because he died here. You can't pay attention to that. How much did you bother trying to find him there?"

"Several times," Ifra lied. "It's no use. I get close and—he vanishes."

"Well, what did you think would happen, coming back here? My father told you to bring us Erris Tanharrow. All he's going to do is send you right back out again."

"I thought he might have a better use for me."

"We need Erris Tanharrow. We can't just go poking around the human land ourselves, jinn. No one else can fetch him."

"I'll try again."

Belin groaned. "You wait here. I'm going to talk to my father. I'll send for you shortly."

Ifra nodded. His heart was pounding. Belin wanted him tied to the throne forever, so that when Luka died, Ifra would belong to him. How long before Luka gave in?

Maybe he should have tried harder to fetch Erris. Yes, he really should have. But he'd been troubled by the thought of disturbing Erris and his family for some reason . . . What was it? His hand moved to his pocket and pulled out the hair ribbon. Violet. Yes. Of course. He didn't want Violet to see him dragging her uncle away.

About half an hour later, a young man opened the door and told Ifra the king wished to see him.

Luka was in bed, his glamour allowing no hint of illness to show through, except that he looked tired and had a cup of strong-smelling tea. He looked displeased, although not angry like Belin.

"Sit down, Ifra. I want you to tell me every detail of what happened when you tried to take Erris. Who did you see, how close did you get before he disappeared, what attempts did you make to find him—everything."

Magic tugged on Ifra, making it harder to lie than he expected. He had never tried to lie to a master before. "I came through the woods. I met a girl there . . . a girl from Tiansher, which was unexpected."

"That must be Nimira, the girl the Lorinarian papers spoke of," Belin said.

"But . . ." Ifra's memory was oddly hazy. "I could no longer feel Erris's spirit there. I searched the area, but I had to give up."

"You said you tried several times. What happened the next time?"

"They expected me the second time. I never even saw anyone, but the same thing happened. When I got close, Erris seemed to disappear." Ifra knew he was speaking a little too quickly, to rush out the lies.

"So you just gave up?" Belin said. "You didn't threaten them?"

"I— No."

"Set fire to their house," Belin said. "Let them know you're serious."

"You told me to bring Erris unharmed."

"Can't jinn control fire? Frighten them." Belin looked at Luka, and Luka nodded.

"Jinn, I want to trust you," Luka said, and Ifra noticed how he was not referring to him by name. "But I'm not sure you're strong-willed enough to do what needs to be done."

"No," Ifra said. "I only thought . . ." The king was right, really. Ifra didn't care for violence. He couldn't bring himself to fight a house full of women to kidnap Erris.

"Father, I told you, we have to bind him to the throne," Belin said.

"Wait! Please," Ifra said. Something else had happened there that would interest the king, but he couldn't quite remember. "There's something . . . My memory . . ." He pulled out Violet's ribbon again. He remembered her anew, and too late he realized, he didn't want to tell the fairy king about her.

"What is it?" Luka said. "What is that?"

"It's . . . a hair ribbon." Ifra looked at it in horror. He'd forgotten her enough to make this mistake, and now he remembered her too much to lie. "There was a girl there."

"A girl? At Ordorio's?" Luka said. "I heard he had a baby with Melia, but they were both killed. Ordorio didn't—he couldn't—the bodies were mangled, so I heard." His voice rose again. "Was it Ordorio and Melia's child?"

"Yes." Ifra wanted to ask more questions about this—how did Luka know?—but it didn't seem the best time. "There's some sort of spell on her so people forget her."

"How'd you get her hair ribbon?" Luka asked. When Ifra didn't answer right away, Luka said, "She wanted you to remember her, did she? Well, well."

"Father!" Belin said. "This could be the perfect solution. I could marry the girl. Then we'd have a Tanharrow on the throne and I can still be king. How old would she be?"

"Fifteen," Luka said. "Yes . . . you're right." He gave his son a sharp look that Ifra didn't quite understand. They were plotting with their eyes now, between themselves.

Ifra wrapped his fingers tight around the hair ribbon. He'd never meant for this to happen. "I'll go back," he said. "And bring her to you."

"Yes," Luka said. "This time I'll make sure of it. I'm sorry, Ifra. I do want to trust you, only—"

"Wait," Ifra said, trying not to beg, trying to ignore the glittering hunger in Belin's eyes. "I'm trustworthy. I did go looking for Erris, just as you asked, and I'll go after him again. I just didn't know how long you wanted me to take."

Luka looked at Belin. "Son, could you leave us for a moment."

"But, Father—"

"I said, leave us. Don't make me argue with you, I'm already weary." Luka waved a hand, and this time Belin obeyed, but he looked upset.

Now Ifra stood alone with Luka. The king's eyes were regretful, tired beneath the glamour.

Ifra dropped to the floor, touching his forehead to the rug. "Please," he said, his voice calm, his insides anything but. "Even as your bound servant, my magic is not infallible, but know that I live to serve you."

"I'm sorry," Luka said. "I wish you were not a kind young man, because these are not kind times. I don't need a good heart, Ifra, I need someone trustworthy, and you are not a good liar. It is now my wish that you will be bound to serve the one who sits upon the fairy throne until the end of your days."

Worse than hearing the words was the feeling that swept over him—a sickening feeling, like a vise clamped around his heart, forcing his will to obey whatever Luka asked of him. He had known this feeling before, when he had to grant a wish he didn't really want to grant, but this feeling was far worse—as if he not only had to grant the wish, but he *was* the wish. Angry, magic heat swept across his skin, but he couldn't release it. His magic belonged to Luka. He stayed on the floor. He couldn't bear to look Luka in the eye.

"I know it must be hard for you, Ifra, but if it helps, know that you are precious to me. I'll care for you. I reward men for a job well done, and I'll reward you too. You'll have anything you want—money, feasts. A lovely wife. When you come back, if you wish, I'll throw you a feast and invite all the loveliest girls in the fairy kingdom. Your work may be distasteful, but you will protect my kingdom and my people, and when you aren't working for me, your hours will be all your own. I have no doubt the people will love you. You'll be a hero."

Ifra took a deep breath, absorbing the words. He could have a wife. He would be a hero. If he had to be bound, most jinn would envy the situation. Was it really worse than his childhood, snatching fun only when his tutor wasn't looking? He got to his feet. "All right, master." He couldn't call him Luka anymore, not when the king had done this to him. "What would you have me do?"

"I want you to bring me Melia's daughter unharmed, and destroy the clockwork body of Erris Tanharrow."

17

The shortest day of the year passed us by, celebrated with music and popcorn and a pie made from jarred summer cherries. The mornings were positively frigid, and the stove wouldn't hold a fire overnight, so I came downstairs every morning to find Celestina bundled in a coat thrown over her long underwear, getting it started so we could all have tea.

"I know you're afraid of magic," I told her one particularly frigid day. "I certainly understand why. But you should learn to warm yourself. It'll make the morning more pleasant."

She didn't resist for long. That cold kitchen, with all the water too frozen to drink, could've motivated anyone to sorcery. I showed her how to draw the warmth from the stove, very slowly, using her breath. It took her several mornings to master, but I saw her eyes light the moment she had it.

"We're going to turn into a houseful of witches," she said with a grin.

Her words turned out to be even truer than I expected.

One day in January, after a week of surprisingly mild weather, with just enough snow to make everything lovely, I heard a soft knock on the door. Erris was outside with Violet, and Celestina was in the kitchen. I was just coming downstairs with some of Ordorio's books—I'd been extracting what kernels of information I could from them.

I supposed I was as good a person to answer the door as any-one. And the jinn hadn't been much for knocking in the past, so I had no reason to assume it was him. Still, I took an umbrella from the stand by the door and held it behind me.

A small woman stood, clad in a black velvet hooded cape, clutching a bag and an armful of books. She smiled. "Dr. Greinfern sent me. I'm the help you requested."

"Annalie?" I bent my head to look beneath her hood. "Mercy me, it is you! Well, come in out of the cold! And the light. How can you be here?"

I had only ever seen Annalie Parry in a room lit by the glowing, firefly-like orbs of the spirits that followed her everywhere. There was no sign of them now. She was out in the daylight like an ordi-nary woman, although with gloves and a hooded cape, which she now pushed back, revealing her thick chestnut hair caught in a loose knot at her nape.

"I didn't really go to Karstor's because he was worried about me. He wanted to see if he could lift the curse, but I didn't tell you in case it failed. I'm still sensitive."

"That's . . . that's wonderful!" I hardly knew what to say. She was the last person I'd expected to see. "Did you take the train up?" What a ridiculous question. Did I think she'd stolen a ride on the back of a magical bird?

"Yes. Goodness. I hadn't been on a train in so long, but it was nice. I sat near the sweetest family. They own a big strawberry farm down south and the little girl told me how to make strawberry cake. So earnest. But then when I got here . . . well, the people here in Cernan are . . . charming, aren't they? They told me Ordorio—"

"Sold his soul to the devil?" I offered.

"Yes, and that some sorcerer was training a coven of witches here." She wiggled her fingers, mocking the ominous warning. "Of course, the fellow looked at me like he thought I'd fit right in."

"No, they don't exactly like us in town," I said. "But we keep to ourselves."

"At least this house is out of the way," Annalie said. I was glad she seemed chatty. Much chattier than she used to be. She hardly seemed the mysterious, almost frightening woman Hollin wrote about in his letters and that I remembered. "And it's a lovely house too. So Roscardian, the stone and the arched windows. And the gloomy interiors." We were passing the parlor, with the painting of the Queen of the Longest Night and all the somber wooden furniture.

"You should see the portrait galleries," I said.

Celestina came stalking into the room, wiping her hands on her trousers—a gesture she immediately stopped when she saw Annalie. "I thought I heard voices. Who—?"

"This is Annalie Parry," I said. "Annalie, this is Celestina, Ordorio's . . ."

"Everything," Celestina said. "I do all the cooking and cleaning and I take care of his daughter, or I used to, before Nim and Erris came along. And I am so sorry I look such a state! Nim, why didn't you tell me if you knew she was coming?"

I looked down pointedly at my own trousers, which had dirty knees.

"She didn't," Annalie said. "I didn't even really know I was coming until I left. Well, I'll tell you all about it over a cup of coffee. I brought coffee in my bag in case you haven't any."

The coffee was exclaimed over, and promptly brewed. Celestina brought out yesterday's raisin buns, warming them and sliding a little fresh butter over their tops to freshen them. Erris and Violet came in while Celestina was placing the afternoon refreshments on the table, and Annalie's presence had to be explained again.

Annalie patted the stack of books she had brought, which now sat before her on the table. "I've been studying magic more earnestly since the events of the past year. Karstor and I have been corresponding about it ever since, in fact. Karstor is much more open with me about magic than Hollin ever was, and he understands the spirit world. I've brought some useful books, but I'm hoping my presence will be more useful. I can enlist the aid of the spirits to create a protection spell."

"How did Karstor lift your curse?" Erris asked.

I should have been the one asking questions, paying attention to this new information about magic, but my mind kept wandering. As Annalie explained some business about spirit gates and something called a "soft exorcism," I watched her. She was out in the world, her curse lifted enough to have freedom, but she looked sad and a little harried. She spoke with a strange note of urgency I couldn't place, and she sometimes glanced up or to the side as if she saw someone who wasn't actually there. I realized, then, that since she was no longer followed around by spirit orbs as she had once been, she must be looking for them, unconsciously perhaps. Her lost spirits. Her friends.

Had Karstor truly done her a favor?

Of all the assistance for Karstor to send. I kept thinking of my letters to Hollin—I'd just had another one in the past week—and the elephant bracelet. Seeing Annalie, I suddenly felt as if I shouldn't have exchanged a single letter with him. What if I held them back, unwittingly, from reconciliation?

When the coffee and buns were gone, Celestina and a curious Violet showed Annalie to her quarters, and Erris leaned over to me. "You all right, Nim? You don't look exactly happy she's here. I thought you two were good friends."

"Well, yes, I mean, we write. She helped me free you, back at Vestenveld. But she's a hard woman to know. I always got the feeling she lived in another world from the rest of us."

"And also, her husband sends you presents."

"That's not . . ." I placed my hand over my eyes. "I wish he wouldn't."

"You could tell him not to write anymore. It's common enough for married people to be friends and correspondents with the opposite sex, at least where I come from, but considering your history with Hollin, do you really think it's a good idea to encourage him with letters? Even harmless ones? Why do you write him, considering what he did?"

This interrogation caught me off guard, and irritated me, perhaps because I had no good answer. "I'm just . . . I'm curious about his travels and what they're having him do in these other countries. We shouldn't discuss this now."

"Why not? The way Annalie's been chattering her head off, they'll be up there for an hour talking about linens. And you know

Violet will want to show off her own room. And, well, every time you get a letter from Hollin, can't you see how it bothers me?"

"Well, you should have said so instead of just making jokes."

"Surely you know I'm not *just* joking. Do you want me to make a big fuss about it instead?"

"You should *talk* to me."

Erris exhaled sharply. "Look. I don't want to get distracted talking about how to talk. I know it's been bothering me since I met you that you'd even give Hollin the time of day. He trapped his wife upstairs for years and told everyone she was dead. I don't care if Smollings made him do it, I don't care if she extracted some happiness from the situation, how can you talk to a man who'd do a thing like that? And then . . . then he asked you to run away with him! Without even telling you the truth. I've tried to be nice about it, to assume you'd figure it out for yourself, but he's a liar." His voice had an edge I'd never heard in Erris before.

"I know he is, but . . . he helped us in the end."

"Because you had a plan and he could see a way to turn the tide and still protect himself. I think he's a coward to the end. Pity him from a distance, because he's dangerous. There seems to be no limit to what he'll do because he's too scared to do what's right. If he wouldn't protect his own wife, then what would he protect?"

I was shaking. I couldn't think of any defense for Hollin, but I hated to hear Erris speak of him that way.

Erris's voice softened just a little. "Why do you *want* to write him?"

I wiped my eyes, running my hands back over my hair, forcing calm upon myself. "Because . . . I'm—I don't know. I'm lonely."

Erris put a hand on my shoulder. "I think we're all a little lonely, but you have us. You have me."

"I worry I might not . . . always."

"It's better to be alone than with a man like that."

I was struggling not to cry, thinking of Hollin's letters. I'd just got one, fat with details about the schools and the people he was meeting, how they needed magic and made it a part of their everyday lives, without the fear and mystery and patriarchy of Lorinarian sorcery. He was changing, growing. I couldn't tell Erris that. He wouldn't believe me. I didn't want to share the letters with him. I knew he was right; I should tell Hollin to stop writing me, especially with Annalie here. What if Lean Joe came in with the mail and there was another package?

"Nimira, I want to understand," Erris said. "But you're crying over him, and I—I don't know what to say. It's hard to believe you don't have feelings for him."

"I—" I swallowed. "That night by the fire, when we kissed . . . I don't think it would have happened if I hadn't taken your arm and warmed you, and told you how tired I was of pretending. I don't have feelings for Hollin in the same way I have feelings for you, but for all his flaws, sometimes he's more open with me than you are."

"Maybe so," he said. "I'm sorry. I've been grieving." His voice was very neutral. I couldn't tell if he was angry. But he made me feel horrid. I knew he was grieving, but I needed him to share his pain with me. Was it selfish? I didn't know when it was appropriate to stop being patient. I had no mother, no parent, no adult at all to advise me.

"Nim, we haven't had the best circumstances, that's all," Erris said. "There's nothing we can do about that. Nevertheless, I don't think I'm asking anything unreasonable when I tell you not to write Hollin anymore." He gave me a brief unreadable look, and then stood and left.

I sat there a moment, my stomach clenching around an odd mix of guilt and anger.

We all gathered around the table again when Annalie came back downstairs. My emotions were shunted aside, at least for the moment. Important business needed attention.

"We must form a plan," Annalie said. "Karstor received all your letters, of course. We talked about it before I left. He suggested I focus on protecting Erris. We felt that it might be easier to defend than to attack."

"I've been practicing sorcery," I said. "I've just managed to move fire. I'm not sure if there's much I can do, though."

"And I've been learning fairy magic with Erris," Violet offered. "But I don't know what help it would be against a jinn either. I can talk to plants."

"She's starting to learn glamours," Erris said. "But we're a ways off from enchantments. *Someone* is not exceedingly disciplined."

" 'Just like your mother,' " Violet mimicked.

"Well, it's true. And not to be maudlin, but look what happened to her."

"Can you draw any protective power from the forest?" Annalie asked. I was impressed by how focused she was. When I last saw her, she seemed barely tethered to the planet, but now she was the most grounded of us all.

"I can," Erris said. "We could work on that in future lessons, although it is a skill for someone with discipline."

Annalie nodded. "I think we should all focus on defensive magic. Maybe together, we can face an attack."

"Are your orbs still with you?" I asked. "I didn't ... see them." I stammered a bit. I was never sure how to talk about Annalie's magic. I'd never felt quite comfortable around her, the way she could hear voices in silence and see things in darkness, the way she seemed content in a situation most people would find a nightmare.

"Not like before," she said. "Karstor had to close the gates so I could walk in the light. But I can summon spirits as a necromancer would, and I have the advantage of long acquaintance with some lost souls."

"I think someone needs to be prepared to be aggressive," I said. "We can't all just sit here and try to deflect whatever the jinn throws at us. What if he tries to harm one of us? Or what if he goes after the house? The forest? Jinns are fire specialists too. We can't protect everything."

Celestina was rubbing her thumb along her palm.

"It could be dangerous to fight a jinn," Annalie said.

"When you and I fought Miss Rashten," I told her, "we were sorely unprepared. You never had time to summon your spirits. What saved us was Linza digging up Hollin's gun. She bought you time. I think we should be prepared for anything. The three of you can work on defense, but I want to take another direction." I glanced at Celestina.

"I'll help you, Nimira." Celestina spoke slowly. "I don't like it, but I think you're right."

The whole notion that we could prepare to fight a jinn when we knew nothing of his powers, besides that they were considerable, felt somewhat . . . optimistic. But I had claimed to be an optimist.

A FAIRY HOUSE

Ifra hesitated, some distance from Keyelle and Etana's door. He didn't want to tell them what he had become and what he had to do, and yet, he wanted to do all he could to right the wrongs he was causing.

Keyelle answered his knock, her green hood drawn around her hair with a pale hand. The cold was bitter this evening. "Yes? Come in. Hurry, you must be freezing."

"Jinn have an inner fire." Ifra had a wool coat and cap thrown over his clothes; he didn't need more. Inside, the stove warmed the cabin, but everyone was bundled up nevertheless.

"I didn't expect to see you again," Etana said. She smiled. "We've already had dinner, but there's a bit left."

He shook his head. "Your stores must be low in winter. I don't need food."

"You don't need heat or food . . ." Keyelle shook her head with a slightly pained smile. "What do you need?"

"Nothing. Air, I suppose."

"You poor thing. I think it must be sad not to need anything."

"Well, there are ups and downs to it, I suppose." He glanced at them—their welcoming, unconcerned faces that remembered him, but not why he had come before. "I have to tell you something important," he said. "Against my will, I've been sent to destroy Erris Tanharrow."

Their faces dropped in shock. He waved down their questions.

"I'll explain everything. I told you once, but I had to make you forget. This time, write it down, if you have anything to write with."

Etana produced pen, ink, and paper. To ask them to write this down was somewhat a breach of Luka's instructions, but not so much that Ifra couldn't manage it. The scratch of the pen felt like pinpricks on his skin.

He told them the whole story, even showed them Violet's ribbon, watched fear bloom on their faces. Only Sery wandered off to play with her dolls, with a child's trust that politics were merely boring and nothing bad could ever happen.

"Ifra, you look awful," Etana said. "There's no way to . . . break free of this?"

"A part of me is no longer my own. I can stop to eat and rest, but if I dawdle too long, I start to feel . . . sick." And worse. Ifra had started to have visions of destroying Erris. He imagined different ways that he could hurt him, his clockwork body blown to bits, Violet snatched from the scene, bound and gagged if necessary. These thoughts came not from his brain—at least, he hoped not—but from some dark, other place, and they were accompanied by a sense of satisfaction. His tutor had warned him that his own thoughts would compel him to grant the most difficult wishes, but Ifra had never really believed, or understood, how bad it could be.

This was how jinns became cruel or, at best, detached, like his tutor.

"Only he can free me." Ifra covered his eyes. "He never will. I'm his loyal servant, and what king would give that up? His son is worse. I suppose my only hope is to restore Erris to the throne and hope he would free me. But instead, I have to destroy him."

"Do you want us to come with you?" Keyelle looked like she was ready to go out the door that very moment.

"We can't take Sery," Etana said, glancing at the girl. She was making a nest from boughs of pine.

"You can't come," Ifra said. "You might get hurt."

"I might," Keyelle said. "Or I might not. But why tell us this if you don't want us to help Erris? Etana can stay here with Sery, and I could alert the other Green Hoods."

"But how can you cross the gate into Lorinar?" Etana asked.

"They let traders cross. I can make up a story."

"Maybe you could sneak across, but a group of you? The humans might be suspicious. And what about the cold? What if another storm comes?"

"Oh, always so sensible!" Keyelle snapped, slumping back into her chair.

"You know I'm right. Ifra is telling us this so . . ." Her gaze moved to his. "So someone will know he didn't want to do this. Someone will know how he really feels."

Keyelle straightened up again. "Is that true? Are you just telling us this so we can sit here, stuck inside for the whole winter, knowing all our plans are crumbling? I'd rather be oblivious! I'd rather keep some hope."

Ifra thought Etana was probably right about why he was really telling them. This was his confession. But there was another reason too. "I'm telling you because, if the worst happens, Violet is a Tanharrow too, and Luka's son wants to marry her. Maybe . . . she could help your cause. She's spoiled, but also unspoiled, in a way, because she's been kept away from politics. She'll need help and guidance. Of course, I don't really know her, or Belin, but within moments I could see that Belin is trouble, and Violet . . . just wants to be loved."

Keyelle groaned and ran her hands through her red curls. "Either way, we're putting our trust in an untried, unprepared ruler. But we're just supposed to give up on Erris?"

Ifra hung his head. "Please don't try and stop me. It'll be even worse if I have to hurt you."

"Well," Etana said. "Erris already isn't quite alive, is he? He's a spirit in a clockwork body. It's possible Erris is doomed either way. Violet is a real girl. And Belin wants to share the throne with this girl. He must think she's young and foolish, and maybe she is, but if our network could ally with her, advise her, rally behind her . . . this could actually be a much better prospect for us."

"I suppose there is truth in that," Keyelle said. "I still just feel so hopeless."

Ifra understood that feeling. Yet, for the first time since Luka bound him, he felt hope. He might not be free, but he could still shape events.

❦ 18 ❧

One afternoon, someone knocked at the door. It was the second Tuesday, normally the day when wizened, wiry Miss Santofair came for our laundry. She was quite late, but as I came downstairs I realized the knock was at the front door and not the kitchen door.

Celestina was heading for it, cursing. "That better be Miss Santofair. My dress is in the laundry bundle. I don't care that she sees me looking so frightful, she's a crazy old loon herself, but if it's anyone else—"

Celestina's younger brother stood on the other side of the door, flushed, panting and scowling.

"Ander? What is it?" Celestina cried.

"There's a bunch of people coming after you." He glanced backward, but the woods were still. "I just ran all the way from town, but I don't want anybody to see me. I'm not about to lose my skin just because you had to mess around with sorcerers."

"Wait. Calm down. Who's after me?" She stepped back to let

him in, because he looked like he'd go into a complete panic if he had to keep standing outside.

"This man came into town this morning—a weird man with funny clothes and gold. A jinn, they said. I don't know what happened. I heard one thing from Louis and another thing from Riley."

"Well, try and piece it together as best you can."

"People have been talking about you all winter, you know," Ander said. "Saying you're hosting a house full of witches." He wouldn't even make eye contact with me. "Like I said, this funny-looking man, he came along and said he's a jinn and he's coming for the guy who lives here with you. Said he's the fairy prince. And some girl named Violet. Said she's Valdana's daughter, but everybody knows his daughter's dead. Anyway, the people in town were saying they'd be better off without Valdana or any of you, and the jinn said anyone who wanted to take down Valdana was welcome to join him. They were all supposed to get their torches and guns and things and meet in the town square."

Celestina had a mixture of confusion and alarm on her face that I likely shared. "Are—are you sure about this?"

"Sure as the sunset."

"What do they mean to do?"

Ander suddenly looked very distressed, close to tears. "Celestina, I don't know! I think they could hurt you! Bad! You should really just get out of this town because people say all kinds of nasty things about you, and I know they aren't true, but you don't want to be here. And I need to go because I don't want them to know I warned you."

Celestina's mouth folded up into itself. Ander moved to the door.

"What about Mama and Daddy?"

"They're at home. They're not going to come after you, but they're not going to stand in anybody's way, either. You know we can't. You could've gone to St. Simona's."

She didn't say anything else. Ander opened the door and ran out into the snow, steering away from the paths.

"St. Simona's?" I said.

Celestina started walking back to the kitchen. "The convent," she said. "They said it was the only way a girl who'd been marked by magic could ever be respectable." She grabbed her coat and thrust her arms through the sleeves. She was crying. It was late afternoon and she'd just started dinner—the kitchen table was covered in potato peelings, a pot of beans was simmering, a jar of tomatoes awaited use.

I knew we wouldn't be eating that dinner.

"Should I find the others?" I asked, trying to sound soothing. Because she was crying, I was focused on staying very collected. Someone had to be collected.

"Yes. Yes. I'll pack some food. Tell Violet to bundle up."

"I will." Now that Violet had recovered to a large degree, she had a tendency to traipse outside without a hat or gloves and come in half-frozen. Erris was teaching her in the house lately— something about growing plants without light or soil. One of the useless little side rooms was slowly turning into a greenhouse, and I found them there now. Annalie was in her bedroom writing letters—I was dying to know if they were to Hollin, but of course I didn't ask. I told them all, as quickly as I could, what had happened and ran to my room.

I was terrified the jinn would burn down the house to get to Erris. I put the dancing shoes my mother had embroidered, all my letters, and the elephant bracelet in my pockets. I briefly considered bundling up all my lovely dresses and stashing them in the shed, but we didn't have time for that.

I met Erris on the stairs. I had started not to notice his limp, but now I realized anew how painfully slow he was. He was clutching Ordorio's journals and a wooden box.

"Mel's jewelry," he said. "It's locked but I remember the box. She'd want Violet to have these things, I'm sure."

Violet gathered all the family photos, in three big leather-bound albums, and a battered copy of *The Poppenpuffer Family Goes to the Sea*. Only Annalie was empty-handed and quiet. Celestina regarded us all with a somewhat frantic expression. "What are you doing? We're running from some sort of jinn-led mob, not emigrating with our most prized possessions!"

"I'm not running away without my photos of Mama!" Violet said. "And Papa gave me this book when I was seven and it's my favorite! Anyway, the jinn isn't going to hurt us!"

"That's very contradictory," Celestina said. "Well, let's just hurry and go. I sent Lean Joe off to stay with his daughter. And I've got food packed." She took a pail from the kitchen table.

We rushed out into the snow, stopping to listen, but I couldn't hear any voices or footsteps, just the vague creak and rustle of the forest. It was already dusk. The forest had an ominous look, dark and foreboding, the ice glistening, the evergreens whispering, as if a sorceress had come along and frozen it to keep it silent. Erris took the lead, motioning us forward with a little restless wave.

"There are people coming," he said. "On horses. We've got a little time, but we need to ..." He paused. "This way. There's a ravine about a mile north. We should be able to cross it, but the horses can't."

We started walking.

"A mile," Celestina whispered. I knew she was thinking of Violet, whose health was never ideal, and Erris's foot, and knowing it was quite unlikely we could make it there before the horses caught up to us. "How far away are the horses?"

"The forest will do what it can to slow them down," Erris said.

We fell silent. Erris was moving faster than I'd thought possible, but his gait was unsteady. The snow appeared blue in the fading light, and it slowed us all down with patches of unexpected depth, forcing us to tread carefully and pick up our feet. Violet was soon breathing audibly, a scarf pulled across her face, but no one stopped and no one looked over their shoulders.

My heart nearly stopped when Erris stepped in a depression in the ground, hidden by the snow. He flailed briefly with his walking stick before crashing forward.

I flew to his side. "Are you all right?" I helped him roll onto his back.

He flexed his limbs. "Fine. I'm fine. I just feel stupid." He groaned and got to his feet.

"Well, slow down a bit. You were being reckless."

He looked furtive. "I don't have time to slow down."

Violet was shivering. "The jinn doesn't really want to hurt us. I know he doesn't. And now Uncle Erris is going to break himself, and we're all going to freeze to death."

"Violet, the jinn doesn't have a choice," I said. "He has to grant wishes. If he has an order to kill you, he'll have to do it."

I started walking again. We couldn't stop and talk, but there was an increasing tension—something creeping and quiet, rather like the cold seeping slowly into our bones. No one really knew where we were going, what the jinn planned, what the townspeople wanted. Celestina had been especially quiet, a pained look on her scarred face.

I tried to summon my inner heat, to warm my cold fingers and nose. I had trouble finding the core of my magic. Panic blurred my vision. What if I was too cold and too scared to do any magic at all? I rubbed my gloved hands together and took a deep breath, sharp in my lungs. Breathe. I had to remember to breathe.

Erris's touch surprised me. He took my hand in his, met my eyes. Gave me a small smile in the darkness.

I smiled back, the fearful pattern of my thoughts broken. I dipped into the magic and sent warmth into his hand.

"You're the strongest person I know," he whispered.

But something about the way he said it brought the fear back, and I didn't feel strong at all.

That was when we heard the voices of the mob.

19

The light of torches flickered in the distance.

We had mere moments to arrange ourselves as we had practiced. Celestina and I moved to face the crowd, joining hands so the
power of our magic would flow together. Annalie and Violet stood to
protect Erris, although it was Erris who put an arm around Violet,
whose eyes were wide. We couldn't expect much help from her, but
I trusted Erris and Annalie. They looked ready.

I had the fleeting thought that Erris had changed since the
day I'd set him free. If I'd grown stronger, well, so had he.

Time moved slow and fast at once, as I forced my mind blank,
ready to fight. My skin had grown hot with magic.

The jinn was as frightening and beautiful as I remembered, still
barely dressed for the cold, still reminding me of gold and fire
made flesh. With my own newly heightened awareness of magic, I
could almost feel him more than I saw him—like standing near the
bonfire where I had first moved heat. The men from Cernan looked

shabby behind him, bundled up and grim. There must have been eighteen or nineteen of them, between twenty and fifty years old. Most of them had a lantern in one hand and a hunting rifle in the other.

The sight of the terrifying jinn and all those rifles made me fight to keep my blood warm. What was I thinking?

"I have no choice in what I'm about to do," the jinn said. His voice was rough but expressionless. "I'm sorry." He shivered slightly, and it didn't seem to be from cold. No one susceptible to cold would wear a mere jacket and no hat in such frigid air.

He flung a hand out at Erris, and something shot from it, like a whip of white fire.

Violet shrieked, "No!" Annalie, however—thank God for Annalie—was perfectly composed, sweeping out a hand to deflect the jinn's magic. Her hair and clothes were shadow-black, but there was a halo of light around her. She'd gotten much faster since we'd fought Miss Rashten.

The men from Cernan watched this exchange, just as we did, and a few of them muttered surprised epithets.

Now one of the older men, a wiry fellow with gray stubble, spoke to us. "Celestina, you've been inviting these witches into town. And that jinn—we're with him only so we don't have to see more of him, or any trouble from the fairies."

"I didn't invite them," Celestina said. "And they're not making trouble."

"We heard that fellow is the fairy prince! What is it next? We're not far from the gate. What if the fairies come here? We need to protect our families." His face was not unkind, which almost made it worse, although I couldn't say as much for everyone. There was a rumbling among some of the men in the back, as if they thought this approach was too soft.

I kept an eye on Erris. The jinn had pulled back and Violet was begging him, while Erris tried to pull her back. I couldn't keep up with that girl if she was going to be so foolish. Of all the men for her to nurse some schoolgirl crush on.

"What do you want me to do?" Celestina said. "They're here waiting for Mr. Valdana to return. None of us have done the slightest thing to bother anyone in town."

The man glanced back at his muttering comrades and shook his head. "We're going to have to ask you to leave."

"Where can we go?"

"I don't know. That's not our business."

"Fairies belong in the fairy kingdom," a younger man snapped.

"Violet!" Erris suddenly shouted.

The jinn had grabbed Violet and was holding her against his chest with one strong arm, like a hostage.

I left Celestina to argue with the humans and hurried over to Erris. Could I attack the jinn and not Violet? My own abilities frightened me—they weren't exactly controlled.

"I have orders to bring her back to the king," the jinn said. "She won't be harmed." He swallowed. "I'm sorry." He winced, as if in pain himself. I had never quite believed that the jinn didn't want to hurt us. He had seemed like a storybook jinn before, emotionless and cold. But now I believed Violet. I didn't think he wanted to do any of it, but he was compelled to, and we had to fight back accordingly.

We were braced for another attack on Erris or Annalie when the jinn did something quite unexpected—he shot a hand out toward

Celestina, and a whip of fire caught her, even as she was shouting at the men of Cernan. Her body was dashed against a tree. It looked so merciless.

Annalie flung out her arms, hissing something. The jinn's fire snapped back. Celestina's body slumped. Flames still licked at her coat.

"Celestina!" I rushed to her, stumbling, trying to grab at the fire with my mind. I doubted the jinn again. Did he have to follow orders so brutally? I was halfway there when I heard the crack of another whip and Erris cried out.

So fast—so cruel. I had no chance to react.

I saw his body thrown around like a doll, caught in the magic, knocked against rocks and trees, and finally dropped in the snow, scorched and twisted. I was as frozen as the icicles that had fallen from the branches. I barely registered the jinn riding off with a howling Violet. Annalie whirled to watch them go, but she didn't try to stop them.

I gathered myself just enough to look back at Celestina. Her clothes were no longer on fire, but I barely remembered putting out the flames. Maybe they had gone out on their own.

I ran over to Erris, but it was clear in an instant that something was horribly wrong. His living glamour was gone. The old wooden automaton face, with its staring glass eyes and sealed lips, rested in a puddle of melted snow. I had almost forgotten the automaton face, and it looked so foreign now that I wondered how I had ever fallen in love with him like that. He was meant to be *real*. I turned away, stricken.

One of the men had dismounted to see to Celestina. Some of the others were murmuring again, but the jinn's abrupt devastation had shifted the mood.

I tried to straighten out Erris's twisted limbs, but it was obvious that the magic was gone. Did his soul even remain in this broken body now?

"Annalie," I said, feeling more desperate than I expected. "Annalie, is he . . . Can you tell?"

She knelt and extended a hand. Her lips whispered something inaudible.

Her lashes lowered. "I don't feel him here."

I started to cry. The air was so cold that my tears felt like ice water on my cheeks. I managed not to cry too loud, but I didn't feel like I could stop, either. I didn't really care who heard me.

Annalie put her arm around me and patted my shoulder, and then went over to Celestina. I was crouched and staring at the ground, my thoughts a whirl.

"I don't think she's broken any bones," I heard the man say. "But she took a hard blow. Could be fractures. You should get her inside, and then—well, look, we didn't come out here to hurt anyone. You let Celestina rest up, but then all of you should get out of here."

"Sir, I was sent by Karstor Greinfern, the ambassador of magic," Annalie said. "All of us were. We are no trouble to you. Rather, *you* volunteered to involve yourself with this."

The men were silent a moment.

The tension surrounded us thick as fog. *Please, just let us be,* I begged inwardly.

"If any of you are willing to help us get the wounded home, we'd be much obliged," Annalie said. "Otherwise, you should leave us. Get warm." The words were kind enough, but her tone was threatening. I wiped my eyes. If Annalie could stand up to this entire crowd of men by herself, I could pull myself together at least long enough to get home.

177

"I'll take Celestina home," said the wiry man. "But we're not touching the . . . that." He waved to Erris. I almost broke down again, but at the same time, I was furious. I couldn't stand here another moment. Erris was much too heavy to pick up, but I grabbed his arms and started to drag him through the snow.

The man took Celestina and rode away, with the other men following. Annalie tried to get Erris's feet, but we couldn't reasonably lift him and move with any speed. We had no choice but to drag him all the way. His body was wet, with the fragments of fallen leaves clinging to his clothes and hair.

But it didn't really matter.

His spirit was gone, and his body had been gone much longer.

THE WOODS, LORINAR

⚜

Ifra clutched Violet tight against his chest, ignoring her shouting and crying and questioning. He rode just long enough for the light of the torches to fade through the trees, and he could no longer hear the men, the horses, or Nimira's sobs. But he couldn't erase the vision of the destruction his own hands had caused.

He stopped the horse, scrambled off its back, and retched. There had been nothing in his stomach but melted snow and a handful of dried apples, but there it went.

He looked at his hands. They were free of marks and blood, which seemed wrong. He covered his face and wept.

"Ifra?" Violet said. "Why are *you* crying? It's your fault all this happened." She let out a broken sob. "Please answer me. Did you kill Erris and Celestina? Ifra! Why? Please. Please take me back."

"Are you stupid?" He grabbed her arm. "I'm a jinn. I told you. I have to do what my master asks of me. No matter what it is. I'm not a man, I'm a vessel for *wishes*."

"B-but . . . do you have to be so cruel?" Violet started sobbing into her scarf again.

He took a deep breath and stroked the nose of his dear, patient horse. The simple sweetness of animals had always been a comfort to him, even at the worst of times.

"I don't mean to be cruel," he said. "No. I'm sorry."

She sniffed. "Then . . . please . . . is Uncle Erris okay?"

He shook his head slowly.

"Is he dead?" Her voice sounded hollow.

"He's . . . Well, I guess it depends on whether he was alive to begin with." Ifra trailed off, knowing it hardly mattered what Erris really was. That dark part of his mind that was no longer his own had taken over more often than not this past day, gathering the townspeople as a distraction, attacking the scarred girl to break the concentration of the woman in the black dress. With his goal so close, he became relentless and cruel. Now that it was over, he was left alone with the consequences.

"I think . . . Celestina will be all right," he said. Even as he said it, he wasn't sure. It was hard to give them names, these people he destroyed.

"Why did the king want you to hurt him?" Violet said, her voice very small. "Before . . . you said he wanted you to bring him unharmed."

"Now it's you he wants. As soon as he found out you were a Tanharrow too, he wanted me to destroy Erris."

"Why?"

"I don't know. But I do know there are many people in the fairy lands who want to see a Tanharrow on the throne. They don't like Luka. There's a group called the Green Hoods, waiting for you or

Erris to return. I presume Luka wants you so he can calm down the people who want to follow a Tanharrow. He wants you to marry his son Belin. Make you queen . . . control you."

"I don't want to become a queen to someone's king," Violet said fiercely. "I want to be queen on my own."

He gripped her arm in what he hoped was a reassuring way. "Maybe you have an opportunity. There are people behind you. People waiting for you. And you'll have me. If you sit on the fairy throne, I can answer to you."

She looked curious. Cautious, but he sensed she found him attractive. His heart was racing. If he managed this right . . . if Violet was on the throne . . . he might finally gain control of not only his own life, but a kingdom as well.

Running beneath his ambition to be free was a dangerous undercurrent of interest in this girl who could become his secondary master. It was never wise to care for a master.

"How?" she asked.

He briefly explained the nature of his enslavement.

"But I don't want to marry this Belin," she said. She shivered a little. The only light they had was the half-full moon reflecting on the snow. Violet, looking tiny and cold, clutched the handful of books she'd been holding on to for dear life even as he swung her onto the horse.

"Think of it not as a marriage, but as a strategic move," he said. "Like a game you're trying to win. I'll help you."

Her breath came in soft, frosty puffs. "Ifra?"

"Yes."

"When you attacked us . . . you kept saying you were sorry. But you didn't sound sorry."

"I'm not really myself when I grant wishes. I can't be. Trust me . . . there is no pleasure in it. Quite the opposite, in fact; it's—it's awful."

She looked at him for a long moment, and whispered, "I'm sorry I shouted at you when you were crying."

"No. Don't be."

He mounted the horse, putting his warm arm around her again, trying to be protective and comforting. It wasn't really hard to think of falling for a young woman like Violet. He yearned so deeply for a loving touch with another person, and her own loneliness was so palpable, so easy to understand.

"If we're going to meet the fairy king," she said, "I want real clothes. Clothes for a lady, not a girl, so they'll take me seriously."

"We can get you some clothes."

She was quiet, then, and a few minutes later she started to cry quietly into her scarf. She cried herself right to sleep, while he rode on through the night. Jinn could go days without sleep, which was just as well when there was no welcoming bed for miles, but unfortunate when dark thoughts chased his waking mind wherever he went.

20

Celestina was in considerable pain when she woke. Without proper care, we could only guess at her injuries. The man who had examined her—I didn't know if he was a doctor or merely someone with a talent for bonesetting—said she had no broken bones, and she could move her fingers and toes, but she couldn't do much else. She could only lie on her back, and she couldn't get out of bed.

I was hardly prepared to take care of anyone.

"I'll see to her," Annalie said. "Why don't you get some sleep?"

"I'm not going to be able to sleep."

"I know. Just rest."

"I don't want to leave you alone to handle all this."

"We are never really alone." Annalie smiled just a little. She had always reminded me of the Queen of the Longest Night herself—something about her seemed much older than her years or her smooth skin implied.

I felt very, very alone myself. I went to Erris's room instead of my own. We'd left his body in the greenhouse room. It had seemed fitting in the moment, to leave him among the green growing things, but now it occurred to me all the plants would probably die without Erris and Violet to tend them. I shuddered at the thought of his clockwork body gathering dust and the plants withering away in the darkness, but I had no intention of opening the door to that room ever again.

The last real conversation we'd had was a quarrel, one where I'd been stubborn. He was right about Hollin. The man had done things I shouldn't forgive him for, and if I felt like I couldn't even tell Annalie about our correspondence, it wasn't proper for it to continue.

I went to the kitchen and fed Hollin's letters to the woodstove. Then I sobbed for a long time, with the cat wending around me, letting out his own sad cries. I didn't know if he missed Violet, or if he just sympathized with the situation. I ended up sleeping curled up with him on the rug.

There would be no letters from Hollin anymore, in any case. The next morning, Annalie came down and said we ought to write Karstor about the situation.

"Lean Joe left," I said. "One of us will have to go to town to deliver the letter."

"Oh, dear."

"Exactly."

Annalie sighed. "Perhaps I can contact him through the spirits."

"Is there anything you can't do?"

Her brow furrowed.

"I'm sorry. That wasn't a good way to word that. I just meant, you've really become good at magic."

"I haven't been like other people for a long time," Annalie said. She was looking at her hands, hands so slender and pale that the most pampered lady in Lorinar would envy them. "Karstor says I don't use magic like trained necromancers. I guess it's all wrong, how I do it. And really, it isn't my magic at all. It belongs to the spirits. I just give them a connection to this world."

"How do you keep the bad spirits out?"

"Oh, I don't even think of it like that. 'Bad' spirits. There are angry spirits, but not bad ones. I guess I just know how to deal with them from all my years when they were with me, whether I wanted them to be or not."

"Do you miss them? Being with you all the time?"

She glanced at me. "Sometimes I do. Yes. I wasn't really sure I wanted Karstor to lift the curse at all."

"Why did you let him?"

"I felt I might be needed. It seemed wrong to stay hidden away forever. Karstor said to me, one day, that I seemed more like a ghost than a woman. And I realized... that was true. I wasn't dead yet, but I was acting like I was. I'd become more comfortable with the dead than the living. Living... frightens me a bit."

What was it, exactly, about living that frightened her? I had my theories.

How funny, I thought, that she would use the same word about living that Hollin used about her. "What about when Hollin gets back?" I asked.

Her lips pinched.

I shouldn't have said anything.

"I bear him no ill will," she said abruptly. "But a life with him is no longer what I want."

"Oh." I hesitated. "I'm sorry to bring up a difficult subject."

"Don't be sorry." She shook her head. "I can't tell if he still loves me or not. He says loving things in his letters, but a lot of them sound silly. Then again, my replies are all wrong too. We've just . . . grown apart. When Hollin returns, I intend to ask for a separation, and continue learning magic with Karstor."

My eyes widened slightly. That was scandalous indeed. "Will you marry Dr. Greinfern?"

"Well, we haven't had a very long acquaintance, but if it would protect his reputation . . . He is the ambassador of magic now, so he'll have to be careful. If he brings it up . . . It hardly matters to me." She sounded astoundingly businesslike.

I wasn't sure what to say. I gaped a bit. I admired Annalie for her power, for her serenity in the face of such adversity, but how could she be so callous about her husband's feelings? About marriage itself?

Annalie looked briefly askance, and then leaned closer. "I mean, you do know, don't you?"

"Know what?"

"About Karstor?" She sat back. "He didn't say anything. Oh, dear. It's not my place, then." She looked slightly anguished. "Of course you mustn't tell anyone."

"I won't." What on earth was it now?

"Karstor and Garvin had a particular relationship," she said. She flushed a bit. "He does not care for women."

I jerked in my chair. He *had* been broken up over Garvin's death, but . . . men often seemed to place more importance on their friendships than on their wives, here in Lorinar, what with all their clubs and leagues and things. In Tiansher, men and women mingled more, shared the same entertainments. "But he's—I mean . . . he's a politician!" I finally finished.

Annalie's lips quirked. "Well. Obviously neither of them would have gotten so far if they hadn't been extremely discreet. Nevertheless, you understand now, there is nothing between us."

I stared at the woodstove. I thought of Hollin coming back to the news that Annalie wanted a separation. His family was gone; he'd be all alone. Would he turn to me ... ?

I didn't want Hollin Parry in that way, though. I could forgive his deceits, but I could not forget them, and I certainly couldn't forget Erris.

"Nim, don't despair," Annalie said. "Just because Erris isn't here, doesn't mean he isn't *somewhere*. The spirits told me you should go here. They told me Ordorio would know."

"Don't." I shook my head. "What can I do about it anyway? How can I even get to the fairy kingdom, or move through it, without Erris? It's too much! I can't keep doing this. I need help, and Ordorio isn't here. I'm starting to wonder if he's *imaginary*."

"He's just abroad."

"With my luck, he'll drop dead on the ship back. He must be at least fifty, and traveling around in all these other countries in the cold ..."

"He won't drop dead."

"Stop being so reasonable!" I shouted, shoving my chair back from the table.

But nothing I said fazed Annalie. She was utterly calm in her black dress, looking at me with a serene sympathy I couldn't bear.

"I know you need time to grieve," she said. "But let it out, and let it go. Take it from my own experience ... you will feel better if you take action, in any small way you can right now. Keep working on your magic."

"My magic?" I snapped. "For all the good it does. 'Oh, Erris, let

me keep you warm while a jinn blasts you into the next world!'"
My eyes welled with furious tears. I didn't know if I was more furious at the jinn or the fairy king or myself—but it was Annalie I
wanted to lash out at, Annalie, who didn't care about Hollin, who
apparently didn't care about anything.

I went to my room before I said things I didn't mean, or didn't
want to say—it was hard to tell the difference just now. I cried
long and hard, but no matter how much I let it out, I didn't know
how I could ever let it go.

THE WOODS, LORINAR

It was some time past midnight when Violet stirred.

"Have—have I been sleeping long?"

"Almost five hours, I think."

She fidgeted. "Ouch! I'm stiff. Where are we going? How long are we going to be riding on this horse? Do you think we really ought to be out in the cold for so long? Don't you need sleep?"

"Not much. You'll be all right with me."

"Well, I'm hungry."

Ifra took from his pocket the last of the dried apples the fairies had sent him off with and put them in her hand. "There."

She unwrapped the paper. "Apples? Can't you conjure a feast or something?"

He shook his head. "Conjuring is only for the three wishes. I could manage an illusion, I suppose, so you *think* it's something else."

She gasped. "Could you make it chocolate cake?"

He frowned. "I don't think I've ever eaten that. How about . . . well, we don't have a bowl, so it needs to be something firm. How about a steamed beef and onion dumpling?"

"Ugh. What about pie? Raspberry pie!"

"I've never had that either."

"You've never had *anything*. Where do you come from?"

"A faraway land without chocolate." He gave the sad lump of dried apples the appearance of a soft, warm beef dumpling. "Try that."

She took a very tiny bite, and then a larger one. "Well . . . all right."

He still was somewhat concerned about what to do with her. He could work his magic on her, like the horse, so she wouldn't need rest or food or heat until he delivered her to Luka, but she wouldn't like it, and even the northern fairy gate was a few days' ride away, with Telmirra another week at best. If the weather held.

He spread his magic, sensing for those pockets of heat in the surrounding countryside that meant life. Much of the inhabited land was behind them now, in Cernan, but there was another town to the southwest, with scattered farms around it. The farms were preferable, he thought—less chance they'd have communication with Cernan.

"I'll find us a place to sleep soon," he told Violet.

She got quiet again. She smoothed a mitten over the books in her arms. "My father will get back and I'll be gone."

"When is he coming back?"

"Spring."

"Maybe everything will be sorted out by then. You can send for him."

She settled a little closer against him. "Ifra, you remembered me. When you went away. Do you remember . . . everything about when we met?"

"I remembered because you gave me your hair ribbon."

"Well, I wanted you to remember me," she said.

"I *think* I remember everything," he said, teasing around the answer she wanted.

She took a quick breath. "They said you were dangerous, though Celestina hardly even saw you. I tried to tell Nimira it wasn't your fault, but she pretty much just laughed at me. And Celestina acts like she knows everything and I don't, but I don't think she's ever had a beau either."

He could identify with her loneliness, but he found her naiveté vaguely annoying. He'd had to work hard and grow up fast—or at least, try his best to grow up fast. Sometimes he felt like he'd done a poor job of it. "They were right, you know. I am dangerous. I don't want to be, but that doesn't change things. I don't want to scare you, but . . . perhaps Celestina and your father had a point in keeping you isolated. The second King Luka found out about you, look what happened. And it could have easily been that Belin brought him a mean and nasty jinn, and that mean and nasty jinn would have a hold of you right now."

"But I wouldn't have given that jinn my hair ribbon."

He sighed.

Not long after that, they reached the farmhouse he'd been aiming for. He knocked on the door, Violet huddled beside him. A dog started barking, then two dogs. In another moment, the door was open and the dogs were barking and jumping on Ifra and Violet while a man with a bushy mustache held up a lantern. "Hello! It's much too cold to be outside! What are you two thinking? Come inside!" He had a merry, rolling accent.

Ifra hustled Violet in. *Calm yourselves!* he thought fiercely at the dogs. Thank goodness, they were eager to please and sat right down.

The man blinked at them. "Mercy. What happened to you boys?" The dogs looked up at him almost apologetically. "I've never seen them behave like that before."

There was no time for introductions before an awful lot of children—six, at quick count—a wife, and a white-haired woman came down the stairs, and they were all very loud, with a lot of religious exclamations. "Saints alive, what's all this?" "Heavens!" "God have mercy, who'd be out in this cold at this hour?" The younger half of the children just seemed to be screaming for the fun of it. The dogs started going again, running around the family, a wagging tail almost taking out the smallest boy.

"My name is Ifra, and this is Violet, and we're—"

"Of course, of course! We'll have none of that! Do you need something to eat? Of course you do! Ma, is the fire still going? Well, we should heat some tea!" The women and the oldest daughter, who might have been sixteen or seventeen, were fretting over Violet at the same time. "You must be half-frozen, child!" "Let me get your wraps!" "Come here, we'll get you warmed up!"

Ifra had used a little magic to dampen their alarm and confusion at the sight of two mysterious strangers appearing at the door in the middle of the night, but this seemed excessive.

The family mostly asked and answered their own questions. "Where'd you come from?" the father asked.

"They must have come from town, Pa! I bet they got lost!" the eldest son answered.

"Happens sometimes, when the snow covers up the landmarks," the old woman said. "Poor dears. Are you new in town?"

"They must be, I've never seen them before. Where are you from originally?"

"They're obviously Roscardian. Are you brother and sister?"

"Sure, look at the family resemblance, Pa. It's in the ears. People look at eyes and noses, but you can always tell by the ears, really. Look at us, we've all got the same ears."

Ifra let them go on thinking whatever they wanted. The truth was quite a bit more complicated. His hands were shaking a little, as if his body knew it finally had a chance to rest.

A cup of tea was put before him, and then a slice of toast. And though he didn't need the food, it tasted as good as any beef dumpling he could imagine.

Violet, usually so chatty herself, looked overwhelmed, and slightly irritated, by the noisy family. Her eyes went wide with horror when the sisters of the family said she could sleep with them.

"You don't have a bedroom for guests?" she said.

"Mercy! You must be the banker's daughter or something. Anyway, it'd be awfully cold," the mother said.

Violet started coughing, looking quite cross. Two of the sisters hugged her, one on each side. "Don't worry!" "It'll be such fun!" "We have an extra nightgown Lissy's grown out of!" Ifra knew he shouldn't smile, but Violet had precisely the expression of a cat being dressed in doll clothes.

They hustled her upstairs.

"And you can sleep with the boys," the father said.

"The boys" grinned at him. Ifra started to say surely he was too old—but no. Of course he wasn't. This man still saw him as a boy.

"I prefer to be alone," Ifra said. "I'll sleep downstairs. If you have a blanket to spare . . ."

"It's too drafty in the parlor! You'll freeze. And we wouldn't dream of asking a guest to sleep in the kitchen!" the mother said.

"I will not freeze," Ifra said softly, meeting their eyes in turn, and a flicker of fear passed through them, as if they had finally noticed that he looked nothing like the people of Cernan.

The mother stood. "I'm sure we have a spare blanket somewhere." The boys dispersed, rough-housing their way up the stairs. The old woman gathered the dishes. It got very quiet.

Ifra waited for them all to leave. He took off his coat and shoes and lay down on the rug before the unlit fireplace. The room was cluttered and a little shabby. It seemed like a wonderful place.

One of the dogs came from the kitchen to stand in the doorway—he heard its nails clicking on the wooden floor. It looked a little shy. He waved it over and the gray beast settled down beside him with a sigh. Ifra wondered if maybe he was the kind of person who preferred animals to people. Maybe he would ask Luka for ownership of his horse, and a few good dogs and cats, instead of a wife. Maybe some chickens as well.

Somewhere in the middle of his dream list of animals, he fell asleep.

He woke to a whisper in his ear. "Ifra?"

"Hmm?"

Violet was sitting behind him. "I thought those stupid girls would never go to sleep. They snore too, at least one of them does. Were you sleeping? I thought you didn't need sleep."

"I *want* sleep." He turned over to look at her. Her hair was down, and all rippled from being in braids. She had a nightgown on that should have buttoned to the neck, but the buttons looked like they'd mostly been torn off by the previous owner, perhaps in some sibling scuffle, baring her neck and the sharp edge of a collarbone.

The longer he looked at her, the less peevish she looked, and the more anxious ... and lovely.

"I'm cold," she whispered.

He rearranged the blanket so he could throw a corner around her shoulder, and she settled down with him, her small body rigid.

"Is something wrong?" he asked.

"It's so ordinary here. I mean ... these people are nice. Maybe a little too nice. And then when everyone went to bed and I had time to think ..." She took a deep breath. "I can't believe ... Uncle Erris might be dead. And I'm going to the fairy kingdom, and ... it doesn't seem quite real. I'm not prepared for it to be real." She turned to him, stricken. "I don't want to be a queen! I want to go home."

"I'm scared, too, but—"

"I never knew jinn could be scared. You must have granted zillions of wishes already."

"Twelve," he said. "I guess Luka's wish for me to serve him was the thirteenth."

"Three wishes times four? You've only granted wishes to four people?"

"Well, I'm only seventeen. I haven't been doing this for long."

"What were the wishes?" she asked.

"I'm starting to forget. When I have a new master, I forget the last ones, mostly."

"How do you become a jinn who grants wishes? It obviously wasn't something you wanted."

"It happens to all of us. On our seventeenth birthday. I wasn't sure what day I was born, exactly, so it was a surprise, but maybe it's best that way. One day I guess I just blacked out, and the next thing I knew, I was waking up to this person holding a golden oil lamp. My first master was young, I remember that. A boy. Wait—a

195

thief. He'd lost a thumb as punishment for pickpocketing, and he asked for it back." Ifra smiled a little. "That wasn't such a bad wish."

"And before that . . . you lived somewhere without chocolate?"

"We didn't have a lot of food. There was grass, so we raised animals, and we had milk and yogurt, but we only had about ten fruits and vegetables. The best time of year was when we'd go to the big market and get spices and tea." His eyes glazed in the dark room, thinking of the colors of the bazaar that were such a striking contrast from the tan rocks and dull green brush he had stared at every day.

"What about your family? Do you have sisters and brothers?"

"No. I don't have a family, not really. My mother is a slave and my father is her master, so a free jinn raised me. I spent the better part of the year on a farm, with a couple that didn't have any children to help with the crops and the animals. I was good with the animals. Plus, if there wasn't enough food, they didn't have to eat as much when I was around, so they never had to starve." That was a good memory too. Sometimes his magic truly felt like a gift. "Why so many questions, anyway?"

"I don't know you. I'm not afraid of you like Celestina and Nimira wanted me to be, but when you came out of the forest, I thought you were immortal and mystical, and you would protect me and say wise things, like in books."

Ifra laughed. "I was never like that."

"All I had to go on were those books. I had a book of stories about jinn."

"Well, what about you?" he said. "I don't know you either. I know people forget you, and your father wants to protect you, and the people in Cernan don't even know you exist, so I presume you don't leave the house much."

"Sometimes in summer, Papa takes me to New Sweeling to buy me new toys and books and clothes. That's it. I was always sick, anyway, especially in the cold months, so I mostly stayed in bed and read books and made up stories with my paper dolls. Nobody knew what was wrong with me. They thought it might be tuberculosis, and that I would die."

"But you didn't, clearly."

"No. Uncle Erris knew what was wrong. He knew things I suppose my mother would have known. I don't know how much alike they were, but when he told stories about her . . . I almost wished he'd stop. I didn't realize, until I heard them, how much I wanted a mother." She paused. "No, that's not true. I always knew it. I just tried to hide it away because Papa would be so sad. He was already sad." She sniffed. "I guess I associate my mother with sadness, but Erris told me she was always cheerful and silly, and she was always getting in trouble, and for the first time I could really imagine her."

She wiped her face, rather dramatically, with her sleeve. "But anyway. I mean, it's no use thinking about that. Except that Erris . . . he made me curious about being a fairy. I wanted to see where my mother came from. And now he's gone too. I just don't understand why the fairy king would want to kill him without even meeting him."

"He did meet Erris, when they were young," Ifra said. "Of course, that still doesn't explain why he wanted to . . ." The word "kill" jarred him. Those were not the words of the wish. "No, that's not right. He didn't want him killed. He wanted his clockwork body destroyed."

"Same thing."

"But . . . it's a funny choice of words. It would have been easier to tell me just to kill him, but Luka was very aware that jinn can twist the words of wishes, and those were the words he chose." The way Ifra kept feeling a wisp of Erris back in Telmirra nagged at him.

Violet's eyes shot wide open. "Death sleep," she said.

"Death sleep? I don't understand."

"We don't know what happened to Uncle Erris's real body. Is it dead? But if it was, wouldn't the fairy king just have asked you to kill him? Wouldn't it be the same thing?"

Violet told him a story about poking around her father's study, finding clockwork mice and a clockwork cat and a clockwork woman, and journals that explained how her father had enchanted automata by putting living creatures in a death sleep and then coaxing their souls elsewhere. "I guess he was looking for a way to raise the dead, but it never worked," she said. "Or else . . . he could have brought back my mother."

Ifra sat up and took from his pocket the cravat pin Luka had given him to aid in tracking Erris. "Maybe that explains why I kept feeling Erris back at the fairy kingdom even while I was supposed to track him down at Cernan. I could never pinpoint exactly where his spirit was, so I assumed it was just because he used to live there, and the strange nature of his enchantment. Like a bit of a ghost."

"No. He's alive. He must be." Violet met his eyes. There was a new brightness to her, an electric sense of purpose. "We just have to find him. And wake him up."

THE FAIRY KINGDOM

Ifra's sense of the weather was not as sharp as his ability to sense living beings, but he had a little warning of the winter storm approaching. They were not long past the fairy gate. He didn't tell Violet—didn't want to alarm her—but aimed for a nearby village. If the storm snowed them in for some days, he didn't want to impose on an isolated family. Maybe they could find an inn of some sort.

"Is there a festival going on?" Violet asked, looking delighted by the main street coming into view.

A bonfire blazed in the town square, with a dozen or so fairies singing and dancing while musicians played merry music. A few brightly painted carts decorated with now-familiar fairy designs of animals, intricate knots, and symbols, sold hot food and drinks, their smells roasty and alluring.

"Ohhh," Violet moaned. "I haven't had real food since the pancakes." After the hospitality of the farm family, including a generous pancake breakfast with the last of their blueberry jam, Ifra felt too guilty to impose on anyone else. He'd accepted a few of their apples and given them to Violet twice a day, enchanted to resemble the best foods he could think of, which rarely pleased her. They slept in sheds, barns, or abandoned cabins.

"Wait here." Ifra dismounted and approached one of the food carts.

"Hello, traveler. Popcorn?"

Ifra wasn't familiar with popcorn, but Violet was clapping her hands. He nodded, digging coins from his pocket. "Is it a holiday?"

The man grinned in a way that was more teeth than eyes. "Have you not heard, traveler? The Queen of the Longest Night's come for the king. He named his son Belin as his successor. They're not even waiting for the first day of spring for the coronation."

Ifra turned back to Violet. Had she heard that? She was petting the horse. "The king's . . . dead?"

The man nodded. "Where've you come from?" He looked cautious, clearly noting the fairy horse and Violet's appearance—Ifra wasn't sure if her fairy blood was obvious.

"Everywhere," Ifra said, trying to calm his shock.

"Everywhere is close kin to nowhere," the man said. Ifra wasn't sure what that meant. He numbly accepted the paper cone overflowing with fluffy white kernels, glistening with butter, handing over a coin in response.

"Is there an inn here?" he said, struggling to keep composed.

"The big two-story building there."

Ifra hurried back to Violet, stomping down the snow. She grabbed a huge handful of popcorn and shot her gaze heavenward with delight.

"King Luka's dead," Ifra said. "This is bad."

"Luka or Belin, why does it matter?"

"Because Luka wasn't as cruel as Belin is. I hoped we'd have a little more time." Ifra swallowed. "I don't want to go back to him. I don't want to serve him."

"You never told me Belin was crueler than Luka! I'm supposed to marry someone who's cruel?"

"Luka wasn't cruel, but it doesn't matter now, not really," Ifra said. "He was sort of ruthless, but not cruel."

"Well, what do we do?"

"I don't know. I need to think. Let's see if there are rooms at the inn."

The inn doubled as some sort of restaurant or pub. Beyond the small foyer with a spiral staircase and an empty desk, an intricately carved entranceway led to a room warmly lit by hearth and candles, full of fairies, singing and stomping.

Ay di day
We'll gather up our swords
Ay di day
We'll gather up the hoards
Ay di day
We'll take to the roads
Down with the rebel king!

Violet looked up at him, her eyes glittering with excitement.

A bird flew from the rafters and off into the pub. Ifra watched it land on a girl's shoulder, and she glanced back at the foyer and mouthed "Oh!"

She walked in, stuffing a rag in the waistband of her apron. "Are you in need of a room? They say there's a storm coming."

"Yes. Please, if you have any."

"We have a couple left on the second floor. Over the pub. I'm not sure you'll get a wink of sleep at a time like this, but . . ." She shrugged.

"That's fine."

Violet suddenly burst out, "Are you really going to take to the roads and march on the king?"

The girl's cheeks flushed. "Oh . . . no, no, they're not serious."

"I'm Violet—"

Ifra covered her mouth. "Let's see our room first and then maybe we can come have a drink."

The girl gave them an odd look for a moment, and then unlocked a drawer and gave him a ring with a key on it. "It's the last one down the hall, on the right. Five silvers. Show them your key downstairs and your dinner is on the house."

"Thank you." Ifra hustled Violet upstairs, hissing in a whisper, "Why were you going to tell them who you are?"

"Why does it matter? They're my future subjects, and they hate the king!" She rolled back and forth on her toes. The music was pounding through the floorboards. "You told me about the Green Hoods and all that, but I never realized what it would really be like—people singing about the king! I bet if I walked into that pub right now and said I was a Tanharrow, they'd start singing for me. Maybe they'd go with us." She gasped. "Maybe we could show up with an army!"

"Maybe that's a *horrid* idea," said Ifra. "What do you think Belin will do to *me* if we show up with an army?" He unlocked the door.

The room was spare but clean, with two quilts on the bed and a rag rug on the floor.

"That bed is far too small," Violet said. "Don't they have any rooms with a larger bed?"

"I'll sleep on the floor."

"But then I'll be cold." She glared up at him suddenly. "Are you ever going to kiss me again?"

Ifra stared at her a moment, and she stared right back, her brown eyes firm and even indignant.

"Are you serious?" he said. "My master is now King Belin. You aren't queen yet. He could change his mind about needing a Tan-harrow on the throne. He could ask me to kill you. He could ask me to attack the Green Hoods, and I might take out an awful lot of them before they kill me. We have advantages, chances to win this, but we must be careful because there is a lot at stake. We have to consider what we're doing. We can't just charge into some town, tell everyone who you are, and get up an army."

"But . . ."

"And you know what else? I am sick and tired of you being so ungrateful for everything that's put before you. You complain about every meal and every bed you're ever given, even when the people offering hardly have anything themselves. I am sorry— more sorry than I can ever express—about what happened with Erris and Celestina, and I know this is not an easy situation for you, but being a good queen isn't about having everything handed to you on a silver platter. A good master wants his servants to be happy, and a good ruler wants the same for her subjects. There is give-and-take for the good of *everyone*."

Violet sat down hard on the bed and started crying. Ifra stayed near the door. He probably shouldn't talk to her like that. She likely *would* be queen, and his only hope of freedom, but, well, all the rules his tutor had drummed into his head clearly hadn't been drummed hard enough.

"It's not that I'm not grateful," Violet snapped. "I just—" She broke off. More crying.

He was finding it increasingly uncomfortable to just stand there. "I'm going downstairs for some dinner. Join me when you feel better."

The singing in the pub had ceased for the moment, but the talk was loud. Ifra found a table with two chairs and showed his key in return for a plate of roasted corn, sauerkraut and apples, squash soup with small red-speckled beans, and a cup of hard cider. The food smelled good enough to get his appetite going even as he fretted over Violet.

He really shouldn't talk to her like that.

But, no, she needed to hear it. The Green Hoods deserved a good queen, and if he *had* destroyed Erris, the least he could do was put some sense into the last remaining Tanharrow.

I'm in way over my head.

He was halfway through the plate when Violet appeared in the doorway. She'd been wearing the same childish dress—gray with black velvet trim—for days. She kept her hair down now, not in bows, but she still looked like a lost child searching for her mother, although Ifra guessed the girl serving him was only a year or two older. Violet caught sight of him and edged over, slipping into the empty chair.

"I'm sorry, Ifra," she said.

"It's all right."

"I never . . . realized . . . I don't know."

He spread his hands. "Join me for dinner."

That put the ghost of a smile on her lips. "I will."

The serving girl brought a plate of food right out to her. The room was even busier now—all the chairs were gone, the bar was full, and some people who had come in after their friends were just standing at tables, holding drinks and talking. Individual conversations were impossible to catch, but the names of Luka and Belin were on everyone's lips.

"We need to make a plan," Ifra said. "And we need to make it carefully. We know what we want. To find Erris, if we can. To put you on the throne. To get the fairies behind you. To get Belin out of the picture. But what does Belin want?"

Violet leaned in closer. She still had that spark of excitement in her eyes—probably a part of her still felt like she was in a story. "Well, it sounds like people aren't too happy with him. He wants me so people won't be as upset, but . . . he must also want to keep me from going anywhere or talking to anyone important."

"Yes. And he'll know that if you're on the throne, you can give me orders."

"Can I give orders that contradict his orders?"

"Sometimes jinn are bound to families, and if that happens, the person usually names a successor, like the eldest son, who takes precedence in giving commands. Luka named Belin as his successor to the throne, so I assume he'll take precedence. But I really won't know unless you gave me contradicting orders, because the commands will tug at me." He frowned. "Try not to do it. I don't want to get pulled in two different directions."

"I'm going to try my best to seem like a stupid little girl who just wants dresses and cake. I'm good at that."

"I bet."

She gave him a withering look. "I suppose I will order you around anyway, in stupid ways. Like, 'bring me my slippers!' Make him think I don't see you as anything but a slave. We don't want him to know there's anything between us."

Was there something between them? Ifra couldn't stop looking at her, even when she was acting spoiled. Maybe even especially then. Not that she ought to just get away with it. "Maybe there won't be, after all of that," he said.

She briefly stuck out her tongue. "What about Nimira?"

"What about her?"

"She and Erris were going to look for Erris's real body in the fairy kingdom. What if she tries to come after us now? Celestina—if she's all right—she . . . she'll be worried about me too. I know she will. She's sort of a mother hen sometimes."

"I don't know." Ifra ran his fingers through his hair. So many personalities to keep track of, and how was he supposed to anticipate what they all would do? "How would she even make it through the fairy gate? We didn't have any trouble, but that's because of me. Would Nimira be able to pass as a trader?"

"I don't know, but I think she's pretty clever."

"Maybe we can send her a letter," he said. "Tell her what our plans are, so she'll hopefully wait it out. I think she'd only be disruptive at the moment."

"Yes."

Violet trailed off. A man with a flute and a girl with a fiddle had walked in the door, playing as they went, which prompted the reappearance of several drums and rattles that had been set aside earlier in favor of eating. Conversation turned impossible, unless they wanted to scream directly into each other's ears. Everyone joined in the old songs about the Green Hoods, songs about heroes hanging, revenge, rebellion.

Ifra felt vaguely nervous, comparing this raucous gathering to the stately hall of Telmirra—they seemed worlds apart. Belin didn't even seem to know how discontented the border folk were, or maybe he simply didn't care.

Please, please don't send me to crush these people. Ifra couldn't even mention these fears to Violet. It was too awful to contemplate.

Violet leaned close enough to shout into his ear. "This is so exciting! Think what they'd say if they knew I was here!" Before he could respond, she added, "Don't worry! I won't." She sat back, hands clapping.

A young man approached her, his cheeks flushed. "Care to dance, miss?"

She glanced at Ifra.

"Go ahead," he said, too fast, seized by an impulse to push her away, to show himself he didn't care. She gave him a slightly impish look and then took the proffered hand. The young man whirled her into the heart of the crowd, packed in the once-open space in the middle of the floor between tables.

The fairy men dressed quite a bit differently from the humans of Cernan. They didn't shy from color. Dark blue and forest green coats whirled and bobbed in the firelight, while other men had stripped to shirtsleeves and embroidered vests. Violet's clothes still looked out of place—too drab and too fussy in the wrong sort of way—buttons and puffs and flounces. But her heart belonged here, Ifra could tell. She looked far away from her concerns, smiling, hair flying, cheeks full of high color.

Ifra finished his cider and stood. He started clapping with the rest. When Violet saw him, she beamed and took her leave from the young man, slipping between two other couples and offering her hand to Ifra. Her best smile seemed to be for him alone.

Ifra took her hand, pulling her against him—you couldn't move in the room unless you were close, but he wanted her there, in any case. They fell into step, feet stumbling because neither really knew how to dance. Of course, Ifra had never heard music like this before, but it reminded him of the dances he'd seen at the bazaar. Drums needed no language.

When the song was done, Violet grabbed his collar and dropped a kiss on his lips. She laughed and went back to her own unfinished cider. Someone had taken their chairs during the song. A new song began with all the wobble of a newborn animal, and then someone came in with an accordion and threw everything off. The musicians were arguing about what to do next.

Violet looked at him over the rim of her cup. Her chest was heaving from the exertion of the dance, although she was trying to play coy.

He slipped an arm around her waist. She put down the cup. He kissed her this time, and hard. She pulled him to her—much more boldly than he expected a girl to move.

"What kind of books have you been reading all these years?" he said.

She clung to him, spoke into his ear. "I just—I've been sick forever, and once I got better, I thought *then* I'd die, because I wanted to experience everything so much. I wanted the whole world. And when I saw you . . ."

She sat atop the table, drew him closer and kept kissing. No one even seemed to notice them. The music had finally found its way again. A faint haze of tobacco hovered in the room.

It was only later, much later, after they had danced again and kissed again, had danced some more, after he had carried a half-drunk and entirely exhausted Violet to bed, that he realized he too had moved far away from his concerns. That night, he had not been a jinn, with all the responsibilities it entailed.

He had been, simply, Ifra.

And a very, very happy Ifra, at that.

⁓21⁓

Every day, I waited to hear the sound of the train whistle on the winter air. Annalie managed to communicate with Karstor through spirit channels and was told he was sending a doctor as soon as possible. Mostly, I heard nothing but branches cracking from the ice, or the wind moaning at the windows. February storms kept the train from running, and even on pleasant days I imagined that Cernan, the last stop on the route, was hardly a priority for the men clearing the tracks.

Celestina grew better by inches. She still couldn't move much or get out of bed without help, but she could sit propped up on pillows without too much pain, making it easier for her to read. Whenever I came to bring her food, however, I usually found her sleeping or simply staring at the ceiling.

I tried to cheer her up, but I couldn't seem to summon the strength for it when I badly needed cheering up myself.

How I missed Erris and his jokes. Sometimes it had irritated me, but now I realized how much I loved him for it too. When he had been trapped at a piano, only able to communicate with our system for matching letters to the piano keys, he had still tried to make light of the situation and cheer me up. I wouldn't be able to do that. I was sure. I couldn't even imagine what sort of bottomless despair would come over me in those conditions. There was something so wonderfully *normal* about a joke, so that even though our relationship had been almost entirely unconventional, I could forget about clockwork gears and fairy royalty, and see him only as himself.

But he was gone, and the only thing to do, really, was work. Annalie did nearly all the caretaking for Celestina, but she wasn't a good cook, so I managed that. Annalie brought Celestina trays of food and cups of tea, dumped her chamber pot, made poultices for the swelling and bruising, helped her change clothes.

I baked bread, chopped vegetables and stirred stews, and washed endless dishes. Neither Annalie nor I had ever known a life entirely devoid of servants. We could manage the simple things easily enough, but we certainly didn't know how to wash clothes, and at some point it had to be done. I took notes from Celestina's instructions.

First we gathered snow to melt, and then we had to heat the water. I didn't realize how much I could sweat in the dead of winter until it came time to stir the clothes, standing over the hot water. Annalie and I took turns pounding and moving the stick around in the tub, then pulling the clothes out.

We'd hardly gotten anywhere, and we were both panting and aching. Celestina always did the hardest work in the house, even little things like grating potatoes for potato pancakes or kneading bread. She did it so automatically that I'd never thought about it before.

Celestina's bell rang from upstairs. She needed something.

Annalie started to laugh, in a spent way. "Ohhh, not now. How do poor women ever manage, with so many things to do and *babies*?"

"I really don't know."

"And there are two of us!" Annalie groaned. "But I really don't want to go up there."

"I'll go . . ."

"No, no, I'll do it. I know you don't like nursing. But maybe you can start taking the whites out and putting the darks in."

"Do you think the whites are clean?"

"I have no earthly idea, but they're as clean as they'll get."

While Annalie disappeared up the stairs, I hooked the sodden clothes on the end of the stick. My arms were shaky from exertion, and the clothes seemed to weigh tons. A nightgown slipped off the stick and fell on the already wet floor. I cursed and hurriedly dropped the rest of the clothes into the wooden tub. Scalding drops of water splashed on my arms. I bent to pick up the nightgown, back muscles screaming, and slipped it in with the rest.

There were still more clothes to be moved. Still the dark clothes to pound. Then the washboard, then rinsing and wringing, and then hanging it all to dry. I had the paper with all the horrid instructions right in front of me, the ink bleeding because along with everything else, it had gotten wet.

I couldn't do it. I just couldn't do it anymore. I didn't care if our clothes were stained and stinking, I couldn't do this. I didn't care if women all over the world, all throughout time, spent their days doing such things. I should be looking for Erris, I should be studying magic, I should be dancing like the old Nimira used to do. I never thought I'd have even a moment of missing my days in shoddy dancing troupes.

When Annalie came back, I am ashamed to say I was sitting on the floor, crying in an urgent, angry way.

"Nimira," Annalie said gently but firmly. "I know it seems overwhelming, but if we just take it one step at a time . . ."

"No," I said. "We're on step one of . . . of I don't even know how many. We can't do it. I don't care. Why do I give a damn if my clothes are clean or dirty anyway?" I was shouting, my throat rough.

She put a hand on my shoulder. "Other women do this. I know we can, and it will feel so nice to have clean clothes."

I turned away from her touch. "I'm tired of everything. I just want to go after that jinn!"

"It would be dangerous to go alone, though," Annalie said. "Maybe when the doctor comes, if he would stay with Celestina . . . Or if she could go to a hospital in New Sweeling . . . we could go together."

"I don't want to wait for the doctor!" I was sobbing, feeling as childish as Violet. "What's wrong with you? How can you still be so dispassionate? Is it something about the spirits; did they drain the caring right out of you? Nothing moves you. You don't even care about your own husband."

I said it and winced. Some part of me demanded to know how I dared to talk to Annalie like that. She'd stood up to the crowd of men from Cernan; she'd taken care of Celestina. She didn't have to help me, but she did, and now I was shouting at her about Hollin, as if I had the right.

"I'm sorry," I said, and I had fled as far as the threshold between kitchen and scarcely used dining room when she spoke.

"Nim. Wait. Please." When I looked back, she shook her head a little. Loose strands of hair floated around her head from the bun she'd twisted it in to work.

"Forgive me," I said, feeling chagrined now that the heat of the moment had gone. "It's not my place to lecture you about Hollin."

"I suppose I did sound a bit heartless, talking about a separation and marrying Karstor for convenience. I just . . . Well, when I was young I did what I was told was best, but it was never best for me."

"You don't think you'll give him even a chance when he returns? He really does seem to be changing."

"What does it even matter to you? Do you think I *need* Hollin Parry?"

"No. No, not that. I think maybe . . . he needs you."

"I don't think I want him to need me."

"Well, no, it's not that either, it's . . ." I sighed. I couldn't seem to explain it to Annalie any better than I could explain it to Erris. "Maybe I just want someone to have a happy ending. Or maybe I just feel guilty about my part in it."

"But it's not your fault, Nim. Not at all! It's entirely his. And I do forgive him for it . . . I truly do. We were already so very distant with one another when you came along. But that's the thing. Our marriage barely began, and then it was over. I'd rather just start again."

"I understand," I said. "He told me . . . he was a little frightened of you."

I expected her to scoff at that, but instead she looked solemn. "I know."

I looked at her a moment, with her disheveled hair, and thought how different she seemed from the first time, when she'd been cursed to spend her hours in a handful of dark rooms, hidden from the world, with the orbs of spirits floating about her like fireflies. "I was a little afraid of you too. Seeing you like this, though . . ."

"Yes, I'm hardly frightening now, not compared to the laundry."

"It's just that you've changed. And he's changed too, I think. But his heart is still with you."

"Did he tell you that?"

"Not so directly, but I can tell, the way he speaks of you."

Annalie smiled faintly, just to herself, as if she didn't mean the expression to be shared. "A part of my heart is still with him too. I just don't want to do anything stupid. I like who I've become."

"I think you're one of the most remarkable women I've ever met," I said, quite truthfully. I had never met a woman whose power you could sense without her lifting a finger! I'd known women in the theater who bucked convention, but it was different with Annalie. There was nothing theatrical or attention-seeking about her, no motive except to be herself. "I'm sorry I snapped at you."

"No, no. It's all right. Whatever becomes of Hollin and me, you and I needed to talk, didn't we? I suppose we can simply thank this awful laundry for bringing it out."

"Are you sure the spirits can't do laundry?" I asked, and she smiled at me ruefully.

22

Hours later, the sun had gone down, and we were running clothes along the washboard. Our hands were red, our skin softened by the water and torn and cracked from the soap and the friction, and every muscle in my body seemed to ache, when we heard the door creak open and boots tromp in. Annalie stiffened. Was it just Lean Joe? Or something worse?

As I cast about for something I could use as a weapon, there was a thump and something heavy dragging along the floor.

Then, "Celestina, are you here?"

I laughed breathlessly. Finally, Ordorio! I was about to run to the entrance hall when Annalie whispered, "What is it?" She glanced around at nothing. "I hear them, but I don't think they hear me. What is it?"

"What?" I asked.

"The spirits are a little restless. But I just—I can't talk to them like I used to. I hear whispers, but no words. I sense things without knowing what. If I want to talk to them now, I have to do a proper ritual." She shook her head with frustration and pushed her chair back from the table. "Never mind. Maybe it's nothing. Let's say hello. I suppose we must break the news about Violet."

Her words made me a little apprehensive, but of course we must greet Ordorio Valdana.

When we entered the entrance hall, my apprehension increased. The man turning away from the coat closet looked a bit haggard, but far younger than fifty. His black hair had a slight curl, and fell to his jawline in an unruly fashion. His face was thin, and too pale, just like his daughter's, with deep-set dark eyes. He dressed, like Karstor, in a necromancer's color scheme—all black with a blue cravat. A black trunk sat in the middle of the floor. It looked a little small for world traveling, but then, perhaps men didn't need as many clothes as women did, especially if he wasn't going to parties.

"You must be Nimira," he said. "And I'm not sure I know you, but you *must* be related to Hansal Swibert."

"I'm his daughter."

"Annalie, is it? My goodness, you look just like him."

He seemed friendly enough, and I'd certainly been waiting months for his arrival, but between his dark looks and strange lack of wrinkles, and Annalie's comment about restless spirits, I felt unnerved. It would be ironic if the townspeople had been right about him all along. Of course, you couldn't really sell your soul to the devil. Could you? Goodness.

He looked at our reddened hands. "What have you two been doing? Where is Celestina?"

"Laundry," I said. "Mr. Valdana, sir, I'm afraid a great deal has happened. I'm not sure if you received any of Dr. Greinfern's letters."

"I do have a letter, as a matter of fact." He was walking briskly toward the stairs as he spoke. "But I'd very much like to hear your side of the story."

"Well, Violet is . . . there was a jinn who is serving the fairy king. Celestina was badly injured trying to save her . . . she's upstairs. We all tried to fight him off, but . . . he took Violet, and he—he hurt Erris, the fairy prince. I'm not sure if you know about him."

"Erris," he said, his tone heavy. "The ninth son. Yes. Of course I know about him."

"What do you mean?" I had to stop myself from exploding with questions.

Ordorio disregarded my question.

"Violet's gone? The Lady's magic should trump a jinn!" He started pounding up the stairs, muttering about seeing Celestina. I started to follow, but Annalie caught my arm and whispered in my ear, "That man is not alive."

"What?" Fear slithered down my spine. "How do you know?"

"There's something about him. I just . . . know."

"Do you think he's dangerous?" As deep as I'd waded into magic waters these days, I was still unnerved by the idea of waking the dead or even talking to the dead. Back home, we had legends of "walking corpses" that ate your soul at night. There seemed to always be a price to pay, at least in stories, for defying the laws of nature.

"Oh, no."

"What does it mean if he's dead?" I was whispering, even though Ordorio had vanished up the stairs.

"I don't know. I suppose we can find out." She shook her head and started to follow him.

Celestina looked as animated as I'd seen her since the accident, which comforted me a bit. She'd known Ordorio for years. He must not seem different than usual to her. She was in the middle of a detailed description of the kidnapping of Violet. "I'm so sorry, sir. We tried to stop him. I don't know how he remembered her, but I will say, Violet seemed to have a bit of an infatuation with him. She's been feeling a lot better this year, thanks to Erris, but she's also been a lot of trouble."

"How long ago did this happen?"

"Two weeks, sir. We've had a lot of bad weather, though. I'm not sure if he could have gotten far with her."

Ordorio ran his fingers through his rumpled hair. "Lady's mercy. I'll have to think on this. I can't stay in Lorinar long. And you, Celestina, are you all right?"

"There's supposed to be a doctor coming..." I could see her struggling to look brave.

"I brought some books back for Violet, but maybe you'd like to look at them. Shall I bring them to you?"

"Oh—yes, please."

Ordorio headed down the stairs again.

"Please, sir, I must talk with you about Erris," I said. "I'm not sure if you know, but he was trapped in clockwork and I'm the one who saved him—in a fashion. He could walk, but he was still clockwork inside, and the jinn ruined his clockwork body, but we found your clockwork woman and animals upstairs—"

"You were in my study?"

"We—we didn't know we couldn't. Celestina had the key."

"No...I never said it was forbidden, I just...Well, Celestina isn't much for snooping, as far as I knew, but I wasn't ready to talk to Violet about all of this."

Any other time, I might have told Ordorio that Violet deserved to know a little more about her situation, but I still kept thinking about him being dead.

He paused. "Do you need to finish the laundry?"

"Eventually," I said. "Please, Mr. Valdana, about Erris . . ."

Ordorio looked at the ground a moment, and then the window. "Something must be done. I can't just abandon my daughter to the mercies of Luka Graweldin. He's a tyrant. But I have never told anyone what happened thirty years ago. It's a shameful, painful memory." He looked at me. "I suppose the time has come. Maybe, with the knowledge, you can save Erris . . . and Violet too."

23

"It all began in school, I suppose. I was studying necromancy, so I dreamed of finding a better way to raise the dead. I'd always been interested in clocks and then automata from childhood."

"The clockwork mice and the cat," I said. "Erris read your note-book."

He nodded. "I tried to keep these experiments to myself. I didn't want anyone to steal my ideas. But, of course, I told my necromancy professor, especially when I succeeded at placing animals into a death sleep and coaxing them into toy bodies. It wasn't raising the dead, but it was something no one had done before."

Briefly, a devastated expression passed across his face. "I had done terribly well in school, and everyone knew my name. I had barely graduated and I had a position in the government, accompanying much more seasoned sorcerers on diplomatic missions to Telmirra. That was when I saw Melia for the first time. I was wandering alone in the gardens outside the palace. She followed me and asked me a few questions. I didn't notice that she was blushing. She told me later how she loved me the minute she saw me, and I always told her she had awful taste, considering I was entirely ready to go to war with her people at the time."

I thought of Violet's infatuation with the dangerous jinn, and how Erris said she was so much like Mel. Indeed.

Ordorio was looking more anguished. "This is where the memories grow painful. Some months into the war, the sorcerers of the council made a bargain with a powerful fairy family—the Graweldins. If they helped us wipe out the Tanharrows and win the war, they would be the new royal family of the fairy kingdom. A secret treaty was signed acknowledging that the humans would control the Great Serpent River, while the Graweldins received generous gifts and concessions.

"However, there is a reason why fairies don't have as much revolution and assassination and all the things you may have read about in our histories."

I nodded. My country had a revolution for independence in my grandfather's time. The king had been assassinated. I had grown up hearing exciting stories about it, but it no longer seemed especially exciting anymore.

"The fairy throne is guarded by ancient trees. Supposedly, they only lend the wisdom of the ages to the true ruler, and if an impostor dares to take the throne, the trees will die. The Graweldins knew the fairy people wouldn't accept them as rulers if the trees died. So they needed a way to get around the ancient magic... such as putting the true king in a death sleep. That was, the trees wouldn't know if the true king was only sleeping. Death sleep isn't permanent... unless, perhaps, the soul is detached from the body.

Or trapped in a false one. The magic I had developed proved to be the answer. It was daring, but ..."

"Are you saying Erris really is in a death sleep somewhere. He *is* alive?"

"I think he must be."

My hands were shaking. I had suspected for so long that Erris was really alive. To have it confirmed by the man partially responsible for trapping him in the first place ... "Where is he, then?"

"I wasn't privy to that information. In the fairy palace, I assume. If his soul has gone back to his body, he might wake up ... one of these days."

"How did you end up with the fairy princess, with Melia, if you were involved in this conspiracy against the Tanharrows?" Annalie asked.

"Well." Ordorio was staring at the ground again. "The Council needed to kidnap a fairy royal, and they wanted the most useless, ineffective heir. Melia seemed the natural choice. She was widely known as a foolish girl, obsessed with boys and clothes and therefore easy to trick. But as I sat there among the men discussing how they would capture this young girl and how they would do this to her, I had my first doubt. I didn't know fairies, except as formal and somewhat hostile diplomats, but I had seen Melia in the garden, and she was just as ordinary as any girl from home. My concerns grew and grew, and I learned that a few of the other sorcerers were troubled by the idea of kidnapping a woman. But if Melia wasn't trapped, she'd most certainly be killed. I arranged to have her smuggled to the far northern tip of Lorinar ... almost two hundred miles north of Cernan. I had a good friend there, a fur trapper who came to Cernan occasionally to visit family. The poor girl spent a few years living in near-total isolation with him while humans waged war on the fairies, and the rest of her family was slaughtered. Many times, later, I wondered if I hadn't made a mistake, saving her.

"Meanwhile, the sorcerer's attention fell to Erris, and he walked into our hands sooner than expected. He actually snuck out of the palace and into the woods to meet a girl or something, a human spy spotted him, and apparently he didn't put up any fight when they tried to capture him. It was obvious he'd lived a pampered life and didn't suspect anything bad could ever befall him. He answered our questions at the mere mention of torture. He kept telling us he was the ninth son, why would we want him? And he barely slept. He cried at night. The other sorcerers disdained him for being so soft, but I wondered if I was any different. I'd never known anything but privilege either."

I was visibly trembling, thinking about my jovial Erris in such a brutal situation.

"Of course, he never suffered physical pain. He was already sleeping when we placed him in a death sleep and his soul into an automaton. The disturbing thing was, the automaton looked different with his soul in it. It looked more like *him*. The men wound it once, and it played some horrible thing—not a song at all, just desperate pounding on the keys, as if he was trying to break free—"

"Stop!" I cried. "Please. I can't—I don't want to hear about it anymore." Erris had never mentioned this to me. I had never realized quite so deeply what it must have been like for him to wake to that, and then go to sleep again for thirty years, without understanding what had happened.

"I'm sorry," he said. "I wish I had . . . done something. Stopped it somehow. But I'd be branded a traitor. So I ran away. Disappeared to the mountains."

"And you left Melia living with some old fur trapper?" I asked.

"Well, I didn't want to see her, considering I'd played a part in doing something so awful to her brother. I didn't seek her out until she was the last Tanharrow alive. There were plenty of rumors that she'd died, but I was still worried they might look for her. I went with the intention of protecting her, and . . . she was different, but she still lit up at the sight of me, and I felt so unworthy. I wanted to devote my life to bringing her joy. I never told her what I'd done."

"Oh, *Ordorio*," Annalie said. "You were never honest?"

He put his head in his hands.

"That must weigh heavily on you," she said.

"It does. But I wouldn't change things. We had many happy years in the woods. I really didn't think anyone was looking for Mel anymore. I guess I got a little complacent . . . sending a few letters, talking to people in town. Violet's first summer . . . fairy men came for us, and I wasn't ready. I hadn't been keeping up with magic all those years. When they found out about Violet, they killed Mel, and when I tried to stop them . . ." He swallowed.

"I am dead," he said simply.

"I know," Annalie said. "I sensed it."

I was not quite so calm as Annalie. "What does that . . . mean?"

"I died, but I couldn't pass on. I could see my fallen body and those men leaving with Violet. It's an awful feeling to die in the midst of a will to live. I feared I would be trapped a lost soul. After I calmed down a little, I called upon the Lady to help me. She said she would grant me life again and protect Violet if I would serve her. She needed a skilled necromancer who could travel the world and deal with abuses of spirit magic. I gave my power over to her, and for nine months of the year, I serve her. I have the summer with Violet. It certainly isn't the life I envisioned for her, but at least she isn't an orphan. I brought Melia here to bury, but . . . well, you saw the clockwork body upstairs. I was trying to find a way to grant her life again, because I knew she would want to raise Violet."

"You are a necromancer," Annalie said. "You couldn't bring her back with her real form?"

"The fairies . . . mangled the bodies," he said curtly.

I was feeling ill, preferring not to imagine all of this. "What are *you*, then?"

"I am a ghost. Just corporeal enough so you don't notice."

Truly, I was glad Annalie was there. If Ordorio had come and I had been alone, hearing these stories spoken to me alone, in the isolated darkness of this house, I might have screamed, but Annalie, accustomed to strange matters of the spirit world, seemed to take it in stride.

"Now, you want to go after your daughter," Annalie said. "And I suppose you can't, because your magic belongs to the Queen of the Longest Night and you are only supposed to be here during the summer."

"You're quite right," Ordorio said.

"I want to go after them more than anything," I said. "I would leave right this moment if I didn't think I'd be hopeless as soon as I reached the gate. But how could I even get in, much less find them in Telmirra?"

"You'll have help."

"Who?"

"You asked me if I'd gotten Karstor's letters. Well, I hadn't, but I heard from other sorcerers I encountered in my travels that he was searching for me to head home. The Lady granted me permission, and so I rushed back. When I got off the train, I stopped for the mail." Ordorio took a bundle of letters from his coat and slid the top one my way. "This letter is how I knew Violet was gone. From Ifra Samra to 'Friends or Family of Violet Valdana and Erris Tanharrow.' I think you'll find it very interesting."

TELMIRRA

The entrance of the palace of Telmirra was draped in black curtains with the royal seal, but Ifra and Violet didn't even make it that far before Tamin approached them, followed by stable attendants to see to the horse.

"Greetings, jinn. I know Belin will want to see you immediately." Tamin had the sort of face that looked perpetually on the verge of a sarcastic comment, even when he was serious and dressed in a drab brown tunic that Ifra guessed to be mourning garb.

Tamin led them around the outside edge of the palace, to the house where Ifra had first visited Belin. Through the bare winter trees, a road cut through the woods where a few groups of fairies went by on horse-drawn sleighs, the bells jingling, and they passed a young woman taking the path by foot, carrying a basket, but the mood was somber, quite unlike the wild mood of most towns Ifra and Violet had traveled through. When they'd stopped at Keyelle and Etana's house, they found a slew of Green Hoods, coming and going and discussing plans, eager to help compose and deliver a letter for Nimira.

They stopped at Belin's door to scrape the snow off their boots, then Tamin let them in. "Belin's been hiding like a mouse since Father died." He called to a frowning servant girl, "Hey, tell my brother he'll want to leave his bed for this."

Tamin took off his coat, looked around for another servant, and made a disparaging sound when the room remained empty. He tossed his coat atop a side table and turned his attention to Violet. "So, you're the Tanharrow girl, are you? *Mmph.*" His eyes had a mocking glint, and Violet edged behind Ifra a bit.

Ifra had stopped in the shops outside of Telmirra and purchased some fairy clothes for Violet—a scarlet bodice with embroidered leaves, and a blue-and-white striped skirt with green ribbon trim. Still, she looked so exhausted from the travel that Ifra supposed she didn't make the best impression for a future queen.

In another moment, Belin was coming down the stairs, his steps heavy. Ifra's stomach tightened with terror before he even saw Belin's face. The new king looked as if he hadn't slept since Ifra left. "You've returned, jinn. This is the girl?"

"Yes, master."

"Your betrothed, milord," Tamin said, with a little bow.

Belin glared darkly at his brother. "*You* may go now."

Tamin picked up his coat again. "You are sorely lacking in servants, brother," he said, and he shut the door hard behind him.

"I am king now," Belin said, as if someone doubted it. "And I suppose you will be my queen." He looked at Violet without much enthusiasm. "You can't possibly be fifteen."

"I am almost sixteen," Violet said, her imperious tone destroyed by the quaver in her voice. "I was born in March."

"Well. You look like a child bride. Maybe humans like to marry children, but here it is considered vulgar."

"Don't marry me, then," Violet snapped.

Belin made a dismissive motion at her. "We will have to make sure it's well-known she is small for her age. Still . . . You might have mentioned this lost Tanharrow is a sallow little thing. I imagined a young woman coming into the prime of her life, not a girl. Maybe something can be done. Maybe the ladies of the court can improve her." He motioned for the maid to whisk Violet away and turned back to the stairs. "Come with me, jinn."

Ifra followed, forcing himself not to give Violet more than a very brief glance. The poor girl looked dumbstruck by this treatment, but if anyone caught Ifra and Violet exchanging even one conspiratorial look, all their plans might go awry.

Belin showed Ifra into a humble sitting room—almost a workroom, really, with knives, tools, half-whittled wood, and pale shavings littering the table. Only the game board arranged by a crackling fire and the bright tapestries hanging from the walls lent it more of a leisurely air. It appeared that Belin himself had carved the wooden animals downstairs; the body of a lumbering bear was beginning to emerge from raw material.

Belin motioned for Ifra to sit, but he himself was restless and pacing. "Well, I'm sure you know my father has died. I am your master now."

"Yes."

"People are whispering that I poisoned him."

Ifra had thought this very thing.

"What are they saying, on the roads? Have you heard anything? I've had reports. Some people think the peasants will take advantage of my youth and inexperience to rebel."

"I . . . am not sure if they're ready to act." Ifra didn't want to give details, but he knew Belin wouldn't be satisfied without them, and his servitude tugged at his words. "It is true that the first village we came to, people were dancing around bonfires and singing about marching on the king, and lauding rebels past. We were snowed in there for several nights, and every time I went to the dining room, I heard talk about you. They think your father was an impostor, and so are you."

"Well, who do they think ought to be king?" Belin asked. "That little waif you dragged along? Do you think she's the hero they're waiting for?"

"No, master. They want a great ruler."

"What does that mean? Was my father not a great ruler?"

Because he had a feeling Belin was on the verge of taking his anger out on him, Ifra said, reluctantly, "I don't know, but that isn't what the people say. If I can be perfectly honest with you, master . . ."

"I demand it."

"You've had me cross this country twice now, and I've spoken to many of your people. They've never felt right about your father's rule. They say there is a disconnect between the desires of the royal court and the common people—that you collect harsh taxes, but you don't protect them. You make concessions with the humans. They think . . . your father seized the throne wrongly and never tried to prove himself worthy of it."

"And do you think that's true?" Belin clamped his hand on the back of Ifra's chair and hissed in his ear. Ifra's heart was drumming, but he forced himself not to flinch.

"Why do you ask me?" he said. "Don't you have advisors? Why are you hiding away here and not at the palace?"

"This is my home," Belin said, with a slightly defiant edge that almost reminded Ifra of Violet. "I have always liked to be alone."

"But you're a king now. A brand-new king. With a lot to do, I'd imagine."

Belin let go of the chair and resumed pacing. "Answer my question. Do you think it's true? I want *you* to tell me because you've been away from court, and a jinn can't lie to his master."

"I think . . . that once things have calmed down, you should go see for yourself," Ifra said. "And in the meantime, you should consider the kind of king you want to be. Telmirra is a wealthy city, and it feels like a protected place. When I go to the villages, the people are free and rough and very welcoming. But they live with hardly any barriers between themselves and the wilderness . . . and it leaves them open to trouble. They're afraid the humans could invade, destroy their homes, drive them away from the woods that they love and the crops they've grown, and they're afraid the taxes will grow higher than they can afford to give."

Belin had paced all the way to the window, and then he turned. "Do you think I killed my father?"

Ifra wanted very much to say no, but it was a lie, and he couldn't lie to Belin.

"*Do* you?"

"I—I don't know."

"Tamin and Ilsin think they should be king. Not me. They're whispering that I had control of you all along, and I used you to trick my father." Belin's voice was taking on a wild edge. "He died so fast, Ifra. I didn't think he'd die this year. I didn't kill him. I spent two years traveling through bleak deserts and getting seasick, to bring you to my father, to prove I could do something better than my brothers, and now they're telling everyone I cheated.

You know I didn't. You know I gave you to my father, and he could have wished to have his health back if he wanted." Belin's eyes were wet with tears, and his whole face was red and angry. Ifra had never seen a master so angry. But he had also never seen a master in pain like this, and that surprised him.

"Master, please—"

"You think I killed him too!" Belin took the half-carved bear and threw it on the ground. He swept his hands across the table, scattering knives and sharp tools, forcing Ifra to fly from the chair to get out of the way. "It doesn't matter what I do, I'm always a failure."

"Belin. Please." Ifra held out his hands and kept his voice mild, trying to soothe Belin like he would a troubled animal back on the farm.

"Shut up!" Belin shouted, voice raw. "I don't trust you either. I've never trusted you. Shut up and don't speak again until I tell you to. And don't write, either. I don't want you talking to anyone. I don't even want to see your face. I just want you to protect me from harm but never, ever talk to me."

Maybe it was all in his head, but Ifra imagined he felt his vocal cords tighten. He shivered.

"Get out of my sight!"

Ifra left the room. He stood in the hall, cold sweat breaking out in patches. What if Belin was losing his mind? Ifra had never imagined that Belin would forbid him from speaking.

He heard Belin stomping around the room, and then he heard a door shut as Belin ventured deeper into his quarters. Ifra took a few calming breaths. It could be worse. At least he didn't have to leave Violet alone or kill anyone. For now. If Belin asked something worse of him tomorrow, he couldn't even beg or plead.

Some time passed. Belin still hadn't come out. Ifra couldn't stand in the hall forever. He didn't have to be within sight of Belin to protect him.

But he couldn't speak. He couldn't even ask the servants where Violet had gone, and when he found Violet, he couldn't tell her anything. If he thought about it too long, his panic started mounting again. Just as a master had never shouted at him before, of course they had never wished for Ifra to be punished himself. The power to speak was one of the freedoms even the lowliest slave enjoyed. Maybe it would only be a day, but what if weeks or months or years went by?

He went downstairs. A servant girl was dusting the carvings. She looked sad, the kind of sad he never saw on fairies outside of Telmirra.

"How is Master Belin?" she asked.

He shook his head, and quickly went out the door, feeling rude. He'd been raised never to leave a woman's presence without a proper leave-taking, but he didn't want to go around miming explanations to everyone he passed.

He walked around the side of the palace, nodding when people greeted him, and entered through the courtyard garden, which was now blanketed with snow. Still, fairies would not be kept indoors. A couple lingered under a bower, and children ran about playing a game. Ifra had just reached the palace door when he realized he couldn't look for Violet. If Belin learned that he cared for her, things would get even worse.

Maybe he could look for Erris. He felt his spirit, teasing at the edges of his sense, and yet—what direction? He couldn't tell. Were fairies buried? Did the Tanharrows have a grand tomb where they might have hidden his body? He wandered down paths, through courtyards, past buildings and groves, but he saw no statues or engraved tablets.

How little he still knew of this place, and these people, and yet it was likely he would be here forever, would never see Arkat and Hami again. Even if he was permitted to write his mother letters, Arkat and Hami couldn't read or write.

His thoughts circled back to Belin's outburst. He had told Violet that Belin was cruel, and as Belin threw things, he thought him mad. But now that he was off by himself, he started to think that Belin seemed more hurt than hateful.

Was he being naïve again? His tutor had told him not to trust anyone, that everyone everywhere was selfish and merely wanted to enslave others and reach for superficial things, and yet he had encountered kindness everywhere—with Arkat and Hami, with the family who insisted on feeding him and Violet the last of their blueberries, with Keyelle and Etana . . . And who was he to Nimira and Celestina? A villain. Maybe it was only a matter of perspective.

He was circling back to the palace again when a woman called, "Pardon me! Ifra? Are you the jinn Ifra?"

"Yes," he tried to say, forgetting Belin's command. All that came out was a strangled sound, like trying to cry out in a dream. The fear and anger he associated with Belin returned in a hot rush as he put his hand to his throat.

"Are you all right?" The woman spoke as if she didn't have time for anyone who wasn't all right, wiping her hands briskly on her apron.

He nodded, then touched his lips and shook his head.

"You are mute?"

Ifra had no idea how to convey that Belin had forbidden him from speaking. He looked apologetic, but his cheeks were hot.

"Well, we've been trying to dress Violet for the king, and she's locked herself in the privy and won't come out. She's calling for you, and I'd rather have her coaxed out of her own free will than find someone with the keys and pry her out."

Violet, calling for him? She was going to jeopardize their plans and he wouldn't be able to say a word! Maybe he could calm her down quickly and no one would think much of it. He started to follow the woman, as she muttered, "It's no way for a queen to behave."

He followed her to a hall with a gaggle of pretty fairy women—some tall and lean, others with an ample, fertile look—clustered around a door. Ilsin's wife was there, and she gave him a familiar smile as if they actually knew each other, brushing her dark curls away from her neck. The women all turned to stare at Ifra, quite a few of them flashing winning smiles, one hand actually darting out to touch the gold cuff at his wrist.

"I've found the jinn, Lady Violet. Please come out at once," said the woman.

"Ifra?" Violet called warily.

Ifra looked around helplessly.

"Ifra?" Violet shouted. "Where is he?"

"He's here. He seems to be mute."

"What? Ifra isn't mute!"

Ifra scratched the door, making a plaintive sound he hoped she understood.

She opened the door a crack, revealing a cross face with eyes and cheeks all shining from crying, and when she saw him, she grabbed his arm and tried to pull him in with her, but he wasn't about to listen to her rant and cry in a privy. He switched his grip to the upper hand and managed to pull her out, past the staring women and into the nearest room, which seemed to be the original site of her tantrum—clothes, shoes, and fabric samples were strewn across couch and rug.

He shut the door behind them and shook her arm, looking at her fiercely. She twisted from his grasp.

"Ifra, why aren't you talking?"

After a few moments of confused pantomime, she understood. "Belin forbade you from speaking?"

He nodded.

"Forever?"

He shook his head, then shrugged, but trying to explain was already getting exhausting. That creeping feeling of violation, which any seasoned jinn should have been able to suppress, seemed to well up in full force. He wanted to talk to Violet, console her and yell at her all at once, and instead he could only stare and gesture. For a moment, he felt like he might cry himself, but instead he shoved aside the dresses on the couch and sat down hard.

"Ifra? Don't cry. Don't cry." Violet put her small, cool hands on his, drew them away from his face, and pulled them against her heart. "Ifra? Is there anything I can do?"

Someone knocked on the door.

"Go away!" Violet screamed.

"We need to dress you for the king." It was the impatient woman again.

Ifra gestured to the door. *You should let them in.*

"They're cruel to me," Violet said. "They said I—I was homely. They asked me why I was so skinny and small."

He smiled faintly and cupped her cheek.

"Papa always said I was lovely like my mother. Was he lying?"

Ifra shook his head. If he could have spoken, he would have told her that it didn't really matter. Violet might not look like the girls who would have been called lovely back home, but he couldn't seem to stop looking at her.

"Belin doesn't like me," she said. "I need to act like a queen if he's going to marry me, but I don't want to marry him. Neither of us wants to marry the other. It's stupid." She put her hand over his again. "Will you stay here? I'll let them in if you promise to stay here."

He nodded, and she let him open the door, but he knew he couldn't stay near her forever.

24

Ordorio asked the Lady to remove the spell on Violet so we would not forget our mission, and we set off with clear skies and the faintest hint of spring, as if you could sense the snow loosening up a bit. We skirted around Cernan for obvious reasons, sleeping in unoccupied buildings, managing to find a house most nights. Many people wintered farther south, and with a bit of summoning, Annalie's spirits could unlock the doors. We were a little giddy and panicked, breaking into empty homes, poking around the dusty parlors of strangers. We didn't dare light candles, in case a passerby saw a light in the window and wondered, so the rooms were gloomy and spooky. But Annalie wasn't afraid of the dark, and my heat magic almost tricked me into thinking we had the company of a fire.

After all the talk of the fairy gate, I rather expected something majestic and imposing, but instead the wooden wall was more like a country fort—built about ten feet tall from sturdy logs, with a row of spikes on the top. Two human men in military uniforms with rifles stood at the gate. Horses were tethered nearby in front of a two-story log house and stable where I supposed the guards lived. On the other side of the gate, we could hear faint music and clanging and clopping, suggesting more civilization on the fairy side of things.

The guards looked a little surprised at our approach. The blond one spoke. "What brings two young ladies on foot and empty-handed to the gate? You can't be traders. I hope you aren't chasing fairy husbands. It's just glamour, you know." He sounded almost flirtatious—they weren't much older than we were.

I decided not to grant an answer, I just handed him my letter from Karstor with the ambassador of magic's seal. The guard looked at it a moment with raised eyebrows, and the darker and quieter guard peered over his shoulder. He held it up to the sun. Then he lifted a horn that hung from a nail in the wall and blew. I looked frantically at Annalie—were we in trouble?

"That's to let the fairy folk know someone's coming through on our end," the dark-haired guard assured me.

Set within the heavy, double-doored gate that was clearly for the passage of carts and carriages was a smaller door, and the guards opened this one for us. I heard one of them whisper something excited about "spies" to the other. My heart was beating at an alarming rate. Ifra's letter had instructed us carefully:

There is a vast group of people called the Green Hoods in the fairy lands who are waiting for Erris's return. They use old ballads for code, to know whether a person is friend or foe. If you must follow us, and Violet insists that you will, go to them, and proceed very cautiously—Belin can ask nearly

anything of me and I don't want to have to hurt
you. I'm told that a number of them even guard the
gate, so when you pass, look for people in green
hoods and say a bit of poetry . . .

Would these be the right fairies?

A hamlet sprung up around the fairy side of the gate—the guard house, a general store, and a small inn, all with brightly painted signs and doors. Two guards were waiting, and not just any guards. These men were so beautiful, their hair shining gold and copper, their skin so clear and their eyes so bright, that I didn't want to trust them.

Just glamour, the human guards said. I had always assumed glamour was for making things more beautiful, but now I understood it could play another role—making things intimidating.

They wore green hoods, however, so when they asked me to state my business, I mumbled, "Ay di day . . . we'll gather up our swords." The words sounded very silly, especially with two unnaturally beautiful men staring at me.

"What's that? Speak up, girl." The red-haired fairy had the rugged bulk of someone who would be comfortable wielding a battle axe, although he only had a sword at his side. I was sure he'd heard enough of what I said the first time that he clearly wasn't a Green Hood. Or maybe Ifra had led me astray. I wasn't sure what to do.

"Please, sir," Annalie said. "Our—our husbands are traders and we're looking for them."

"Do you have permits to trade here?"

"We have a letter from the ambassador of magic," I ventured. Ordorio hadn't thought it would work for passage into the fairy kingdom, but I wasn't sure what we had to lose at this point.

"We don't care about a letter from *your* ambassador." Even his voice was charming and threatening at once.

As he spoke, a man—also in a green hood—had stepped out of the general store with a sack of potatoes, and now he was walking our way. "Why, is that Nirima?" he said, quite as if he knew me, except that he had my name slightly wrong.

He was a fairy too, of course, but I didn't think he had any glamour. He wasn't particularly good-looking, with a cut on his chin, maybe from shaving or maybe from something more . . . wild, with a very lean face and a mischievous air. I wasn't sure if I could trust him, either, but I said, "Yes, that's me."

"Are they with you?" the fairy guard said.

"That's right, my friend."

"What's your business with them?"

"I'm escorting them down south to work as teachers."

"Yes," Annalie said. "That's where our husbands work as traders."

We all nodded, and then I wished we hadn't *all* nodded—we looked like players in a bad production.

"It's just a couple of girls," the blond fairy said. He looked rather bored and had taken a pouch from his pocket, maybe tobacco or snuff—he had the look of someone wishing for indulgence.

"Hmph," the red-haired fairy said, but he stepped aside and let us pass.

"Let's be on our way, girls," the man said, grinning. He led us down the path, past the inn—not much activity there at the moment besides the sign swaying in the breeze and a woman selling pickled vegetables from the back of a colorfully painted carriage.

I had always imagined the fairy lands to be lush and green, but of course even fairy gardens went to bed for the winter, and this place looked just like Cernan, except that the buildings all had the brightly painted accents, and the fairy clothes were brighter too. The man walking beside us had a red coat under his green cloak.

"How did you know my name?" I whispered.

"I'm one of the Green Hoods, milady Nirima. The word traveled among our numbers that you might be coming."

"It's—it's actually Nimira," I said, shy at correcting him. "And this is Annalic. Thank you for helping us with the guard."

"Not at all. My apologies about your name! I've always been terrible with them. I'm Rowan, by the way." He bowed slightly to each of us, without breaking his stride. "I'll explain more once we're away from the village. We should move out and off the roads as quickly as possible, but we'll wait until we're out of sight and we've crossed the bridge."

I glanced around nervously, and then forced myself to look ahead, thankful for the hood obscuring my face. It was probably obvious I was a human, and I didn't want to draw any attention to myself.

The path winding through the forest sloped down to a small bridge crossing a creek that was running fast and swollen from melting snow. Once we'd passed, Rowan motioned us off the path.

"Hungry?" Rowan took what looked like meat jerky from a pouch at his waist and handed it back to us.

"Oh, yes," Annalie said. We'd eaten the last of our dried fish the previous afternoon, and now we were down to dried fruits and corn cakes.

She looked puzzled when she took a bite. "What is this?"

"Dried and smoked mushroom."

"Ohhh."

"Do you not care for it?"

"I just didn't expect it to taste so . . . fungal." She took one more bite and handed it to me. She was right, it tasted very strongly of mushrooms, but I was hungry enough to eat several good mouthfuls.

Rowan grinned and nibbled on the rest as we walked. "We don't eat much meat here."

"Yes, so I'm told," I said, thinking that was one part of living in the fairy lands I would not care for.

"Now, I bet you'd like to know the plan," he said. "I'm taking you to meet with some of the other Green Hoods. We should be there before nightfall. Is it true that you were actually with Erris Tanharrow, in his clockwork body?"

"That's right."

He whistled. "Now that's a situation I don't envy. How did it all happen?"

My history with Erris certainly made for a good yarn to fill the time as we walked along through the soft snow and the still air. I had just reached the point when Erris and I left to find Ordorio Valdana when we heard voices ahead in the distance. The land rolled in gentle, forested hills, so you heard people quite a bit before you saw them. Rowan glanced around at the barren winter forest. The snow was full of our tracks.

Rowan paused a moment, with the same expression Erris had when he was listening to the forest, then he motioned us sideways. I could see an open space ahead indicating another creek or ravine, but I wondered about the tracks.

"I can hide our tracks," he whispered. "At least for a ways. Once they've passed, we have to hurry along to the camp, just in case they're looking for you."

We ran forward to overlook a brook making tiny rapids over the rocks below. I shivered just looking at it, but it had rocky banks with enough room to hide. I was mostly concerned with getting down—from where we stood the best way to get down to the river-bank, as far as I could see, was to slide down the slope. It would be dirty business, and Annalie was wearing a dress.

"You go first," Rowan said. "I'll create a glamour on the tracks. I do apologize, ladies."

Annalie, with a slight frown, tossed down her pack and gath-ered up the hem of her skirt, which was already dirty and wet from the snow, baring her wool stockings. "Well, do be a gentleman and turn away." She made her way down, using her arms and legs to keep from falling in the steeper portion, and I followed the same way, the dirt turning to mud as we reached the bottom and the snow runoff. My gloves and the seat of my trousers were now black with grime.

"What a mess," Annalie muttered. "This whole voyage is mak-ing me feel quite the pampered princess. I should have worn trou-sers like you, but I just wouldn't feel right in them."

"It doesn't matter," I said. "Look, at least your dress hides the dirt better."

"Shh!" Rowan dropped down beside us, somehow managing not to dirty himself at all. I hadn't noticed how lean and lithe he was while he was tromping through the snow, but now I thought he was probably quite skilled with the knife at his belt too.

It actually made me a bit cross, to think that after all I'd been through, this stranger was escorting us to the Green Hoods and I presumed they would lead the rescue. My role felt almost an after-thought. What use did they really have for me?

I had a fleeting wish to break away from Rowan, and even

Annalie, and steal away to Telmirra to find Erris myself, if he was somewhere to be found. My fingers traced the outline of his key beneath my shirt.

With the water rushing over the rocks, and the hill we had just slid down muting sounds from above, we could no longer hear the voices. Rowan had his hand pressed against the dirt, obviously trying to sense when they had passed. Annalie sat down on a rock to rest while I paced.

"All right," Rowan finally said. "They've passed. Let's hurry on before they find the tracks. We can travel down the riverbed for a time."

And so we resumed our march, nibbling corn cakes and dried mushrooms along the way. A mile or two down, the riverbed narrowed and became too treacherous to continue down, so we had to scramble back up the embankment, getting even dirtier in the process. What a sight we would be to the Green Hoods.

"Rowan, when we get to the camp, what will happen?" I asked.

"I don't know," he said. "We'll have to discuss it. We learned of you from the jinn, but he has to do whatever the king says, so we'll proceed cautiously. We just need to hurry along now and worry about all that later. We want to reach the camp before nightfall."

Despite Annalie's obvious exhaustion—she had, after all, spent most of the past few years cooped up in a handful of bedrooms— we managed to reach the camp before dusk. A tall, athletic woman with a stern expression was mending arrows, while a man was tossing more of the strong-tasting mushrooms—goodness, I was already getting sick of them—in a pot half submerged in the ashes of a cookfire. When we appeared, they both looked up. The woman remained stern and went right back to her work, but the man stood and grinned.

I had somehow expected more people, and more of an excited air about the Green Hoods' camp. This place had the feeling of a party nearing its end.

"You found them." The man approached us, and suddenly Rowan grabbed my hands from behind, while the other man took Annalie.

Or a trap!

Action came to me before thought; I jerked from his grip hard and fast, but it wasn't enough. He still had me, but I kicked backward, trying for the most painful place, although I couldn't quite see. He deflected my kick with his leg, and pulled me closer.

"Sorry, Nimira. Nothing personal, just my job," he said, but I was furious at him for daring to apologize and call me by name even as he betrayed me. How ironic that the humans at the gate had thought us spies and instead, we walked right into a spy's trap!

All the while, the fairy woman was replacing the heads of broken arrows, without seeming to care what happened to the rest of us. Clearly, she was so confident the men had it under control that she wouldn't even bother. That angered me too, when in a rush I thought of Ifra attacking Celestina to break our attention. I reached with my magic into the cookfire—my body was already blazing with anger, and the connection came with surprising ease—and flung it at her, a ball of red flames that caught her hair and clothes.

She screamed, and now—now I kicked again, managing to plant my heel between Rowan's legs. He let go with a howl, but I heard a knife slip from its sheath.

Oh God. I didn't want to get cut with a knife.

I ran around the other side of the cookfire, which was still blazing as if I'd taken nothing from it. The woman had rolled in the snow to staunch the fire. She'd acted quickly enough that she was barely scorched and was already back on her feet—at least she didn't appear to have any arrows at the ready—and the other man still had Annalie.

The fire was my only asset, but I couldn't fling fireballs at all of them at once—it took too much time, and the fire didn't last.

Could I touch the heat, now that I had a connection with the fire? I'd never tried it before, but it felt like something that could work, and, backed into a corner as I was, I was desparate. I grabbed a smoldering stick from the fire, and sure enough, it seemed the same temperature as my own warm hand. I threw the stick at Rowan, and before it even reached him, I lobbed another at the girl. Both managed to dodge. These fairies were clearly experienced at their business, and one winter hadn't turned me into a great sorceress.

Of course, if I didn't know that already, I wouldn't be in this mess.

I shouted, "Who are you? What do you want with us, then?"

"I've been undercover with the Green Hoods," Rowan said. "But really, I work for Prince Tamin. When I heard you might be coming with word of Erris, I knew he'd reward us handsomely for you and your companion. That's it, really, and I do feel badly because you spun such a tragic tale, but I have a family to feed like anyone else...." He trailed off, glancing at Annalie. The firefly lights of spirits had appeared around her. They still lacked their full impact in the blue light of dusk, but suddenly she seemed to melt out of her attacker's hands, black sleeves flowing behind her. She rushed to my side.

"Do you know what to do?" she whispered in my ear.

"I can throw fire at one if you can handle the other two."

"No. There are three of them. They have weapons, and they're fast."

"So what do we do?" I hissed.

"Surrender. For now." Her eyes darted to the woods. "I don't think we're alone."

I didn't dare follow her gaze to see if there really was someone watching us, for fear of alerting Rowan and his friends.

"I hope you're right. What if the king wants us dead?"

"There are worse things than death." She shook her head, even now with an infuriating air of serenity. "But I don't think any of that will happen."

As I lifted my hands in concession, I wished I had Annalie's fearlessness toward death. It seemed like it would make life a great deal easier.

TELMIRRA

Without speech, Ifra quickly became a shadow. Word swept through the castle that he was Belin's silent guardian. Theories varied as to whether it was so he couldn't betray Belin's secrets, or so he couldn't betray Belin himself, but of course no one spoke to him directly anymore.

During the day, Ifra managed to distract himself with the routine of the court. The waking days were hardly dull. The sumptuous suppers were full of unfamiliar foods, even fresh citrus and raw salads that seemed an unimaginable luxury near the end of winter. Balls happened almost every night, with bouquets of fresh flowers and dozens of musicians providing a backdrop to the fairy women with their long hair and gossamer gowns shining by glowing magic lights. Belin liked Ifra to stay close, but not too close. Belin didn't seem to really want anyone too close. Whenever he could slip away from the palace to his old home and lock himself away, he did so.

At night, Ifra wandered the lonely halls, unable to sleep. How long would it be before Belin asked him to perform some task? What about when Belin married Violet? How could Ifra endure even that event? He couldn't console Violet. He barely even saw her. The ladies of court pulled her to and fro, presumably teaching her what a queen needed to know. Whenever he saw her, she reminded him of a small animal being slowly pecked to death by crows.

One morning, after a sleepless night, he staggered outside, dreaming of escaping into the woods and never returning. He was such a failure of a jinn. For all the kindness of Arkat and Hami, who had treated him like a son, and the excitement of kissing Violet, maybe his tutor was right all along. He was better off without ever tasting love.

Even now, it tore him up to think so. It took a long time to get his heart to slow to a normal rhythm. And even then, he couldn't seem to empty his mind of anger.

Anger had never come easily to Ifra, but it made him want to seek comfort. It finally led him to the stables. The old wooden door swung loudly on its hinges as he entered, announcing him to a pair of curious stablehands. Ifra recognized the boy who had brought him his horse before, but it was a woman who approached him. She was broad-shouldered and freckled, dressed like the boy, with pants tucked into mud-crusted boots, her hair pulled back in a messy knot. "Hello, sir."

"It's the jinn," the boy said.

"Ah." She smiled. "Well, you know, I'm so removed from court gossip."

Ifra waved his hands a little. The woman looked confused, and the boy said softly, "They said the king made it so he can't talk to anyone."

"Oh." She looked as if she'd been struck. "No. I didn't know. Why?"

"Well, *I* certainly don't know," the boy said.

The woman frowned enough that the barest beginning of wrinkles appeared around her mouth. Ifra made the motion of brushing a horse.

"You don't have anything better to do than brush a horse?" the woman asked him, now lifting an eyebrow.

Ifra shook his head.

She started to walk, and he followed. "Do you want to take him riding, or are you just looking for something to lose yourself in?"

He nodded.

"Lose yourself?" she confirmed. Her voice, in contrast to her rugged appearance, was really rather sweet and soft.

He nodded again. He thought she was being remarkably patient with all this stupid nodding, but she kept looking at him, and she seemed upset. "I don't understand how the king could forbid you from speaking. What a horrible way to treat another person, I don't care how much trouble he went to find you." Rows of stabled horses looked at her rather placidly as she ranted.

Do you know the king? Ifra wanted to ask. She seemed unusually indignant about it for a woman who worked in the stables. Had Belin—

No sooner had he thought this than he noticed a little carved bear hanging from a leather thong around her neck. He recognized the same bear form Belin had been carving in his work room. He pointed at it, mouthing Belin's name.

Her fingers flew to cover it. "Oh—yes. He made it for me."

Tell me more. He motioned outward from his mouth.

"It's nothing," she said, trying to sound curt, but he heard heartbreak there. "I guess it doesn't matter if I tell you. Everyone knows the gossip, but it's long stale now. When I was young, the king, that is to say, Belin and I—well, he loved horses and spent a lot of time here in the stables and we . . . Of course his father didn't approve of the match. And even then—well, Belin's ambitions came between us."

Why? he mouthed, for lack of being able to ask better questions.

"Oh . . . well . . ." She looked around as if making sure no one would catch her talking. "Belin just—he never had Tamin's charisma or Ilsin's talents. Belin does have talents of his own, but . . . he's good with animals and plants. Making things. Not people. His family and the court just didn't value him, and it tore him up. He really wanted his share of the accolades his brothers receive. I can't entirely blame him, but those ambitions of his . . . they don't take him to the best place, I think. So that was that." She sighed, clearly done with the topic. "Do you know how to brush a horse?"

Ifra knew how to brush horses back home, but he let her show him the fairy grooming tools. His mind was no longer on the horse, however. It was naïve to think he could persuade Belin to step down from the throne and go back to his horses and a girl in muddy boots, but such an insight into Belin's character was a treasure.

But what good were insights when he couldn't speak? He kept circling back to that trouble. Belin had given him such hope earlier, and then shut him up again. It was almost impossible to reason with someone who would choose to silence anyone who said the slightest thing he didn't like.

Ifra felt almost as if he had become the embodiment of Belin's own conscience, so that when Belin ordered Ifra around, he was really just shouting at himself. Maybe all jinn felt this way when they were bound to one master for life—maybe it was their lot in life to reflect some aspect of their master. Of course, there were no other jinn around to ask.

———⊗⊗⊗———

Another night, Ifra wandered to the Hall of Oak and Ash. A guard paced outside, but when Ifra motioned that he wanted to go inside, the guard cracked open the door for him. "It's always been a tradition that when our people are in need of wisdom, they may sit beneath the ancient trees when the court isn't in session, but it's been a long time since anyone came."

Ifra lifted his brows, wondering why.

The guard didn't quite understand. "You can go in. I don't think it matters if you aren't one of us." He paused. "Watch out for ghosts. Some say it's haunted. They bury the old kings beneath the trees."

Ifra's heart beat a little faster.

It was a cloudy night, and the trees blocked much of the feeble light coming in through the windows. Even the keen night vision of a jinn was nearly useless. Yet, Ifra heard the trees rustle and sigh in an imperceptible wind, as if they were speaking to one another. Ifra didn't feel any wiser. In fact, he felt considerably unnerved. He recalled the time his tutor had asked him to bring a parcel to the family that lived past the Ujer River. On the way back, Ifra was reluctant to return home, so he wandered down another path that led up into the hills. He intended only to go to the summit and see what the land beyond looked like, but the path led not to the summit, but to a burial cave filled with ancient bones. Some were arranged as if nestled into sleep, others were in disarray, bones left at strange angles, skulls set off by themselves, yellowed paper and broken fragments of wood and bone tools and bowls strewn around. There were remnants of a fire, and from the scattered objects, he guessed that at some point over the ages, someone had looted the burial cave. The walls were covered in faded paintings of unfamiliar figures with staring black eyes, and he felt as if they were the faces of the dead, demanding to know who had disturbed their bones.

Ifra had turned around and started running for all he was worth. Death was a part of life on the farm, but not like that—not heavy and ancient death.

Now a forest, in a throne room, with the air of a tomb.

And yet somewhere, amidst the whispering darkness, like a faint light in the distance, Ifra thought he sensed a small pocket of warmth.

He followed it to the throne itself, a solid mass of stone on a dais formed from equally solid stones. The heat seemed to grow almost nonexistent when he drew near, but it was close. He crouched. Beneath him. It was beneath the dais. The heat of life.

Erris? It had to be Erris.

Buried alive, under the throne? At least, hopefully alive.

Ifra pushed and pried at the stones with his fingers, but they were too solid to move.

Erris? he mouthed.

Even though Ifra couldn't speak, the trees whispered back. They whispered without words, and yet, somehow he felt like he caught a wisp of meaning. He stepped off the dais behind the throne, onto the flagstone, and he felt a slight sense of hollowness when his foot touched down. He wouldn't have even noticed had he not been looking for it. He got on his hands and knees. Behind the throne, under the stones supporting it, was a hole, just the size for a snake to slither beneath.

Ifra stepped off the flagstone and dug his fingers around the edge. It was two feet wide, solid and heavy, but with effort he was able to move it aside, revealing a narrow passage. He could hear the echo of the space within. He summoned a little flame to the tips of his fingers. Summoned flame didn't like to sit still; he had to keep twitching his fingers to keep it alive, but in the flickering light he could see a cramped, dim little chamber beneath the throne. The entrance was barely wide enough to fit Ifra's shoulders. He stripped off his shirt to avoid getting suspicious dirt on it, and squeezed feet first into a space not quite tall enough to stand upright in.

A narrow hall extended on either side of him, off into darkness, sometimes sloping down to avoid the massive roots of trees poking through ceiling and walls. Even from here, he could see niches where skeletons rested in eternal repose, clad in tattered, ancient garments. Was Luka buried down here? Ifra wasn't about to follow the paths and look for him. He didn't want to spend another moment in this place. But what caught his attention were the rather substantial-looking feet visible in a hollow just beneath where the seat of the throne would be, almost eye level with Ifra.

Ifra could sense life in those feet, which were clad in embroidered shoes with red heels. Hesitantly, he touched the stocking-clad ankle, and his fingers met cool, soft, living flesh.

He jerked back. His hand was dusty and dirty.

Ifra put out his fire to free his hands. His breath came choppy as he grabbed the ankles and pulled—dragging out calves, sliding his hands up to knees, now supporting Erris's legs with his right arm and sliding him out, his utterly limp body uncomfortably intimate in the utter darkness as Ifra rested him on the ground and crouched beside him. He flicked the fire in his hands alive again.

Erris was pale as a corpse but still gently breathing, clad in gaily embroidered frock coat and breeches of a cut no one wore anymore, and seemed shockingly young to be trapped in such a hideous way. He was covered with dirt. Ifra brushed it away from his face and then gave his shoulder a little shake. Even though Ifra couldn't speak, he whistled softly, trying to reach Erris through some sense or another.

Nothing Ifra did provoked even a change of breath or a twitch of the eyelids. When Ifra lifted Erris's hands and let them go, they flopped like a doll.

Even if Ifra did wake Erris, what could he do with him with a guard standing at the sole exit?

The catacombs reminded Ifra of the ruins of the jinn, where he himself had rested, waiting to be woken by his next master. He took a deep breath. He hated to leave Erris here, but Ifra couldn't stay with him forever. The guard might grow suspicious.

Ifra crawled back up, replaced the flagstone and his shirt, and left the room on shaking knees.

The guard saw him, and pitched his voice low. "Did you see something in there?"

Ifra glanced back at the door, warily and curiously, hoping the guard would elaborate.

"My friend Gwydain . . . he saw a ghost once. The ghost of the queen." His voice dropped to a whisper. "She was calling for Prince Erris. During the war, you know, he disappeared, and his body was never found."

Ifra nodded, but he knew now—that wasn't true.

TELMIRRA

Ifra could not stop thinking of Erris, trapped in the eerie Hall of Oak and Ash, nearly every moment. He wandered every inch of the palace and its grounds, searching for any underground entrances or secret passages where he might smuggle Erris out, and found nothing. He couldn't ask any questions. He still hardly saw Violet, except briefly or distantly—passing in the hall, exchanging fleetingly desperate looks, or at the dinner table, next to Belin, picking at her food. He couldn't even visit her at night; four ladies-in-waiting slept in an outer chamber, with her bedroom beyond, and he didn't dare try and sneak past them.

For that matter, he saw little of Belin. Every day when Belin met with his council, he asked Ifra to stand guard, but he forbade him from standing near the door, so Ifra's only sense of what was going on came from snatches of conversation he heard in the halls or at dinner. Ifra remembered how Luka had promised him the life of a hero when he returned from that awful mission to destroy Erris and kidnap Violet.

Instead, he was mute and isolated. His only interaction was that with the servants who changed his linens or brought him breakfast, or the passing glances of the court—intrigued, nervous ladies, frowning men. His silence seemed to make him more ominous, more suspicious.

One day, after Belin's meeting with the council, he approached Ifra, looking cross. "Follow me, please. I need to speak with you."

Belin led the way to a sitting room, a more sumptuous space than the room with the wood carvings—the walls were painted a luxurious creamy color, with a massive imported rug on the floor. Flowers obviously aided by magic grew from fussy painted china containers. Ifra's own lamp sat atop the mantel.

"Please sit, jinn."

This time, when Ifra sat, Belin took the chair across from him.

"A week from now, I am having a ball for Princess Violet. I have invited every lord from every corner of my kingdom. My purpose in this is to give the people what they so desperately want—a Tanharrow on the throne. She isn't the impressive figure I hoped for, but she *is* a Tanharrow. We'll see then if they really think ancient blood is all you need to rule, or if they're hoping for something that doesn't exist. But Tamin feels . . ."

Belin drummed his fingers on the table, frowning. "He feels we should also send a stern message to the people to quell any potential rebellion. We have a man in prison, one of our own, who led an uprising against the tax collectors and killed two men some months ago. We think he's one of the leaders of a rebel group called the Green Hoods. Tamin wants to hold a public execution."

Ifra couldn't help the shudder that ran through him, and then the way every muscle in his body seemed to calcify. *Don't make me kill him, please . . . please . . .* It wasn't a command yet, but he was perhaps seconds away from that wish becoming a part of him. Ifra's body would kill while the desires of his heart and soul would vanish until it was done.

Tamin, he mouthed, grasping at anything. Belin said Tamin wanted the execution, which must mean Belin himself was unsure.

Jinn weren't supposed to persuade their masters, weren't supposed to clutch their master's arm and meet their eyes, but Ifra did those things. He mouthed words, made wheezing noises. He was starting to sweat.

Belin jerked back, looking disturbed. "Speak, then," he said. "Speak softly."

Ifra was so overwhelmed by the things he wanted to say that he was briefly rendered speechless. He had to be very, very careful.

"Master, I went to the stables the other day," he finally said. "I met a girl who wears a carved bear around her neck."

Belin looked so angry that Ifra made an effort not to flinch. "Why were you poking around there in the first place?"

"I'm trying to understand you," Ifra said. "My life—no, not even just that—my *choices* are in your hands. And so I want to know what you will choose. I want to know what sort of person you are. What sort of king you will be. Compassionate? Cruel?"

Belin frowned at his hands, and then frowned more fiercely at Ifra. "What kind of trick are you trying to play now?"

"Nothing! Why do you always think I'm trying to trick you?"

"When I was in the city of the jinn, everyone warned me about your kind. If I managed to capture one, they would do anything to trick me into setting them free. Why should you be any different? If I were in your shoes, I'd do the same thing."

"I do want to be free," Ifra said. His heart was still beating fast, but he had a gut feeling that he needed to be honest to get through to Belin. "If I knew how to trick you into letting me go, I would, but I don't. I'm seventeen years old—"

"Old enough," Belin interjected. "My brothers and I were well versed in manipulation at a younger age than that."

"Maybe it's just not in my nature. I spent part of the year with a tutor who tried to train me in dealing with my masters... how to serve them, yes, but more importantly, how not to grow attached to anyone or anything. I understood, on a logical level, but I couldn't feel it deep down, because I had people who loved me and I loved them, and I couldn't *not* care."

"Who do you love?" Belin asked. "I don't even know where jinn come from."

Ifra resisted answering. When he thought of his mother, his tutor, Arkat and Hami—all the people of his childhood—he felt anger at them, that they couldn't have somehow protected him or prepared him for this. At the same time, he missed them so terribly. He didn't want to tell Belin about the people he loved. Belin could have his magic and his strength, but not his memories. "Please," he said. "Don't force me to answer that. They're so far away, it hurts to remember."

Belin was looking at his hands again. "People must think I didn't love my father, if they think I could kill him. Sometimes I was angry at him, but I would never kill him." He looked at Ifra as if daring him to deny it.

"I believe you," Ifra said.

"Never," Belin repeated fiercely. "Why would I spend years of my life trying to bring him a treasure if I wanted him to die?"

Ifra felt unsure of what to do next. What did he really know of Belin's relationship with his father or brothers, or even royal families in general? It seemed terribly competitive, and if Luka was the kind of man who could imprison Erris . . . Well, he was ruthless indeed. It would be hard to be the son of a man like that, trying to please him and live up to his expectations on one hand . . . and perhaps knowing, deep down, that it was wrong all the while.

"Why did you go to such lengths to be king?" he finally asked. "Why didn't you allow Tamin to have the throne?"

"Why should Tamin have the throne? I brought home the greatest treasure."

"Yet he thinks he deserves it, doesn't he?"

"Yes, and that's why I wanted to prove him wrong."

"And you did."

"Yes . . . I did." Belin said it without satisfaction.

Ifra suppressed an urge to push his hair from his eyes. He felt as if the slightest wrong movement could sent Belin off. "What will you do now, master? What will you accomplish, as king?"

"You keep prodding at me. What is it *you* want me to do, jinn?"

Back to this again. Ifra was beginning to suspect Belin didn't trust anyone, or else why would he ask Ifra's opinion one moment and accuse him of having his own agenda the next? If he trusted someone, he would be talking to that person instead. "I'm trying to help you. I think you know your father was a flawed man, and Tamin would be just as risky. Why do you think this man in your prisons took up a rebel cause? Why do you think your country is full of people wishing for the return of the Tanharrows? It is in your power to be a great ruler, Belin."

Ifra had his doubts that this was true, but he had been advised to always flatter his master. He continued, "The trees in the Hall of Oak and Ash"—Belin's head shot up at the mention, and Ifra stammered—"they—they lend wisdom to the ruler of the fairies, don't they? Maybe you should let them advise you. Not me. Not Tamin, but the ancient trees."

"Certainly not Tamin," Belin snapped. He was on his feet again. "But the trees don't talk to me. Just like the rest of this world, they're waiting for a *Tanharrow*." He motioned to the door. "I've heard enough from you. You're no help at all. Be silent again, and go away."

Ifra stood up slowly, feeling as if he'd been struck. He could try so hard to talk to Belin, make an attempt to understand and help him, and Belin could dismiss him with a word. As if he had no feelings at all.

I wish I had no feelings.

Every few days, exhaustion overwhelmed Ifra and he managed to fall asleep. The tall bed and thick mattress were too soft for his taste—he'd grown up sleeping on the ground, and that was where he slept now; on the floor with a blanket wrapped around him. He quite liked the pillows, however, and when he felt the pillow being jerked away from him in the dead of night, he instinctively clutched it before even wondering *why* his pillow would be jerked away.

Violet! Violet was staring at him, frowning, and when she saw he was awake, she said, "You're finally in your room. I keep coming in here and you're never here."

Why? he tried to say—at times he still forgot he couldn't speak—and sounded like he was choking on a fish bone instead.

"Oh, Ifra, I never see you anymore and it's awful! I didn't think it would be like this. In fact, I don't even see Belin. I thought I would have to order you around and everyone would think I was silly, and I'd surprise them all after Belin married me. Instead, they treat me like a child and it's even worse than Celestina because at least she liked me *some*. They don't like me at *all*. That woman who came and found you when we first came? Wista? She's so awful, and I can't even do anything about it. The other day I found a beetle and slipped it down her dress when she wasn't looking and she didn't even scream, she just shook it out and put it outside. What can you *do* with a woman like that?"

Ifra made a sympathetic face. He wasn't sure if she could even see much of him in the dark. The moon was just a crescent out the window.

"Oh, it's just awful. I didn't think it was possible to hate any-one as much as I hate Belin, and . . . one of the ladies told me that the night I marry Belin, I'll have to lie with him. She told me what it means, and I will never, ever do that. I would rather *die*."

Ifra suspected Belin wouldn't press her into consummating the marriage. He didn't seem to find her attractive in the least. But he couldn't calm Violet down and tell her to behave herself in the court, just long enough . . . He couldn't tell her Erris was trapped under the throne. He couldn't even tell her to go back to bed and stop prowling around at night looking for him—heavens, how many times had she given her attendants the slip, and how long until they noticed?

So many things he wished he could tell her. Perhaps, most of all that feeling that he was losing himself, becoming a silent sym-bol of Belin's own lost self. The nights he had spent traveling with Violet felt so far away.

He reached for her hair, that long soft hair that flowed freely across her shoulders now, smoothing his hands along her head, trying to comfort her and himself at once.

She was, as always, a girl of many frivolous words but decisive physical action, smoothing her hands down the V of his chest bared by his shirt, clutching his collar, melting her lips into his.

Her kisses made him feel free, at least for that moment.

After the kiss was over, she curled against him, pressing her forehead to his collarbone like she wanted to hide away inside his skin. When he put an arm around her, she started to cry, but she choked it back quickly, as if ashamed.

"I know you can't cry right now, Ifra," she whispered. "I won't cry either." She took a deep breath. "Some people are saying Belin poisoned King Luka."

Ifra shook his head.

"What would happen if one of his brothers took the throne instead? They're already married! What would happen to us?"

She knew he couldn't answer, so she didn't ask any more questions. He let her stay with him for a long time, running his fingers through the fine strands of her hair, feeling her heart beat, before he forced her back to bed. He didn't get any more sleep that night, but he felt a little stronger in the morning nonetheless.

THE DINING HALL, TELMIRRA

⸎

"Ifra Samra, Jinn of the Court."

Ifra was announced, in line just behind Belin, his brothers and their wives, and Violet. Usually Ifra sat apart, but at the feast for Violet, Belin had him playing the part of the exotic and dangerous bodyguard. He suspected this might be Ilsin's wife's idea, because when she saw him, she smiled in a slinky way and said, "Oh, yes." She nodded at Belin. "Your jinn dresses up so nicely."

Ifra, of course, had been at the mercy of the servants that morning. They decked him out in a heavy necklace of gold plates, put his hair in a topknot with a golden ornament that looked like miniature stag antlers, and gave him a sword to wear at his left and a knife at his right. His shirt bared his chest. All the women in court looked at him as he made his way around the periphery of the room to the chair at Belin's right hand. The attention made his cheeks hot, but he felt more like a character than himself, and he felt a bit of sympathy for Violet, being told she was plain and sickly.

If one had to look a part, it helped to feel you could do a good job of it.

Of course, the trouble with Violet was that she hadn't mastered the art of glamour like the other fairies. On a night like tonight, everyone was more beautiful than usual, even the servants. The fairy women wore gowns with trailing sleeves, their long necks bared like swans', their hair gathered up with feathers or beads or streaming in waves of red or black with flowers in a contrasting color. Some men wore their hair shoulder-length and loose, others cropped it like that of the men of Lorinar, and some tied it back with more feathers and ribbons.

They came from all over the fairy kingdom, even the bearded lords of the wilder places wearing furs bedecked with beads or hide capes with painted patterns. One group of women wore knee-length dresses with skirts made from dozens of filmy layers; another group wore only green, with even green paint on their eyelids.

Violet, meanwhile, looked out of place sitting on Belin's other side in a gown that bared her neck. She kept slouching, and Ilsin's wife, who sat across, would whisper, "Violet!" and then lift her own chin. Violet would straighten half-heartedly. Ifra didn't dare look at her too much, but he suspected her expression was sulky.

She wasn't the only one, though. Clusters of beeswax candles arranged in centerpieces of holly and ivy gave a flattering light to faces, but among the many lovely, wild fairies, he noticed expressions of skepticism and hostility. Once seated at the six long tables that mirrored the rectangular shape of the walls, groups whispered to each other. The room was full of so much chatter that Ifra couldn't hear a word of conversation beyond the fairy royal family sitting around him. Attendants, wearing vests in the deep royal shade of green, poured wine from an endless number of flagons.

There was whispering at Ifra's table too, much of it from Ilsin and Tamin. They watched every person as they entered, scrutinizing, appraising: Did *they* look loyal? That one should be watched, he had never been loyal; that one was weak and you could see it in the way he carried himself. Ifra didn't catch every word, but he got the gist. Belin himself wasn't included in the conversation.

Tamin and Ilsin laughed.

"You two troublemakers," Ilsin's wife said, sipping her wine. Ilsin whispered in her ear, and she wrinkled her nose, but they both looked amused.

Ifra glanced at Belin. Belin pretended to be interested in making sure his silverware was absolutely exactly straight.

Almost every chair in the room was full now. Tamin looked at Violet. "Are you ready to be presented?"

Violet said nothing. She was clutching her wine cup with two hands but not drinking.

"It will be interesting to see what the court thinks of you," Tamin said. "Your human blood is so obvious."

Violet glared at him.

Ilsin's wife smiled a bit. "Oh, now, you must admit, she's adorable. Such a naïve little thing."

"Well, what would her human father know of our ways?" Ilsin said. "I hope you're being patient with her, Elsana."

"Don't you talk about my father," Violet said. "Do you even know who my father is? He does the bidding of the Queen of the Longest Night herself. He's the greatest necromancer in the *world*."

"Tamin," Belin said, still looking at his forks, but his tone was low. "You'd best not provoke her. She *is* my future queen."

"Very well." Tamin briefly raised his eyebrows. "Such enthusiasm you have for her too. Of course, I can see why. That's the trouble with being king, I suppose, you have to marry based on strategy, not beauty or intelligence." He took his own wife's hand and kissed it. Her smile looked a little forced. Tamin's wife was very quiet, and Ifra sensed she wasn't entirely comfortable with the brothers' bickering.

Understandably so. Why was Tamin being so merciless to poor Violet? Ifra didn't even want to meet her eyes, knowing how all this must be tearing her up.

Belin stood. "You take that back, brother!"

The noise in the room immediately died down as all heads turned to see the source of the commotion.

Tamin glanced around the room, adopting a sudden expression of confusion. He stood up and put his palms together. "Belin, Belin. Calm down. No harm was meant."

"You slandered my future wife."

"Belin!" Ilsin said. "Tamin was only expressing concern about her complete lack of familiarity with the court, being raised in the human world by a human father!" His voice was loud enough for everyone to hear.

Ilsin was a good actor, Ifra realized. Both brothers were. And they were trying to make Belin look like a fool in front of the entire court.

"I know you've been sensitive ever since Father . . . died so suddenly," Tamin said. "It is funny how you seem to snap at us whenever we make any attempt to touch upon the subject."

The whispering in the room increased once more. Belin looked furious. "I didn't kill him!" he hissed.

Ifra cringed. Belin's anger did nothing to improve his image. Belin might have claimed to be skilled at manipulation from a young age, but Ifra wondered about that—it seemed that he succumbed to emotion first and sense later. Ifra gave the hem of Belin's coat a gentle tug, but it went ignored.

Tamin threw up his hands. "I would not dare make such a harsh accusation!"

"But it is awfully suspicious," Ilsin said, rubbing his forehead, blinking as if he were hovering near some deeper emotion. He suddenly stood up too. "As soon as you bring Father this fine gift of a jinn, he *dies*. I know Father could be a cruel man, and some might say he deserved a taste of his own medicine, but he was still our father."

Tamin gently squeezed Ilsin's shoulder, and he sat back down and buried his face in his hands.

"I didn't," Belin protested. "He'd been sick for a long time. I'm wondering if *you* killed him to blackmail me."

Tamin gave Belin a long, hurt look, and then he said, "If you'll pardon me, brother ... I just need a bit of air."

Ilsin rose to join him.

"My apologies to the court. Don't let me disrupt your dinner," Tamin called on his way out.

As they left, the whispering rose back into a roar of conversation.

25

Before we reached our destination, Rowan blindfolded us, so we stumbled over uneven ground, a guiding enemy hand at our elbows while our hands were tied behind our backs. It was already getting dark, and I couldn't even see much beneath the edge of the cloth. I was beginning to have grave doubts about the assistance Annalie had supposedly seen or sensed in the woods, but I'd had no chance to ask her anything more about it.

We should have tried to take them, I kept thinking. There would surely be even more guards at the prison, and what if the king locked us away before we had a chance to spread his secrets? What if he did something worse? I kept thinking of Ordorio's story of Erris trapped in the automaton, and how the fairies had mangled his and Melia's bodies, and I could hardly bear the panic crawling over my skin like ants.

Suddenly my feet were on the packed ground of a path again,

and then the hand guiding me stopped to knock at a door. I heard the door swing open.

"Found them at the gate," Rowan said. "This is the girl who was with Erris Tanharrow, plus some witch."

"Nice work," said a gravelly male voice.

Rowan grunted. We were led across a threshold, wooden floor, and then carpet. The room smelled rather like wood, offering no particular clues, but I had only taken a few steps in before Rowan said, "Stairs ahead, ladies."

Now we were led downward. I kept my elbow against the banister for some stability. When we came to the end, Rowan removed my blindfold, revealing nothing but a small, dark room. A man was sitting on the ground in bored repose, with metal shackles tethering his ankles and wrists mere inches apart.

"Oh, good. Company," he said in a droll voice.

"I wouldn't get too comfortable," said Rowan's male cohort, sounding grim. Rowan moved to the door. The woman was behind me, and I heard the clink of chains. She handed a set of shackles to the man, and he crouched to put them around my ankles.

I stepped back instinctively. I didn't want to be tethered and bound—like Erris to the piano—helpless.

"You'll make things worse if you don't hold still," Rowan said. The man took a firmer grip on my ankle.

Don't be stupid, Nim, I thought wildly, only I wasn't sure what the stupid act was—to let him shackle me or to fight it. Of course, if we couldn't fight them before, we couldn't now, but what if this was our last chance? I kept imagining my regret if I was dragged out to a guillotine or a hangman's noose—how did fairies execute people anyway? No, it probably wouldn't be anything fancy and public. They wouldn't want me screaming about Erris before I died. Maybe someone would just come slit our throats.

Upstairs, the door opened, followed by a thump and a strangled cry. Rowan looked behind him.

"What was that?" the woman asked. The man clamped his sweaty hand over my mouth. The woman shot Annalie a sharp look and took out her knife, pointing the tip at both of us in turn. "Either of you make a sound and you're dead."

Rowan hurried up the stairs, taking out his own knife. My heart was pounding.

Rowan shouted, "Both of you come up—"

He never finished the sentence and he never came downstairs. In a rush of adrenaline, I gathered my heat magic and blew out a hot breath, forcing the man to take his hand from my mouth. Annalie slipped her hands easily from her bonds, and I realized she must have gotten her spirit friends to loosen them for her.

"Hey!" The man grabbed my arm. "Don't you try it!"

Annalie was left to fight the woman, and I saw her hand move with the knife, heard Annalie scream, but I had my own battle to pay attention to. I quickly moved the heat from my lungs to my skin, shooting it up the man's arm—just as I had warmed Erris so many mornings, only now the magic was too hot, and the man howled with pain and took his hands off me.

The room was cold, however, and it was hard to keep up my magic without a source. My hands were still tethered behind me, and I took a step back to the wall, quickly noting that Annalie was still on her feet—sleeve slashed and arm bleeding—but she seemed to be merely grazed. Could I burn away the rope? But I couldn't seem to make fire. I was too panicked.

But now whoever had initiated the attack upstairs was coming down the stairs—a man in front with a sword at the ready, a red-haired woman with a bow and arrow poised to shoot—both in green capes.

"Drop your weapons *now*, you lot of traitors," the woman shouted. "Two of your comrades are already dead and there are ten of us here with more on the way."

"You call us traitors? You're traitors to your king," the woman shot back, but she sheathed her knife.

"We're waiting for the true king," the Green Hood woman said. "Or queen. Whichever it may be. Now, lift your hands and come up."

I went over to Annalie. "Are you all right?"

Her hand was clamped over her upper arm, but she nodded. "It's just a scratch. A nasty scratch, but not much worse than the Captain's given me on occasion." The Captain was her old cat, and having encountered him once, I could believe it.

Tamin's spies went up the stairs in surrender, and the two Green Hoods came down to us.

"I'm Keyelle," the woman said, untying my bonds. "And that's Esmon. Ifra, the jinn, he told us to expect you. I'm not sure he really had all of this in mind, but we couldn't wait for a convenient time to act. You've come looking for Erris, haven't you?"

"Yes."

"I'm sorry it took us so long to intervene," she said. "We thought Rowan was one of us, and he volunteered to go to the gate and look out for you after Ifra told us you might come, but we know there's been a traitor in our midst because that's how Calden was captured." She nodded at the man in shackles. "Another one of our people who works the gate suspected Rowan, so we've been following him, hoping he'd lead us to Calden."

"Nice work," Calden said. "I hope there's food around. They've been giving me nothing but porridge."

"You've got bigger worries than porridge. There's a rumor that Tamin wants to have you executed at Belin's ball this very night," Esmon said. "And we'd better clear off right away. We're only half an hour from the palace on horseback and we don't know who's watching the place."

"Where are we?" I asked. "We came blindfolded."

"You're in Tamin's lodge. He comes here in the fall for his royal hunt," Esmon said.

"Half an hour from the palace," I said. *Half an hour from Erris's body*, if my hopes and suspicions were correct. I could almost taste both success and failure. "Where will we go now?"

"Ifra told us to be very careful coming after Erris or Violet," Keyelle said. "But Belin's hosting a ball to introduce Violet. He's hoping his engagement to a Tanharrow will calm everyone down, but a lot of them are Tanharrow sympathizers, and . . . well, if we could sneak in tonight and find Erris . . ."

"Do you know where he might be?"

Keyelle glanced at the men.

"I've some idea of the layout of the palace," Calden said. "But I'd rather not have anything to do with this, if those Graweldin brothers are out for my head."

"I confess I was hoping you might have an idea," Keyelle said, looking at me.

Just as Keyelle glanced at the men, I glanced at Annalie.

"The spirits might help," Annalie said. "But you might be able to help too, Nim. Your magic has improved so much, and you know Erris's spirit better than anyone. I wonder if you'll be able to sense him."

"Well, let's get away from this place and figure it out then," Keyelle said, waving her hands. "My family is already upset that I just had to go put myself in danger, but if I end up getting ambushed at Tamin's house, it will be particularly mortifying."

When we came upstairs, I laid eyes on Rowan's corpse. It was just there, on the ground, eyes open, an arrow in his chest. One moment he'd been leading me down the stairs and now he was dead.

Maybe I wasn't supposed to cry for him. He'd kidnapped me and been a traitor to the Green Hoods, but when he told me he needed money and had a family to feed, I believed him. I didn't think he deserved death.

"Don't bother," Esmon said, sensing my mood. "He was a traitor."

Annalie squeezed my hand. "I understand," she said. "I don't think he was a cruel man."

Keyelle shook her head. "He took a dangerous job for financial reward and paid the price. That's why I hate war, and I hope to be done with it as quickly as we can."

I couldn't agree more. It didn't seem fair at all that King Luka, the one who inflicted such torture on Erris, had died in his bed past the age of fifty, having seen all his sons reach adulthood, while Ordorio held on to life by a thread so he could see his daughter in the summer.

THE COURTYARD GARDEN, TELMIRRA

"I'm really doing you a favor, Belin," Tamin said. They stood beneath the bower. The stars were beginning to come out above them, and all the fairies were still in the dining hall except Belin, his brothers, and a shivering Violet.

"A favor?" Belin cried. "How can you possibly say you did me a favor? You just implied to the entire kingdom that I killed our father!"

"As if they aren't already wondering," Ilsin said. He opened a case tucked in his waistcoat and took out a cigarette.

"I keep telling you, Belin, a king can't simply hide off in his own house and carve deer. Especially us. Father was ruthless, and you've got to be ruthless too, and that's all there is to it. If you can't stand up to me, how are you going to stand up to the half of the room who want to follow a Tanharrow?"

"That's what *she's* for!" Belin clapped Violet rather roughly on the shoulder. She jerked away and shot him a fierce look. Ilsin chuckled.

"That isn't enough, and you know it. You know the rumors. There are more uprisings . . . talk of a whole network of rebels. They may have started here and there without much threat besides singing some old ballads, but look at that man Calden. He killed two of our tax collectors. Sure, the old ballads make such a deed sound heroic, but I doubt their widows think so. Father wouldn't have tolerated that. You need to show them you won't tolerate it either."

"I'm supposed to drag him out here and have him killed in front of all those people after you made them think I killed Father?" Belin's voice was quite a bit louder than Tamin's. Any lurking spy would have had no trouble with him.

"So what if you did kill Father?" Tamin said. "Not to sully his memory, but think about the things Father himself has done. If they don't fear you, you won't last a day. None of us will. Ilsin and I will follow you if you show us it's worth our while, all right? But we're not going to let them get rid of us and put this imp on the throne." He gave Violet the briefest condescending look.

Ifra dreamed of strangling Tamin. Belin could say the word, and Ifra could wipe that smug expression off his face in a moment.

Violet's bottom lip was trembling.

"Oh, don't take it personally," Tamin said. "It's just politics, you know."

"I'm not marrying Belin!" Violet burst out. "I don't want anything to do with any of you! I don't care if every fairy in the world rots! I just want to go home!"

"Shh!" Belin jostled her again, cowing her into silence. There were three men, so much older than her, none of them sympathetic. And silent Ifra. He couldn't even let them see that he cared for her. He just had to look to the distance, a silent bodyguard.

"All right," Belin said. "Bring Calden. My jinn will kill him."

Ifra's fingers coiled into fists. It was all he could do not to show further reaction.

"But if I hear even a whiff of betrayal from you again, my jinn will kill you next."

Tamin actually grinned at this. "That's exactly what I want to see." He turned to go, while Ilsin lingered, but Belin shooed them both away.

Violet started crying, but Belin didn't pay her any regard. He watched his brothers walk away. Tamin left through the side of the garden, while Ilsin strolled slowly, smoking his cigarette, glancing back a few times as if to make sure Belin wasn't going to change his mind. Time seemed to crawl, so slowly, and Ifra forced his mind blank. He would not think about killing a man in front of hundreds of eyes. In front of Violet.

The door shut behind Ilsin.

Belin was pacing the garden path, but now he turned to look at Ifra. "I thought this was what I wanted," he said. "To be king. How grand it sounds. A chance to make everything right. But I can't, can I? It doesn't matter what my father did right. My brothers and I can never be good kings because of what he did wrong."

Master, Ifra mouthed, a silent plea. Did Belin finally understand?

"Erris?" Violet whispered, looking between them. "Are you talking about Uncle Erris?"

"Yes," Belin said. "Father wanted me to kill Erris after I married you, and . . . Tamin doesn't believe I'm ruthless enough to do it. Well." He looked to the door of the Hall of Oak and Ash. "He's right."

26

The lights of the palace of Telmirra loomed ahead through the dark woods. I recalled how Hollin had described this place to me so long ago—an attractive city with gardens but no gas or electricity or other modern amenities.

Telmirra, in fact, hardly seemed like a city, surrounded by miles of woodland. I assumed the residential and shopping districts were removed from the palace so the nobles could have forest to roam in, but it gave it the feel of a storybook castle one might stumble across, except that it wasn't stone like a storybook castle, but wood. Elegant silhouettes of spires and neatly stacked stories were dark against the moon, but golden light shone through windows.

Five of the Green Hoods had accompanied us, including Keyelle and Esmon. We stayed off the paths, and when we heard horses pounding nearer, we crouched behind brush. A rider on a lovely white horse, much like the one the jinn had ridden, was heading the way we had come, followed by four more men. They carried magic lanterns, casting a soft light that caught the fair flax and copper tones of their hair but did not reach us. I hunched still lower.

"That's Prince Tamin," Esmon whispered. "They must be coming for Calden. I hope he's had enough time to put distance between them. That means we have to hurry."

"Do we have enough time?" Keyelle's eyes gleamed wide in the moonlight.

"Yes, yes, let's just go," I said. I could hardly bear looking at the palace where Erris had grown up, knowing I might be so close to finding him. I crept forward, and the Green Hoods moved with me.

We hovered at the edge of the woods, taking stock of the situation. A guard roamed the side of the building, and perhaps more looked from the darker windows—we had no way of knowing. The guard paced, occasionally glancing up at the moon.

"How do we get past him?" I asked.

"A diversion?" Annalie said.

"Nothing that will attract too much attention," Keyelle said.

"King Belin invited people from all over the realm to this feast," Esmon said. "Do you think we could just pretend to be latecomers?"

"Not the way we look!" Keyelle said. "Glamours?"

Esmon shook his head. "No, they'll be trained to see through them, or what sort of guards would they be?"

"I could divert him with my spirits," Annalie said. "Diverting one man is easy. If there are more guards watching from the windows, then I can only give you that long. But I might be left behind, and I won't be able to help you find Erris."

I shut my eyes a moment, almost in prayer—begging my magic to become a beacon to Erris. Familiar frustration crawled over me—that I had to study magic on my own, that I had no teacher and few books, that even if I wanted to learn magic in a proper way I would be forbidden from practicing. I had to grope and claw my way through each technique, learning more often from desperation than proper instruction.

The first spell I had ever done had come with my breath. I had learned to move and summon heat and fire, even to warm Erris. I could so imagine how it felt to share my own warmth with him, the warmth of my life. I had touched him then. If only I could connect with him now.

If our hopes proved right, he was alive here. He would have his own warmth and life. Could I feel it? Could I find it?

"Nimira?" Annalie said. "Are you all right? What do you think?"

"I can't feel him," I said, feeling as frustrated and angry as the first day I tried to move flame. I kept thinking how the jinn had tracked Erris, and how jinn magic was supposed to come from fire. Of course, he was a jinn, and magic came easily to him, but it maddened me, how my own powers didn't come to me.

The jinn. I had *felt* his magic once. Could I draw from it? Even if I could just sense him, maybe he would know where Erris was. It was terrifically risky, considering he was the same person we had come to fear, but I needed to take some action. I didn't want to die, but we were *here*. Something had to be done.

I closed my eyes again, inhaled and exhaled, and reached for Ifra.

THE HALL OF OAK AND ASH, TELMIRRA

Belin pushed open the heavy carved doors.

"Your Majesty? Aren't you wanted in the dining hall?" the guard said.

"Did my father pay you to ask him questions?" Belin snapped. "I need a moment to speak with my betrothed." He pulled Violet into the dark room. Ifra followed. Just as before, the room was almost pitch-black with the thick branches of ancient trees blocking the scant light the windows might have provided, and the whispering of leaves was even thicker than the darkness.

"We have to hurry," Belin said. "I don't know if I can trust those guards anymore, and as he says, they'll be wanting me to start the dancing soon enough."

Violet suddenly clutched Ifra's hand in the darkness. "What is this place?"

Ifra hoped Belin couldn't see her hand clutching his. "The Hall of Oak and Ash," Belin said.

"Can you hear them?" she said, her grip almost painfully tight.

"The trees?"

"Yes. They're sick. I've never heard anything like that," she said. "Oh no. Please, hurry, where is Erris?" She sounded almost frantic. "It's awful. They want to die and they can't die, and we can't *let* them die." She sniffed. "Won't you let Ifra talk now?"

"Not yet," Belin said, making Ifra feel almost as frantic as Violet. For a moment he'd almost forgotten about Belin lifting the wish, and he subconsciously assumed Belin had too, but apparently not.

"Jinn, can you make a light?" Belin said.

Ifra extracted his hand from Violet's grip and summoned a flame, casting ghostly shadows along the massive trunks of the trees.

"Follow me." Belin rushed to the throne, which was at the far end of the room, in front of two of the massive trees. He went around the back—Ifra and Violet following—to the farthest edge near the wall, and started prying up the flagstone to the underground passage. He was having trouble on his own, so Ifra quickly moved to assist with his free arm, the one that wasn't holding the light.

Just as they moved the stone aside, Ifra had the sensation of someone touching him—or looking over his shoulder.

He turned to look at the shadows behind him, but wherever he turned, he felt the presence just behind him. It wasn't a body, he realized, but the feather-light touch of a warm spirit. He prodded back.

Nimira. It was Nimira. She was tugging at him from somewhere nearby, with uncertain little magical tugs.

He didn't know what to do. She could be in danger, wherever

she was, but how would Belin react to her? Of course, Belin was freeing Erris, but Ifra still didn't quite trust him. Even so, Belin was surely safer than Tamin.

Ifra exhaled sharply, making an alarmed noise to catch Belin's attention. Belin was climbing into the catacombs. Ifra tapped his shoulder and then ran to the door, tracing Nimira's spirit.

"Is it Tamin?" Belin was struggling out of the passageway again.

Belin's question tugged at Ifra, demanding an answer, and yet, Belin hadn't told him to speak, so Ifra had to leave the request unfulfilled. He ran out into the garden just as Nimira came through the side door that led to the forest, an expression of considerable alarm on her face.

27

The moment I slipped through the garden gate, I was greeted by the sight of the jinn running up to me, and guards off to the left and right, posted at doors. I could have turned around and dashed back, but obviously I'd already been spotted, so instead I froze, praying Ifra was a friend now.

It was terribly hard to shake the image of him destroying Erris.

He put a finger to his lips and motioned with his hands. Was he asking me to be quiet? I was confused. He'd certainly had no trouble speaking the language before, but now he seemed tongue-tied. He motioned for me to follow him, back to the door at my left, set in a wall covered in climbing vines.

"Who is that?" the guard demanded. "What's going on?"

Ifra opened the door and shoved me into a dark room. He didn't follow, just shut the door on me.

"Who's there?" a man called. "Ifra?"

"He's—he's still outside." I reached behind me, finding the door handle, but I didn't think fleeing would do a bit of good.

"Ifra?" Now, that voice I recognized.

"Violet?"

"Nimira?" I saw a shadow flutter, and Violet threw her arms around me as if we'd been the best of friends. "Why didn't Ifra come back in?"

"Well, the guards were asking who I was . . . Maybe he's . . . taking care of them. What's going on?"

"Erris is here!" Violet cried. "Under the throne. In the death sleep. We have to help him before Tamin gets back—Tamin's one of the other princes—and Belin's the king and he's going to set Erris free so we can show him to the people, and the trees are dying!"

I was quite confused, but I understood one thing: *Erris.* "Take me to Erris. Please. Now. And why is it so dark in here?"

"Ifra has the light," Violet said. She gently nudged me aside to open the door and look for him.

"We don't have time for this!" the man screamed. Was that King Belin? "If the guards know—and Tamin's coming back . . ."

"I don't understand," I said. "You want to free Erris?"

"Yes," Belin said. "My family . . . we can never be great rulers as long as we've taken the throne by such means."

I didn't care for Belin's tone, but he was willing to help Erris, that was the important thing. "All right," I said, just as Ifra returned, flicking his fingers to summon a flame. We hurried to Belin's side, and now I could see a narrow passageway leading underground, and my heart was drumming so hard I could barely breathe.

Belin shimmied down and waved for me to follow.

I couldn't summon any fire myself. I was too shaken with

anticipation. Was Erris here? I couldn't see until Ifra came down, and then . . .

Erris was lying on the ground, mere inches from my feet. It was absolutely my Erris, through and through, even dressed much as I had first seen him, with stockings and breeches and heeled shoes like someone in an old book. He was pale and dirty and I dropped to my knees and started to shake him.

"Erris! Wake up! How do we get him to wake up?"

"I don't know!" Belin said. "I always heard people wake up from a death sleep eventually."

"Eventually!" I cried. "Well, what if this isn't eventually?"

"There are skeletons in here!" Violet shrieked, once Ifra had helped her down. "Let's bring him out!"

I couldn't believe I was really looking at Erris. It was as magical and terrifying as the moment when I'd freed him from being trapped at the piano. I put my hand on his chest and I could feel skin and muscle and bone there; I could feel him breathing. I knew that now, of all moments, I needed to keep it together, just a little longer, but I couldn't even seem to care that Belin and Violet and Ifra were there. My jaw was trembling, so close to tears. I wanted to touch him, kiss him, whisper in his ear.

"I can wake him," I said. "Please, I know I can. Just leave me alone for a moment. Please."

"In the dark with the skeletons?" Violet said.

"Yes."

"Hurry," Belin ordered, as if he had any better ideas. Erris was right, these Graweldins were an irritating lot. They all climbed back out, and I blocked out the sound of them talking above me. I blocked out everything except Erris, there before me. I pressed my forehead to his, pressed my hand to his heart, and felt not the tick of clockwork, but the beating of a heart.

"Erris," I whispered through tears, running my fingers along his soft hair, brushing away thirty years of dust. "Wake up. Please wake up. This is how fairy tales end." I kissed his lips—dry with disuse, but alive, so alive—and I flooded him with all the warm magic I could summon.

The lips parted, with a soft crack just audible in the silence. A hand slowly lifted to touch my face.

"Nim?" he croaked, and then he coughed a cloud of dust into my face, which was not very much like a fairy tale at all, but I didn't even flinch. "Am—am I dead?"

"Oh, no. No. It's just dark. We're in the palace of Telmirra—"

"In the catacombs . . . under the Hall of Oak and Ash?" he whispered. His hands moved to my neck and my shoulders and then back to my hair, and he clutched me close. "But I must be dreaming. How did you get here?"

"I'll explain later. King Belin wants to speak to you."

"Wait a moment, wait a moment." He held me close.

And then he started to cry.

And I started to cry too.

We'd both tried so many times not to cry, and now it was okay. It was okay.

"You did it," he said. "You saved me."

"I had help."

"But it was you. And you know it. You needed help; it was an impossible task, but *you* saved me. And my heart is beating so fast. I haven't felt that in so long. I'm really alive."

I touched his cheek, put my face close. "Kiss me."

"Kiss you now? No, not yet. I haven't cleaned my teeth in years and it's really— Let's just wait."

I laughed, with a catch in it, and I kissed him anyway, although not like I'd kiss him later.

At least, once we were safe.

Above us, I heard some muffled shouting, the sudden commotion of an opening door. More shouting.

I helped Erris struggle to his feet on stiff limbs before Prince Tamin could find us.

TELMIRRA

The door burst open, and there was Tamin with fury in his eyes, and his men behind him, two of them holding a woman dressed in black, the other two holding crossbows. They had Annalie, Ifra realized, after a moment of connection. She looked so serene that the men kept jostling her as if trying to get a reaction.

"What are you doing?" Tamin hissed. "Do you want to put our entire kingdom in jeopardy?"

"I want to free Erris," Belin said.

"But what does he know? How is he fit to be king? Are you so desperate to go against me that you're willing to let him have the throne?"

"Tamin, we can't do this," Belin said. "We're making the trees sick. Father did this to us, decades ago, and it hasn't made us stronger. Only weaker. I agree, Erris may not be fit to rule now. But we could help him."

"Oh, well, I see. You're going to make a hero out of yourself now? Somehow I don't think you intended to bring Ilsin and me along. I mean, you've got your betrothed! She is a Tanharrow! A rightful heir! She would have fixed it all with the old magic and you would have been the one looking to the future, so why bring Erris into it at all? I just don't understand. I don't think you're really doing this for any noble purpose; you're doing it to spite me."

"Maybe I am," Belin said. "In part." He glanced at Ifra. "But the jinn . . . he asked me what sort of king I wanted to be. He told me I could be great ruler. And I thought then, that I would like to be that sort of ruler. But I can't. None of us can. Because of this."

As Belin spoke, Erris Tanharrow himself appeared, crawling rather shakily out of the catacombs. He looked like someone recovering from a bad bout of influenza, all pale and wasted, but he was up and alive, and even Belin looked a little startled.

Ifra seemed to sense the danger before he saw it; he looked at Tamin and saw the shock and anger in his eyes, saw his fingers gesture an order, saw the crossbow. He dived to cover Erris, taking the bolt in his side, gasping with pain, unable to cry out.

"Ifra!" Violet screamed.

But it took more than that to kill a jinn. Jinn couldn't even take their own lives with ease—not that Ifra had tried. But he knew poison, knives to the gut, hanging ropes, and even fire were all useless. The curse of a jinn was not death, but to live at almost any cost.

"Ifra, kill Tamin, *now!*" Belin shouted in his ear.

Yes . . . that was the curse. Living at any cost, a life that was not his own. The wish roared through him, drowning his sense, overwhelming right and wrong and everything but a sudden surge of energy that made him spring to his feet and sweep his arm toward Tamin. Another crossbow struck Ifra and he hardly noticed. The Green Hoods pushed through the doors; he saw Keyelle's familiar face, but it didn't matter. Tamin's body flew into the air, slammed against a tree with force, and Ifra felt the crack of his bones and the crush of organs. He had had to break Erris, and now he had to kill Tamin. There was no choice.

Tamin's body slumped to the ground. Most lives were so fragile.

Ifra dropped to his knees, buried his face, and wept soundlessly. He'd never killed before. He'd done everything to get to know Belin, talk to him, convince him to choose a noble path. He didn't like Tamin, of course, but what did that matter? Now he'd never wipe the sight from his eyes, never shake the feeling from his limbs of that power overcoming him. Why did he have so much power, even now, even without three wishes? It wasn't fair. He didn't want it.

The commotion in the room died down quickly. With Tamin gone, and the Green Hoods there, Tamin's men didn't fight back.

Violet's hands, small and cool, were touching Ifra's shoulder, his head, then gently probing wounds he barely felt. "Ifra. Ifra."

Violet couldn't console him either.

"Ifra, it had to be done," Belin said.

Violet sprung to her feet. Ifra slowly stood behind her. "It had to be done?" she cried. "What do you mean, 'it had to be done'? Then why didn't you do it? You're a coward, an awful coward, to ask somebody else to kill your brother!"

"I couldn't do it like Ifra could."

"But you're the one who wanted it!" Violet picked up a fallen branch shed by one of the trees and struck Belin with it. "You should have seen Ifra after what you made him do to Uncle Erris. It made him *sick*. He took care of me and was pretty much the kindest person I've ever met, and you wouldn't even let him *speak*. You made him do an awful thing he'll have to live with for the rest of his life."

Belin's brow was bleeding, his eye rapidly swelling. "I know . . . it seems harsh, but Tamin . . . just tried to kill Erris. He's ruthless like Father. If I had put him in jail, I could never have rested. None of you grew up with him, none of you really knew him like I did. But I couldn't wave a hand and kill him. It was my last wish. Ifra— I'm sorry."

Ifra would not forgive Belin that. No. He didn't even let Ifra speak, and now Ifra knew why. Belin couldn't bear to hear Ifra beg or plead when he made that wish, maybe he didn't even want to hear Ifra cry afterward. It was easier that way. Easier to pretend Ifra wasn't mortal.

But Ifra himself had wished, for a moment, that Belin would ask him to kill Tamin. Just as jinns twisted the wishes of their masters, Ifra felt Belin had somehow twisted his own unspoken wish. Was it somehow his fault?

And then: "I wish to set you free now," Belin said.

Ifra had dreamed of this moment. He would fall to his knees in gratitude. He would cry with joy.

But now, all he could say was, "I'm glad you gave me that."

Then he took Violet's hand.

He turned to Erris. "I will serve you, Erris Tanharrow, as a free man."

28

Erris looked so pale and overwhelmed that I feared he might collapse. He probably needed food, for one thing. "Well," he told Ifra, "why don't you have a good rest first, before you go pledging yourself anywhere."

"You're going to need loyal and powerful men," Ifra said.

"Yes . . ."

"You will have all the Green Hoods," Keyelle said. "We've been waiting for you for a long, long time."

"I will try to be worthy of it." Erris glanced, uncomfortably, at the fallen form of Tamin.

"I know you probably don't care for my support, after all this," Belin said. "But you have it nevertheless."

"No, Belin . . . you set me free," Erris said gravely. "I know these weren't easy decisions. I'll need your support."

"I will tell you, tonight I've gathered nearly every fairy noble in the land, more of whom would have you as king than me. They're waiting for the ball to begin, and if I introduce you, I assure you the palace will erupt with joy. We'll worry about the dissenters later."

"Yes," Erris said. "Dissenters."

"There will always be dissenters," Annalie said. "Don't worry. After all, you know Karstor will be on your side, and that should help a great deal of the tension."

Erris licked his dry lips. "Would all of you mind . . . stepping out for just a moment?"

"Of course, Your Highness," Keyelle said. She was beaming. In fact, all the Green Hoods were beaming. Tamin's men gathered his body, and all of them left the room with a respectful silence and speed, already treating Erris like a king, even leaving two torches in holders by the door so we had light.

He turned to me, with countless emotions playing across his face. He held his palms open to me, and I placed my hands in his.

"Look at you," he said with a slight smile. "Even more rough and tumble than the last time I saw you."

"Well, I was kidnapped while looking for you, and I had to eat dried mushroom–based cuisine for two days, which was just awful, if I'm being honest."

"Oh, dear. I'm concerned about you assimilating around here."

"Does even the queen have to eat dried mushrooms?"

"Well, the king hasn't eaten in thirty years and is pretty unsympathetic."

"I bet there is something else the king hasn't done in thirty years, so he should be indulgent of the queen."

"Oh?" Erris's smile looked a tad more genuine.

I gave his lips a peck. "I mean *that*, you rogue."

"Of course you did. I knew that. I'm a perfect gentleman, you know."

Erris pulled my hands against his heart, looking serious again. "Nimira . . . I'm scared. All these people have been waiting for me for thirty years, and I really don't know how to be a king. They may be happy at first, but when the celebrations are over, they'll realize how hopeless I am."

"I know it's scary, but you won't be alone," I said. "Belin may be awful when he isn't rescuing you, but he can also tell you things, and you have Ifra, and the Green Hoods, and Karstor, and . . . you have me. I know I'm just a dancing girl, but—"

"No, no," he said. "You are a sorceress, Nim. But are you sure you really want to step into this mess with me?"

"I've got my boots on," I said, sliding my arms around his neck and pulling his living body a little closer. "Let's go."